Chris Danill
1982

Virgin Kisses

Gloria Nagy

1978
CHELSEA HOUSE PUBLISHERS
NEW YORK, LONDON

Copyright © 1978 by Gloria Nagy and Chelsea House Publishers, a division of Chelsea House Educational Communications, Inc. All rights reserved. This book may not be reproduced in part or in whole without express written permission from the publisher.

LC: 78-56873
ISBN: 0-87754-068-3
Distributed by Atheneum

CHELSEA HOUSE PUBLISHERS
Harold Steinberg, Publisher & Chairman   Andrew E. Norman, President
Susan Lusk, Vice President
A Division of Chelsea House Educational Communications, Inc.
70 West 40th Street, New York 10018

To Wende Hyland. To Keven Bellows.
And my children and my friends, who are my life.
And to Dr. Gertrude Harrow
And the Hole....

I

Pygmalion saw so much to blame in women that he came at last to abhor the sex and resolved to live unmarried. He was a sculptor and had made with wonderful skill a statue of ivory, so beautiful that no living woman came anywhere near it. His art was so perfect that it concealed itself and its product looked like the workmanship of nature. *Pygmalion* admired his own work and at last fell in love with the counterfeit creature. The festival of Venus was at hand—a festival celebrated with great pomp at Cyprus. Victims were offered, the altars smoked and the odor of incense filled the air. When *Pygmalion* had performed his part in the solemnities, he stood before the altar and timidly said, "Ye gods, who can do all things, give me, I pray you, for my wife—" he dared not say, "my ivory virgin," but said instead, "one like my ivory virgin." Venus who was present at the festival heard him and knew the thought he would have uttered. When he returned home he went to see his statue and leaning over the couch, gave a kiss to the mouth. The virgin felt the kisses and blushed, and opening her timid eyes to the light, fixed them at the same moment on her lover...

The Age of Fable
Bulfinch's Mythology

1

My name is Dr. Arthur Freedman. Psychiatrist and killer. I make fifty-thousand dollars in a good year (more in a bad one). I drive a Mercedes-Benz sedan. Have a lovely home. Lovely wife, son same. I am almost brilliant. Witty. Charming. Immaculately tailored. Esteemed by my peers. Well read. Civilized, and have a raised social conscience. I play tennis, chess and backgammon and am a good party guest and excellent host. I am respected for my sanity, calm, cool and control.

I am also a snob, a prick and a phony, cunt-sniffing asshole. A hypocrite, a sadist; a cold, self-absorbed schmuck. Tense, anxious, alienated, drowning, unfulfilled, weak, pretentious, smug, half-latent fairy boy. A liar, a bad doctor—and now, a murderer.

I am, in sum, the American wet dream.

You (whoever you will be—I haven't decided yet) who are listening to this tape may be disturbed by the above statement. You may be wondering why I would admit such transgressions of character—not to mention a hanging offense—when it is not necessary. Well, fuck you and your wondering. Because I don't yet know why. It may in the end turn out to be a pure matter of ego. For I, *I* have fulfilled the Mind Men's dream. I have murdered a patient without ever touching her. I have killed her with skill. I have used what I know about infantile, regressive, manipulative, sociopathic paranoia—and the sham of medical science. I have probed, pushed and played with the fleshy body and feeble mind of the most meaningless human being I have ever encountered (an honor very hard for a psychiatrist to bestow on a single soul), and I have let her die and never told my secrets. I have not yet told you—you too will have to wait. I will tell all, fifty minutes at a time, for as long as I choose. And then you will know... and I will know. And then I will decide what to do with this unwinding: burn it, bury it for the Bellevue archives, turn it over to the APA (ha) or— well, we will see.

And now I must stop. A patient is waiting to be misled. (I am smiling.) I must tell you things like that—give you the eyes I want you to have. And you will believe me—because you know nothing else.

I say I am smiling. And it may be a lie. I may be crying. I may be sticking my tongue out. Or playing with my cock. But you will believe I am smiling.

2

Testing...testing...always testing....It is me again. I have been avoiding you. But no more. I have made a decision. It is now six o'clock in the morning, the first of October, 1977. Very close to my fortieth birthday. I am sitting here at my desk in my plush, overly understated "patient environment." I have canceled all but one appointment for the day (guilt). And I am committing myself to you—one Mother tape—to tell my story.

I will sit here as long as necessary. In front of me are various bottles of amphetamines (uppers) and barbiturates (downers). I have my cocaine spoon filled and two Colombian joints rolled; a quart bottle of Johnnie Walker Black Label Scotch, three fine old Cuban cigars, four packages of Benson and Hedges 100's; eight packs of Trident gum (spearmint), a large bottle of Perrier water, a pot of coffee, and in the fridge—hidden under my desk ever to perpetuate the illusion that I, the Profound One, never eat (bathroom hidden behind a grass-clothed wall, etc.)—in the fridge are: a nicely ripened Brie, two apples, a pear, a tin of domestic caviar, a loaf of cocktail rye, a jar of marinated herring filets, a fresh strawberry tart, a slice of goose liver pate and two boxes of Oreos (which I will separate individually and lick off every last drop of icing, obsessively); two Twinkies, three Diet Pepsis, a six-pack of Coors and a Hebrew National salami. (The Jew in me refuses to die completely, still squeezing spastically in the supermarkets—wretched reachings into my amputated past. An arm shoots out of my elegant, assimilated, non-sectarian sleeve and clutches a kosher salami—will I never be free of it?)

I have a box of Kleenex, six Snicker bars and a pint of Korbel brandy. I am set. I will remain in here until I have finished with you.

Oh Mother Tape.

First, before I introduce Her, my victorious victim, I will let you know of my life through my work. I will play some tapes that will explain things better.

August 14 1972

Mr. Davis, your internist suggested that you come and talk to me. Do you know why?

Of course I know why.

Would you like to tell me about it?

I don't care—you can't make me do it.

Do what?

Shit.

Shit?

Yeah, shit.

They tried. I didn't shit for three months—and then I got sick and they put me in the hospital. But I still wouldn't do it. And it was beautiful, man —I mean all these dry pussy nurses and faggot doctors running around— "But Mr. Davis, you must defecate or you will get very toxic and very seriously ill"—and I'd just smile at them, my fuck-you smile, man...and drive them crazy. And then one night this little prick intern comes in with three of the big honcho residents and he's just started his surgery rotation or whatever it is—and I'm like his first big "case" and the honchos are hyping him,—"Yes, Dr. Schwartz, this is Mr. Davis; Mr. Davis is toxic; he has not defecated in ninety-two days"—and the guy is trying to look real cool like "oh another one of those, oh of course"—but his eyes are flying around in his head, and I'm starting to go out of it, all doped up, and this dialog is going on, and I'm tuning in and out and all of a sudden I get it— that these dudes are setting this turkey up to shovel the shit out of me...!! Ha! I was his first surgery, man! I passed out and they took me into the operating room, and in comes "Young Dr. Schwartz-Putz"—took him all night, digging into my asshole with his hands—four years of college, four years of med school, year of internship...every mother's fair-haired boy— a fucking shit shoveler. "Oh yes, Mom, Dad—had my first big case last night, saved a man's life." He took twenty pounds of crap out of me, worked all night—the guys did a first-class number on that dude. Ha! Probably still washing his hands—ha!

How did you feel about that?

Fucking good. I felt real good. I had absolute control and nobody could make me do it. And now they're trying to make me do it again. And now I'm really driving them nuts because I won't pee either. That really freaks them. "But Mr. Davis, the bladder must be voided. It is physically impossible to prevent urination indefinitely; the damage to your kidneys can be severe and irreversible." "Suck sand," I tell 'em—"Oh yeah? Watch me." They can't make me do anything I don't want to do ... and I'm not going to shit and I'm not going to pee ... I'll make the news. Walter Cronkite will do a bit.... I may start Pee-Ins all over the country, my own protest movement—supreme meditation, man.... See, I don't care if I die, so they can't hurt me.... When you don't care, that's the only way you beat 'em... ha!

Mr. Davis was right. I have always had a fondness for Mr. Davis, who never came back. I told my wife about him. She didn't understand. She recommended Ex-Lax. And diuretics. Mr. Davis controlled her too.

November 23, 1973: Group Therapy Session

Okay, who wants to start?

(You are hearing nothing because no one said anything... everyone dying to spill some seething event that has consumed them all week, but every session, every single session I will say "Who wants to start?" and no one moves... and then we play "silence is okay" and fidget in our chairs for fifteen minutes of my time and their money.)

Bruce, how about you—did you and your wife go on that church weekend?

Yes.

Everything go well?

Yes, the kids loved it. The mountains were beautiful ... but ... Okay, I'll start. I got jealous again.

Okay, put it in the present and tell us about it.

Okay, well, everything is going just fine. And Jane and I are really communicating. And it is good. And then it's Saturday night—one of the counselors that came to help with the kids comes in.... He is very young, maybe twenty-two, and tall and very good-looking...and he and Jane start talking about kids...he's interested in social work, and you know that's her career.... I go to get a drink and when I come back they're gone and I feel this terrible rage. It's like I'm just going to burst into tears, right there in the lodge. I almost can't stand it. And I want to kill her and that kid—well, about ten minutes later they come back in. They'd taken a couple of the children for a walk, and I feel so ashamed.

Okay, let's try something. Move two chairs together. Sandy and Lowell, help him please. Now try to be Bruce—little Bruce. Be five years old and talk to Jane as your child-self.

(Bruce, who is six-feet-three inches tall, crouches on the floor in front of an empty chair containing the ghost of his wife. He is very embarrassed—but consumed with emotion.)

Okay, Bruce, take your time with it.

(We sit in silence, all eyes on him, struggling to be five years old. Suddenly his arms swing up above his head and crash into his phantom wife with such force the chair topples over, just missing my crossed leg.)

I hate you...I hate you!... You went away and left me all alone.... How could you do that to me when I need you so much?.... You're out there laughing at me...making fun of me...with a grown-up. I trusted you and you laughed at me—I hate you...I hate you!

(Bruce is sobbing. Lowell and Sandy and Mrs. Peterson touch his back in support. I recross my legs.)

How does that feel?

Better.

Okay, want to be grown-up, Bruce, and talk to Jane?

Okay.

(He takes a deep breath and wipes his eyes. The men in the room look away.)

> Okay, Jane. I know you love me. I was angry at you when you went outside with that young guy. I felt jealous and scared. But I'm a grown-up and I can love that child part of me and accept those feelings and not be paralyzed by them. I love you and I trust you...and I can tell you that I felt jealous because I trust you. I feel good....I feel much better.

> Good, Bruce.

Bruce is a highly successful forty-five-year-old television writer, married for fifteen years and the father of three children. I am his sixth therapist.
We lapse again into silence. People light cigarettes and sip cold coffee. Bruce is content. He has forgiven himself for last Saturday.

> Uh, isn't anybody going to ask me about Mexico?

It is Lowell. Lowell is a millionaire. He dabbles in B movies. He has been in Mexico producing one. Lowell is fifty-eight years old and has had a stroke. It left him with a paralyzed left leg, and he walks with a cane.
Everyone asks him about Mexico in unison.

> It was great. Beautiful women, beautiful...uh, I have a question to ask...not a problem...just a question I've been thinking about....

> Okay, Lowell.

> Well, I was at a party and several people were talking about their sexual fantasies and I realized that I'd never had any and I wondered if that was normal. I don't want to sound like I'm bragging but I've always been a real cocksman.

(Sandy and Mrs. Peterson eye his crotch unconsciously.)

> I mean women have told me, even at my age, that they've never been with a man like me. I mean I could always keep an erection for hours. I never let a woman go home unsatisfied. Never. Could screw all night—twelve hours straight—and not come, or come five, six times...and nothing embarrassed me. I was a real sexual acrobat. I really liked to please women. I mean I never had any problems that way...never... and, uh, but since the stroke, I, uh, well I can't get into some of my favor-

ite positions and I feel awkward so I, uh, find that I just don't make love anymore. And a couple of times I've tried and I can't. The night I had my stroke—you know, I woke up and there was this terrible pain and my wife woke up and I said "Jesus, I feel funny—terrible." And then I lost control of myself and the next thing I remember I was on the floor and I had vomited on myself and everything, and you know, being out of control like that it scared me; and well, I made it, but now I'm divorced and, I mean, I can have all the women I want, like I said before, but I just wanted to ask if it's normal for a man not to have sexual fantasies, because I've never had them... that's all—I just wanted to ask.

There is no "normal," Lowell.

(I am still thinking about his twelve-hour erections and am jealous and feeling glad that he is old and has had a stroke and is not so threatening. And I am also wanting to tell him that he is full of shit and has terrible performance anxieties and is probably a lousy lay, desperately insecure and totally dishonest, egocentric and self-absorbed. But I say:)

Anyone want to contribute anything to Lowell?

Mrs. Peterson, who is pushing fifty and whose husband has left her for his (yawn) secretary and who is so horny she can hardly keep her legs together, says:

Lowell, every person is different. Fantasies are not important—you obviously don't need them; but speaking as a woman, it really isn't so important how many positions you know or how acrobatic you are. It's for a woman, knowing that you want to please her, being warm and gentle. You shouldn't be so afraid of letting someone see you without your big front. Anyone that cares about you won't care if you can't perform like a twenty-year-old all the time. I wouldn't care.

Lowell winces. She is trying to help. She isn't. He is imagining a world of withered trysts with matronly, sex-starved widows and divorcees, when he wants eighteen-year-old starlets and all-night erections. He will not hear her. And he will not get better. And eventually he will stop coming.

No one else wants to contribute. Time is almost up. We finish the session in throat clearing and cigarette lighting. I have just made two-hundred dollars.

3

I am opening my beautiful, tongue-luscious, almond-amber, pussy-licking, gut-stroking, thick-rich bottle of Johnnie Walker Black Label. It is now 6:45 a.m.

I am pouring a neat water glass full of tummy honey. You will know this is true because you will hear the change in me for yourself. Unlike the twitch-tick-smile-frown syndrome—you will know this without your popeyes... hah, haahhh, good.

Now, for a moment, to digress, to put off where I must next move—I would like to talk about pain.

I, you see, have not felt it for years. Gave it up for the good pop psycho life. Gave it up to treat it (can't have it and treat it at the same time... same reason no one's ever licked sin, I imagine).

Pain. It hurts (thank you, Doctor). People pour in here dripping of it. "Help me, help me. If I've ended up HERE"—(HERE being a noxious reference to the place I live most of whatever life I have left in—"if I've ended up HERE I must be close to the end"—close to the point of breaking, of NOT BEING ABLE TO STAND THE PAIN!

I am the Lion in this Lair—the Island no man is. I am the jumper's ledge, the razor's strop, the eye's tear, the wino's dime, the Last Chance Saloon. "HELP ME!" they cry—defenses shatter, crash to the silent, thick-piled floor... "help me, please/oh God, THE PAIN!"

Sure, sure, sure, fella—why not, what the Hay—I'll help ya. Want a little wine into water or vice versa? How's about my Snake and the Stick number?.... Sure, sure, sure... I'll get rid of it for ya... tell me 'bout the childhood—motherloveya?... fatherleftya? Snap—gone... feelbettah? "Oh, the PAIN."

Easy. Dr. Freedman, Witch-Bitch Doctor of Pain Removal, will stop it.

"I hurt. They hurt me, they scare me, they reject me, they manipulate humiliate - castrate - exacerbate - flagellate - fornicate - potentate - violate -

hate-placate-me."

They. They. Them. The They is moving. It's the MARCH OF THE THEYS—the Army of the Pain People—moving against the sickly little souls thrashing on my brown corduroy self-welted couch. An Army of People Eaters coming for, summoned by Himwho—just to get them?

Germ of the earth—bug in the bed—ant on the pant—puck in the pot—monster in the mirror—me..."they came to get *me*"...to take all the why-me's to the Great Macerator in the Sky.

The Army marches—travels through space and time—(crashes EST meetings) all to get the *me's*. Sinner of sinners, jokes of the universe, giant pygmy? Albino coon? Wombless mother, juiceless lover—misfit —me. THEY CAME JUST FOR ME!

Oh Luscious Pain Goddess, I'm getting drunk. I am feeling—something—something is stirring. I am feeling what?

I traded in all of that "feeling" stuff years ago. I rose above the pain-paralyzed thrashers on my brown corduroy. I gave all that pain shit up! Ha! The laugh is—was (I didn't get it then, cockiness of youth and egomania and all)—that the laugh would be—losing it all. Can't get the pastrami without the rye—lost it all. No more pain: romance-laughter-silliness - softness - love - joy - compassion - crying - ecstasy - passion - high - low - melancholy - crushes - touches - moo...moooo...oods... firepipeanslippers. Ha!

Gave it away. For a good impression. I make a very good impression. The PAIN PEOPLE are very impressed. I impress the shit out of 'em... They admire my lack of it—while they cry and scream and fuck and suck and drink and sink and go all the waay uppp and alll theee waay doooown and leave me—"thanks Doc—still hurt—never be like you— but it's okay, it's better"...leave me.

And I'm still here—in this Last Train to Fucking Burma...I'm the only one left here. Shit.

I am drinking coffee now. Mother Tape is rewound. I will fill in as I sober—with more Pain People.

May 21, 1974

Welcome back, Paul. How was Tahiti?

Great. Really fine. Hate to be back. I've got cases piled up on my desk, as if I was the only bankruptcy attorney in the world.

I can imagine. So, what's going on with you?

(Paul sighs deeply, removes his glasses and rubs his pale blue eyes.)

> *Everything is dynamite. Well, I mean, you know that I really came here to try and save my marriage—and now, really, since the divorce—I don't really need to keep on. I realize that it was just living with a bummer—with someone so inappropriate for me—that was causing the problem, and now, really that's solved. Frankly, it's just too much bread to put out to talk about my vacations. You know what I mean?*
>
> I understand what you're saying. If you're in a good place with yourself and want to terminate...

(Paul tightens slightly at this word.)

> ...we can discuss that. Or would you rather spend the hour on something else?
>
> *Well, I just wanted to let you know that I've been thinking about stopping. I haven't decided definitely yet, but I really am great now that Bonnie's gone. Life is really beautiful... You know I took someone with me to Tahiti...*
>
> Oh yes, someone you seemed quite impressed with.
>
> *Yes; beautiful, very bright girl. An advertising account exec. She's divorced too. I thought she was really different. But she turned out to be, well, too neurotic. I keep thinking there are women who aren't really screwed up—I really thought this one, Monica, was different—but she wasn't.*

Paul's face is clenched. His blond brows furled. (This Scotch coffee is bringing back tons of tender details like that.) He is wearing a blue three-piece suit, with lapels reflecting Eastern prep school anality—too narrow. A yellow shirt and striped tie. He is short. Handily constructed. Most likely smug about a large organ which unfurls before his conquests—in Mighty Mouse glee—as they silently squeal in gladness at the small man's surprise. Father a dead—former alive—drunken radio writer. Mother an organ-playing (oh god, the symbolism) music teacher and intellectual. Only child. Little Paulie. Worked way through Yale Law School. Married early and well. Divorced too late and badly. Spineless. Ruthlessly ambitious. Got the mother-loved-me-and-blew-my-balls-off ba-lue-ues.

> What happened that made you change your mind? You seemed to feel that you knew her rather well.

Well, it was nothing really. I mean it was really trivial. We got along beautifully—fantastic on the rack—I mean the sex was too much. And bright—we really had a good rap going....

Okay, put it in the present and tell me about it.

God, I hate that gestalt number—it makes me feel ridiculous.

I know. But let's try it. Take your time with it.

Okay. Well, everything is going really well. And I mean she really turned me on. And it's Sunday morning, the day before we're coming home—and we wake up and smoke a joint and we're like really loose and stoned and Jesus, I must have fucked her for two hours and she's just popping over and over and finally she—not me—she says "please stop—I can't come anymore." So I'm feeling great and we order a huge breakfast and we're eating and we smoke another joint and we're talking about our childhoods and I am feeling funny, as if I can trust her. And I start talking about something I have never told anyone. Not even my wife. She was...

In the present...

Okay. She is talking philosophy. I mean human philosophy about trying to survive and still care about people and the responsibilities you accept with parenthood and that kind of thing. And then there is a stoned silence and I hear myself saying from nowhere...one time when I was in high school I had a hall pass during class and there was this girl in the junior class who was crippled. She had a withered leg and she wore a brace and had to use a cane to walk with. And everyone was nice to her and all but she was not a big attraction, if you know what I'm saying. Anyway, I always felt really uptight around her. She just gave me the creeps. And so I have my hall pass and I'm walking down the main hall, which was very very long and with high old vaulted ceilings. And I'm all alone. Well, this girl comes out of a doorway at the other end of the hall and we're walking toward one another. The only two people in the entire place. And because the ceilings are so high, the acoustics are unreal and I can hear her brace clicking on the tile and I'm getting nervous. And all of a sudden she loses her balance. She stumbles and her books and crutch go flying and she falls on her face on the tile. And I am only a few feet away from her by now. And she looks up at me, really scared and embarrassed and she can't get up by herself and she's just lying there helpless with her skirt up almost to her underwear and the crutch out of

> *reach and she's looking at me—waiting for me to help her. And I just couldn't touch her. I wanted to help her but I just froze. I was repulsed, and now she reaches out to me. And then—I didn't see it because I looked away from her—but I felt she saw into my mind because she lowered her hand and started pushing herself along the floor, trying to reach her crutch. And I turned and ran away.*

(Paul's hands are threaded together in white-knuckled prayer formation. He avoids my eyes while he puts his facade on again.)

> *Anyway, I was—I am stoned and I'm telling this story to Monica, confiding my weakest moment in her and expecting, because I think she is different, not another demanding bitch, that she would really understand—and she didn't say anything... she just sat there, kind of stoned—quiet—and I felt her disapproval: like he's not a strong man—something like that whole ball-breaking number—men can't make mistakes—just like my wife did. She didn't say any of that. She didn't say anything. And finally I was getting pissed, so I said "so what about your weakest moment" and she said "I never allowed myself any—I always had to be the grown-up"... bitch.*

Did she explain that?

> *Yes. But I wasn't listening anymore. I mean she made me feel really bad. We finished the trip okay. But I felt the change. But now I feel like I was really lucky—because if I hadn't told her that, I wouldn't have found out what a cunt she was—is.*

(We went on. Paul hit Monica's ghost with a pillow to work out his rage—he talked to Paul as Monica and Monica as little Paulie and to little Paulie as big Paul and watched me for signs of disgust, which I did not feel, being much like him in many ways myself... let us all pull up our pants and show our braces... all together now... Brooks Brothers would be out of business. We worked on his feelings of rejection—poor defensive little bastard that he is—was—and he finished, again convinced he was a perfect and lucky man to have exposed another wormbrained witch posing as goddess. I fantasized about calling Monica myself—she'd never hear my "hall" story and she would love me madly—pop-pop-pop.)

4

Sometimes I run my tapes backward and all of my patients sound like Donald Duck. Here's a good one: I once spliced together bits and pieces of years of interviews with women patients who mixed together in my mind. Husbands' names, children's names—their names whirled around in my brain and confused me. And them. Once in a while I would use the name of a loved one on the wrong woman and she would not even notice. "Does Ralph mind your coming here?" I would offer. "That bastard is so wrapped up in his work he doesn't care what I do," she would reply, not noticing the fact that her husband's name is Richard. I am taking one more hit to wash down the dregs of my Scotch coffee. It is now 8 a.m.

Monday, April 23, 1970: Danielle Levine

We had another fight yesterday. I told him I was not raised to have a life like this. I was raised to have a lovely home and a maid and he was going to just have to take care of me and the girls by himself. I was not going to work anymore. I thought that if he really understood that I expected him to support us without my help and I refused to help, he would have to start getting better clients and making more money. I've invested fifteen years in him. I put him through school. Everything. And now I'm almost forty and I don't even have my own home. He's got to do it. We have one jar of peanut butter left in the icebox and I don't care. I'm going to make him do better. I wasn't raised to live like this.

Wednesday, August 3, 1969: Audrey Miller

We had another fight and I told him that he couldn't afford to write screenplays, that he was a lawyer and I worked to put him through school and now it was my turn to be taken care of. He just screamed at me that he was trying, that he just couldn't get the clients, and I don't believe that. Anyway he slammed out of the house. The children were crying, and about one hour later he came back, and he was white and shaking all over, and he went into the bathroom and stood in front of the heater, crying and shaking like a child. I'm thirty-eight years old and I've spent fourteen years with him and he's still a spoiled, selfish mama's boy.... Something's got to change—he's got to start making some money. All of his friends—all of my friends are married to men who have made it and they're not as smart as Jerry. He's just not a pusher, he's a terrible businessman. I told him to go with a big firm...not out on his own...he wouldn't listen...he never listens...and now he's falling apart and we have no money and I will not go back to work.

Friday, January 15, 1972: Marilyn Jamison

We had another terrible fight. I got so angry I threw a book at him and he went crazy—he was shrieking at me, "You want to see mad? I'll show you mad"—and he picked up a lamp and hurled it through a window. It was awful. I told him that he is just going to have to keep his job whether he likes it or not. I keep my job—I hate what I'm doing; I want to stay home and write a novel, but I drag myself downtown every day while he dreams and schemes and quits jobs every time someone smiles at him crooked. All of our savings are gone on his goddamn hobbies and bad investments. I'm a nervous wreck. He makes me feel like a ball-breaking bitch and it's just not fair. He is going to have to grow up and face reality. It's been sixteen years and he's still a child.

Here is my work-of-art reel:

I'm having paralyzing migraine headaches and I haven't slept in a month.

I've got a bleeding ulcer and my jaw is so tight I have trouble opening my mouth.

I sleep all the time—sixteen hours a day—and I can't do any housework.... The dishes are piled up all over the kitchen, the laundry is all over the floor and I can't even open a can of tuna without bursting into tears.

I scream at the kids all the time and hit them and I'm just angry at everyone all of the time and it's scaring me.

My clitoris is so bad the doctor is afraid they'll have to operate on me and I'm scared.

I can't eat at all. Every time I look at food I get sick. I've lost twenty-five pounds and I have malnutrition and it's scaring me.

I have no sexual desire. I can't stand him to touch me.

I'm anxious and tense all the time—my nerves are so bad. I'm afraid I'm going to have an accident or something.

I'm so tense my hair is falling out.

I've got asthma—at thirty-eight—all of a sudden I've got asthma.

I feel like I'm suffocating all the time.

I can't swallow—I feel like my throat's closing.

I can't breath—I feel like I'm in a cage.

I've broken out in boils and hives all over my body.

I throw up every day.

I don't want him to touch me.

I feel like I'm going to kill my kids and I can't sleep anymore.

I'm tired all the time.

I'm anxious all the time.

I've stopped menstruating for no reason.

I've got palpitations and I swallow air.

I can't relax.

I can't stay awake.

I don't want to make love any more.

I cry all the time.

I feel numb inside.

I feel so lonely.

I feel so empty.

I'm scared of everything.

I feel trapped.

I hyperventilate so bad that I pass out.

I'm having fainting spells.

I have headaches.

I have stomachaches.

I have diarrhea.

I'm constipated and I grind my teeth all the time.

I feel like I'm floating above my body...disconnected.

I hate my body.

I'm so fat and I can't stop eating.

I can't swallow.

I have no energy.

I'm tense all the time.

My skin's breaking out.

My hair's falling out.

I don't want him to touch me.

I'm depressed all the time...sad all the time...tense all the time....I have colitis...ulcers...headaches...can't eat...can't sleep...too fat ...too tired...too angry...don't touch me....

My Ladies Lament: Splice of Life I offer into evidence.

5

I may give you, Mother Tape Goddess, to N.O.W. and let them publicly burn you...reeling off tales of such radical antifeminimism from the soundproof lagoons of my mind pool. I, however, for the record, would like to remind the listener that I just push the buttons, ma'am—it is not my chauvinstic woman-loathing self that spewed all that forth. It was an army of emancipated, sophisticated, youngish matrons. Closet why-me's changing into their Wonder Woman gear by day, whining out a cornucopia of psychosoma and betrayal-delusion-tension-anger and denial of reality by night.

Men wanting them to do *it*—THEM wanting the men to do—here, you do *it*—no chance—baby *you* do *it*—but I thought you were supposed to—no way—you are...unh-unh—uh-huh! But Mommy said I'd get someone handsome and strong and perfect to take care of me—oh yeah, well, *my* mommy said I was her angel boy and she would always protect me and take care of me—so there—well—SOMEONE HAS TO DO IT,...unh-unh—uh-huh. They stand up at their consciousness-raising sessions ranting and chanting of freedom and take it on home and hit ol' Momma's Pride in the balls with it—and he escapes—withholds—cheats—blows his money—screws his best friend's wife or his wife's best friend—plays golf all weekend and puts down her cooking...stops listening.... If she's not going to do *it*, fuck her—if he's not going to do *it*, I'll make him.... The women trudge on—trying to pull the poor prick into shape...he just disappears inside his own little tootle-dee-doo-block-out...he tootles on and she scratches and thrashes and makes her stomach hurt. He tootle-dee-doos on and then his heart just breaks open. Or something. Nobody wants to do it. Jesus H., there's got to be someone who wants to be the grown-up. It's not that tough a job, is it? Don't know, really never get to meet anyone who's accepted the position. Present company included. AH...one more before I get on with the gruesome business at hand. My Supreme Damsel tape:

Saturday, September 25, 1975, 3:30 a.m. (emergency session): Lolly Baines.

(I meet Lolly at my office. She is drunk. She has called saying she is losing a ten-hour struggle to keep her hands off the OD bottle. She is a southern beauty. Forty years old. Looks ten years younger even at three-thirty in the morning—drunk, pale, her fine hair wild and black-rooted. A Dresden-cool cameo woman: fragile, tall, hollow, thin body. An actress by affectation and avocation. Saucer-blue eyes. Baby face. Lilting tones of the Carolinas. A Blanche DuBois cast photo. She is staggering, her mouth twisted to the side in self-mocking instability. She is barefoot. A sea-blue nightgown and peignoir peeking from a trench coat. She stumbles. I take her arm and lead her to the couch. It is our first meeting.)

Do you have a drink? Ah need a drink please, Doctor.

No. I think we'd better talk first. We'll see about a drink later.

(She stares at me in animal-eyed despair. Nodding, woozy. Deciding not to fight me. Tears begin to fall aimlessly and unheeded down her face.)

Ah'm so sorry to bother you lak the-iss, in the middle of the naght—but Ah knew if Ah didn't talk to someone Ah'd never make it to mawning. And Ah had no one else to call. No one.

(She wipes at her eyes and running nose with the pale cream back of her wrist. I am thinking I have never seen a more feminine gesture.)

Okay. I understand. Just take your time. I'm here and I'll stay as long as you need me.

(She nods. Swallowing tears. Nodding off in bourbon haze and fragments of memory. I am not bored. I want a drink. I sit quietly. A woodsman before a doe.)

Do you know how to get a deevorce? Ah have to... Ah must have a deevorce, and Ah don't—Ah don't know how—Ah can't think of how to do it all alone. Can you help me, can you?

Well, why don't you tell me why you want a divorce first.

(She nods again. Womanchild in periwinkle-blue nylon and running eyes. I am beginning to anticipate: another chapter for my Ladies' Lament spool: "he didn't, he won't—he drinks—he stinks"—something that will leave me bitter and having reduced her, magnolia petals and all, to "another one of those," and I will bill her double for emergency service.)

Rudy, mah husband, Rudy...

(Oh God, Rudy and Lolly Baines—doth warm the heart of a big-city Jewboy.)

...mah husband is a transvestite...

(She has blinked herself clean. She is dry-eyed in the confessional. I blink myself clear—my smug rug having just tripped me. I start to speak—then think better of it. She has opened the can herself. I am now invisible to her—a receptacle to receive the beans. That is my role here—I will be used.)

He—you see, Ah'm an actress and Ah was married to a wonderful beautiful man—a screenwriter—a very very famous writer who was blacklisted—you know 'bout all that—and it was hell, so anyhow we had gone East to live...and then things got bettah and there was work for James in Hollywood and we came back here and bought a house, an' you know, the day before we were going to move into this beautiful wonderful house, Ah went over there alone to measure some windows and Ah got the strangest feelin' Ah was pregnant with our child and Ah felt this house is evil, this house is bad luck, and Ah ran out and went back to James and pleaded with him not to move there but he just kissed me and made a joke about it and—Ah sure would like to have a drink...well, we moved in there and mah baby—mah little girl was born dead—and then three months later mah James had a heart attack and he died...and Ah was an actress, you know—well, Ah lost mah part, mah best part, and Ah couldn't work and had to get out of that house so Ah went back to Carolina and had a nervous breakdown...and then Ah finally was able to leave the hospital and I went to New York and I met Rudy. And he seemed so kind and strong and I needed someone to help me—to take care of me—and I married him and—and he used up all of James' money —everything—and then one night about a year after we were married I was in the kitchen—and I hate to cook—never liked to do any of those things—I'm an actress, an artist—anyway I was in the kitchen and— and he came up behind me and I turned around—and he is a very big man, over six feet four and very skinny, and conservative—always wears a tie and all—and he is standing there in the kitchen wearing mah best evening dress and all mah makeup and high-heeled sandals and his eyes all crazy... and he takes me by the shoulders and tells me—he tells me this awful thing—he makes me listen and he's all mad-eyed—he had been married before me and he has five children—and all of that time he was hiding this thing—and he, he...

(She is sobbing; again mucus oozes from her nose unnoticed.)

...he married me—he married me and used up James' money and he didn't tell me. God—God, I have no place to go. I have no one left. James is gone—my baby is dead, my parents are dead, my two best friends killed themselves three weeks apart, and I am not a stable woman...

(She turns mocking—sneering through her haze—eyes get mean—I see other sides—my neck heats.)

...I slashed him—he was drunk and I was drinking and he was serving me dinner. You see, it's been five years—I have lived with Rudy for five years since then, and you see we have a cute little routine. Every evening he gets himself all dressed up in my clothes and puts on his makeup and his wig—or sometimes he wears a cute little bonnet—and then he puts his apron on and he cooks me a big fancy dinner—when it's all ready, and the wine is open and the candles are lit, he calls me in and I sit down and he serves me dinner—never eats with me—he just trots around like Ichabod Crane in drag and serves me dinner. Tonight I watched him and he was drunk and I guess I was—well, no, I was just having a few cocktails but he reached over to serve me some asparagus and I just went crazy and I grabbed his wig and pulled it off and I slashed his face with my fingernail—blood just gushed out of him—I slashed him so deep. I could feel the bone all the way down, from his eye to his chin. I had skin and blood caked up my nail—I—he would have killed me. Then I saw his face all bloody and with makeup smeared all over and his wig hanging off and he was crazy-eyed, completely wild, and I just ran and locked myself in the bedroom...I was so frightened....

(She cries quietly now, her mouth open, idly brushing at tears and mucus with her fingers. I hand her a Kleenex.)

...Ah was always so pretty—it's always been very important to me to be pretty. I'm not pretty now. I'll never be pretty now...I have nowhere to go and I—I just can't be alone...I'm so frightened of being alone.

(She stops crying and blows her nose. She seems to be getting drunker—by herself. She laughs—bitter, wheezing laughter.)

I'm sorry, but it really is so funny, and I've never been able to talk about it before. You should see him. I mean he is the biggest stick-legged ugly woman you ever saw...ha...and he clumps around with those huge hairy feet—clump, clump—and he wants to go to Sweden and have a sex change. But of course we don't have enough money to pay for it....Poor duck...he expects me to feel sorry about that—clump, clump...and by day there he is going to work in his three-piece suit and his pipe. Sometimes, oh God, you don't know how bad I want to jump up in a restaurant or at a party—when we're being so loving and refined and cuddly and he calls me "pig" and I call him "poo"—couldn't you vomit?—and I get drunk a bit and I want to jump up and scream out his secret: RUDY BAINES IS A CLOSET-QUEEN-IMPOTENT-SCHIZOPHRENIC-DRUNKEN-TRANSVESTITE WORM! Clump, clump, clump. But he is really a very gooooood cook, I must give him that....

(She is silent, lost in secret corners, and again the tears come tearing out of her past.)

I have no place to go—he—I can't stay there anymore but I can't be alone. I'm so frightened. Oh please...he will murder me, he will...

(She stops. The hard mad center of the soft blue eyes returns—taking ration—I feel her moving away from drink into something deeper; paranoid breakings or...?)

He killed my baby girl, you know. He did. And you see what he wants, don't you...he wants me dead. You do see that. Don't you...you do understand that. He wants to be me. And I have to die for that. Only one of us can be me. One of us will have to die.

(It is time now for me to trade roles. She tries to stand up and falls on the floor. A blue and white deflated cloud of pain. I straddle her, pulling her up by the shoulders, thinking of what-did-you-do-today-dear vignettes....She slops against me, half-conscious, giggling in Deep Southern huskiness. I am thinking that she has probably not been made love to in years. I am wondering about their sex trip, what happens...I am aching to ask. I sidestep her—in silent-movie rhythm—to the couch. I pour coffee into her. I do not give her a tranquilizer or any medication. I know when she leaves she will drink, maybe for days. I ask her who I can call, where she wants to go—she has done as much as she can do. I play the odds—training telling me she will not harm herself... just pulled the ol' child's trump card to get the stage—she has performed well. She insists on going home. Unwise, for a potential murder victim. I weigh it, accepting certain responsibilities I do not wish to accept (why-me why-me)...I call a taxi and give her address. I close up—pouring myself at last a good stiff drink. I go home. It is 6 a.m. I think about her all day. She does not call. Two days later she does:)

> Hello, is this Dr. Freedman?

> Yes, it is.

> Oh, Doctor. This is Lolly Baines. Ah hope Ah'm not disturbing you. Ah just had to call and apologize to you for mah shocking behavior the other night. Ah had just lost a close friend...

(They seem to go like flies around her.)

> ...and Ah was just crazy drunk...and Ah do apologize. You were so kind and dear...and anyway Ah'm fine now and Ah won't be needing to see you again. Just forget anything Ah said. It was just whiskey talk.

> Okay, Lolly, but if you change your mind please feel free to call me.

> Oh, thank you, Doctor—you are very dear.

(I feel betrayed. I was ready to throw my glen plaid coat before her bony white feet—fragile, demented lady of the night. A case to reckon with. Not a why-me. But she slipped back into costume. Picked up DuBois in the third act. Sealed her fate. And we both knew it. No dummy, this one. The fear got her. For I also knew, and she knew that I knew—knew—knew that she had told the stone-straight truth...and gone back to toe dance in the quicksand. Scared herself to death... ranting and panting toward her terror and—joke—her total aloneness. Goddamn cop-out damsel—never ever get to lay my glen plaid down.)

6

So now you know a bit about my work. Maybe even enough to despise me. Or pity me. Maybe not. I am lighting another joint. I will pause now for a deep long drag...and another. I want to be absolutely cooled out to perform the task at hand. The introduction of the main player in this one-sided little dramatique. The victim. The deceased. My own rotted masterpiece. My Rose. My Rose Liebschitz.

Ms. Liebschitz: It is not a human name. It is the name of a thing. People who are worth dealing with do not have names like Rose Liebschitz. John Dean, John Chancellor, Barbara Walters. Holden Caulfield, Wernher von Braun, Paul Newman, Neil Armstrong, Doris Day. Rosie Liebschitz is not a name bestowed by anyone on anyone destined to be seriously considered by the elitists (in which group I have normally claimed membership). Christian tradition had much too much class to give out such slop as a calling card. Jesus Liebschitz never came.

I am taking a very deep hit...Let us trip on, my Rose...

Frozen in 1947 like a bug in ice, this creature; wandering through the seventies in black-penciled eyebrows and orange-netted curls. A small rounded woman. Wearing a turquoise blouse with ruffles down the front. Tiny waist. Cinched with gold elastic. Short skirt. Matching turquoise seamed stockings...Springalator shoes...small white breasts peering through the coyly unbuttoned ruffles. Lacquered bangs pressed against their will into the creases of her forehead. Brightly rouged.

Give her your drink order and send her back into the darkness: Rosie the Riveter. Betty Grable poster in the barracks washroom. Pushing at fifty from the downhill side. Sucking on invisible candy drops. Baby doll revisited. Lolita—a lot later. An atrophied child-woman cut down mid-flight, fallen in the middle of a rhumba—slaughtered on her way to the USO—frozen alive in '47.

She must have been a beauty—was still, behind the insanity of her self-image, a good-looking woman. Cream-skinned. Sexy, squirmy-fuck-loving body. A dumb cunt. A giggler. A compulsive "truth" teller. Vain...silly...selfish...sleazy...guileless...delusive...Fairy princess in her own cobwebbed fantasy. Ignorant. Compulsive. Common. My Queen.

I did not tape my first encounter (perversely romantic phrasing—oh, lovely weed-high) with Rose. I'm not exactly sure why. I think I probably thought, here is the consummate why-me—and I've got enough of those. I do remember my state of mind that fateful day.

I am pausing here for a very long drag. Beautiful "teenage" thrill...a middle-aged pseudosmart cock with my thinning hairs trailing down on my gold-chained neck, Gucci-loafered feet jauntily crossed on my Swedish-modern desk—turning on, but staying scrupulously clear of hip talk, never a "man" or "all right" pushing forth from my mustachioed lip. Not like all those other thirty-nine-year-old Machiacs (coined that myself on a coke trip). Machiacs: middle-aging boy-men trying to flee truth, jogging and arteries clogging—denim leisure suits—Porsches—divorces—eighteen-year-old blondes with tight pre-baby cunts. Asshole city. See them—shuffling around rock concerts: "heavy sounds, man," "right on, brother"—middle-class mama's boys playing Black Dude, playing Hip Man—playing loose—cool and enlightened. The backbone of every EST seminar: "clear my space, man," "I'm in a good place, baby"—BULLSHIT, I shout, held back from joining my brothers by self-consciousness and fear. No eighteen-year-old hole for Arthur. Arthur is a good boy. Arthur will get old gracefully. No caftans for Arthurla. I am wandering in the same grass.

Oh, I remember. I was talking about weed being a silly, dishonest experience for middle-aged people. Yes, it is. We—they (I am the exception)—are not acculturated for mind tripping...CONTROL YOURSELF, OTHERWISE YOU'LL SINK...They look silly, sloppy, not lazy-eyed and sensual like the strong young hairy heads with tilted-up mouths and fuck-me eyes. We just look red-rimmed and slack-lipped. And worse—we never got to be like those big sexy mothers, even when we were young. That sort of style wasn't in then. We got to be durky little overachieving bastards: polishing our Chevys like they were silver pricks and "studying." Planning for "the future." Jerking off 'cause all the good girls were home planning for *their* futures, saving themselves for THE DOCTOR-THE LAWYER-THE PROFESSOR. No one of them wanted an Elton John—no one really even wanted Johnnie Ray or Frank Sinatra—not "that" way; not groupie gangbang I'll-do-anything-for-a-high—that seventies way. No way. Hadn't been invented yet.

So there we were: I—were, heh, polishing away—get that fucker to shine—polishing and jerking off and trying to play baseball well enough to get a letter sweater—shiny car and letter sweater oughta get ya a handful of tit sometime—and studying for college...Good Boys. Never got to go to school in my crotch-crushing jeans and a sleeveless tee shirt with a pair of parted lips painted on it and a beard and hair (that I had then) in a ponytail (love it!)....*Oh hi, Mom, new look—all the guys are doing it*....Jesus, what a picture in 1953...what a thought. Anyway, we never got to be *that* kind of young. And now here are all the Machiacs trying to make up for it. And that is sad. They come in here thinking they're neurotic because it is not happening, and I either take their money and listen to myself or I don't. But I have never told them the truth—too close and too painful. They aren't crazy—they're just dying. Heavy trip, "like blows me away, man"...ha...okay...I am not getting where I need to go with this grass high. So I am cutting a lovely little piece of cocaine with my trusty razor blade, putting it on my shaving mirror, chopping liver....Now we take the finely chopped white powder and place it in the little spoon. Raise spoon to right nostril, inhale deeply and repeat. Sit back and feel great. Feel absolutely fantastic. Relaxed and energetic. Optimistic *and* insightful. Passionate and serene. The drug of contradictory emotions: The I-can-do-anything-feel-it-all-because-life-is-loverly...better than speed...no really deep comedown...floats you along and lets you down easy. Reality comes back softly...sort of sneaks up on you...no speed thud. I would turn on all my patients if I had the money. "Here, take a hit of this and go home...forget that sibling shit..."

Okay, Rosie-baby:

I did not tape her that first day but I remember everything: I was sitting at my desk waiting for her, my next new patient to arrive. I was feeling terrible. My parents had just died—and I was glad—and scared to death about that. I looked around and I was free. I had survived. But they were gone. Too early and badly. Burned to death in their brand new Cadillac. Crash—smash.

God had heard me after all....*Excuse me, sir, I really didn't want you to hear that—couldn't you reconsider? Do you have to be so goddamn efficient about granting a little kid's wishes? I also, if you remember, asked for a pair of roller skates—along with wishing my parents dead. Could have given me the roller skates instead*...BUT I WAS SO GLAD they were gone.

I sat in my office absorbed in guilt-forgetting all the years of brain-picking, all the sage advice, all the healing of guilt-splattered minds. Fuck that—He did hear me—I did do it. I killed them, and now something terrible is going to happen to ME—I must pay! Now calm down,

Doctor—ha! I was slipping into a huge pit of panic—the ol' panic-pit syndrome. I remember taking a tranquilizer—I remember thinking: they are gone; I should release the guilt and rage. But I am still here and she (my wife) and he (my son) are still here and I can't stand them either—will He hear that too? How many car crashes can I get away with? And my work ...can He get me out of here? Can He? Old Himwho in the sky—O answer to our prayers—Goddess of we'll see, spark of life—old Himwho—can he get me out of all of it—let me run in the fields with flowers in my wispy hair?.... What will I have to pay for that? What?... Anyway, that is where I was...wallowing.

The tranquilizer calmed me. The secret door buzzer sounded. My new patient sat waiting, leafing through *Psychology Today*. I stood up and walked to the door.

Yes, Miss Liebschitz. I'm Dr. Freedman. Won't you come in?

(She stood up teasingly and smiled. I thought, she's going to giggle. She followed me into my office. I felt smug. Superior. Tranquilized into strength. I motioned for her to sit anywhere, guessing she would sit on the couch. She did. I snickered to myself. As I said, I did not tape our first encounter. But with the help of my fine white powder I will reconstruct my impressions.)

She did not so much sit as grind herself into the couch, carefully crossing her too short, somewhat thick-ankled aqua legs at the calf. Like a congressman's wife. She folded her small, surprisingly soft-looking hands in her lap. But her ass kept resettling, grinding around on my seven-footer like it was a great big tufted prick. She sighed. And then she patted her orange bangs and reached inside her ruffles to fix her bra strap. Nervous, I thought. Sleazy and nervous.

I felt suddenly a thrusting blast of contempt. I noted this rather strange over-reaction. I asked her some routine questions and got unsatisfactory answers. She was having stomach problems (how original). Her doctor could find nothing physically wrong so he suggested she see a psychiatrist. But she wasn't crazy. (I felt reassured...ha.) We went on something like this:

Your full name is Rose Liebschitz?

(She squirmed.) *Well, not really. I mean I don't use that name socially. Socially I use Randi Laine. Laine was my married name but then I went back to my maiden name when we divorced. But then later I started using it again, so I guess either name is okay.*

Fine. Have you been recently divorced?

(Giggle.) *Oh no. I was just married for a year. A long time ago. You probably wouldn't believe how old I am. Anyway, I only lived with him a year, and then he wanted to have kids, and I told him my figure is my best feature—I won the Most Perfect Back YWCA contest—and I didn't want any babies ruining my body. So we fought about it, and I went back home to live with Mama and Papa. And I lived with them until they died—which was two years ago.*

(I make mental notes charting correlations between her stomach gurgles and the above information. Somewhere, however, I am thinking: she is too dumb to be neurotic. Though of course I know this is ridiculous. I smell her perfume. Too sweet. A floral. I am, however, not bored. Here before me is this over-fifty kewpie doll: a grown woman who has never met the world yet seems totally and simply connected into it somehow. Too naive to pretend. No consciousness raised enough to invent a more acceptable reason for not having children than I didn't want my body bothered, baby. Not at all defensive about living with Mommy and Daddy until they moved off to the Great Bagel in the Sky. Flirting with me. Totally oblivious to my thinly veiled sneer. Prattling on:)

Oh, maybe you should know: I have insomnia. I take sleeping pills. I've always had it. But it doesn't bother me so much now. I read the National Enquirer and drink hot cocoa, and usually with my pills I can fall asleep by four or five, and then I put on my sleepy mask and so the light doesn't bother me. And I sleep till two most days. Need my beauty sleep ... (Panting ... giggle.) ... but now with this stomach trouble, sometimes I have to keep getting up and going potty ...

(She blushes. I am amazed and still not bored.)

... so I've been real tired lately. I even missed my hair appointments last week, and I haven't done that in ten years ....

(She repeats her routine: hair is patted—bra strap is snapped—ass wiggles deeper into my cushion. I am not doing anything I should do. I let her prattle on. I study her. She actually runs her tongue over her teeth like Marilyn Monroe in that poster number. She is posed for effect—totally contrived to turn a man on. Her body is good. Not fashionable, but basically the kind of body we beasts like. Round thighs. Sturdy, easily spread legs. Titties rather than breasts. Small waist and hips. Nice, slightly too fat ass. Squirmy. That word keeps coming back. White skin. Clean cunt, this one. Talcum powder and sachet pockets in her lingerie drawer. High, girlish voice. Blushy, teasy smile. A moving, breathing dirty joke, this one. I have never talked to one like her. I sit transfixed.

> I guess I should tell you about myself. I'm a Scorpio. You know what they say about us....

(Lewd half-smile—tongue moistens lips.)

> ...my parents were Russian immigrants. I'm Jewish....

(Naoooo!)

> ...I have a brother and two sisters—had—one of my sisters died of cancer. I could have saved her. I sent her every single clipping from the National Enquirer on cancer resarch—all the drugs they use in Mexico and everything—and my other sister, Louise, who is sort of psychic—she was going to try to heal her. We did get lots of vibrations...if she had gone to Mexico or Rumania she would still be alive....

(She sighs—her tits move tight against her blouse.)

> ...Anyway, my brother Morley is very, very religious. Very Orthodox. So were Mama and Papa. They lived to be eighty-six. Papa adored Mama. She didn't leave the house for thirty years. She had arthritis and she got senile. Someone said she was a hysteric. I don't really know about that. But Mama just sort of gave up. She was a very beautiful woman in her day. A seamstress—a dressmaker really. She sewed for the Rockefellers and the Carnegies. Papa was a grocer with a mustache—and when he came from Russia he went to New York to look up my mother. Someone in Russia gave him her name, and he fell madly in love with her. She didn't like him at all. She said, "You are fat and you sell groceries and you have a mustache and I hate all those things and besides I don't want to get married and have children—I want to be free." Anyway, Papa would not give up. He followed her for years. He lost forty pounds and shaved off his mustache and sold the grocery store. And then Mama got sick, and he had worn her down. So finally she married him. And he moved her to Alabama. But then he got fat again and grew another mustache and bought another grocery store. We grew up living in back of pickle barrels and dried fruit. Anyway, Mama had us four and then something happened and she just stopped going out. She was always beautiful though. I have her skin. Even at eighty-six not a wrinkle on her face. I took care of them. After Mama died Papa really had no-

thing to live for. They left me their house. Well, actually it's not a house, it's a small apartment building. I live in one. My sister lives next door. And there are two apartments upstairs. It's a lot of work. But at least I can support myself. I can't work. I'm too nervous. I was a manicurist, for the studios. Met all kinds of handsome guys. I love big curly-haired men. Young ones—no one believes how old I am. They all think I'm thirty. They wanted to put me in the movies a couple of times. Here—I brought some pictures of myself. These were taken by a boyfriend I had, a photographer. He wanted to marry me. He was gorgeous—beautiful build.

(I am in a rage, a short balding man's rage. How dare this nitwit—this sleazy whorey old bitch—pass over someone as wonderful as myself in favor of curls and bulk? How dare she think she has the right to choose?...Thirty, huh...I could level you right this minute, bitch. She hands me a manila folder with stacks of yellowed photographs. She is nude, except for some sort of taffeta cloth draped around her privates. She is lying on her side in front of a plastic replica of a Grecian pillar... kissing the pillar...lying perpendicular to the pillar. The guy got off with the pillar. Then there are photos of her in a black slip with, again, that tongue dangling between her overpainted lips. Photos of her doing some form of ballroom dancing—wearing a costume that looks like something from Carmen Miranda's garage sale. Photos of her French kissing some slimo with center-parted slicked-back hair and a pencil mustache.)

That's Frederic Chateau—he was an actor and a dancer and a bullfighter. He was the best dipper. I love to dance. We won hundreds of contests. He did a perfect tango and he could dip all the way to the floor and up again without missing one beat.

(She went on. I heard what she had for breakfast. How many poopoos a day since her stomach trouble. Her favorite kind of ice cream (peppermint with chocolate sauce—for the biographers). My god, I have total recall. I am my own Sony portable. Wooowoo woo, what a little cocaine can doowoowoo....Okay, I have recalled enough of her. Let's talk about what happened to *me* that day:)

As I said, I was not bored. That fact being exceptional in itself. So here I was, hanging onto the edges of professionalism by a pulled thread. Full of guilt and manufactured tranquility. Me in my role and this "girlie" bumping around on my couch talking about the Big Dipper. I do not recall much more of what she said then because of this extraordinary thing that happened to me.

I was sitting looking—leafing, actually—through this plethora of yellowed egoism, these Pillar Pictures of Rosie baby, and suddenly with total free will my cock pushed forth into absolutely the hardest, horniest, most convulsive erotic erection I had ever had. She babbled on. I sat behind my desk (mercy me)—my face set into its familiar mask of bovine cynicism. My right hand idly holding a Pillar Pic. My left hand resting casually on the arm of my leather swivel. My legs comfortably crossed. And my prick poised like some fucking Polaris missile threatening to blow me out of my chair (or at least out of my French gabardine slacks).

I was unnerved. My mind flashed on a what-if fantasy: what if this sort of thing started happening to me all the time—a victim of my prick blasting out during lectures, group sessions, dinner parties? I'd never be able to go anywhere, have to give up my practice. I wafted off in panic waves for several moments. And stayed hard, harder, hardest. No shit. Then I surrendered to it. Because it was agonizingly beautiful. And new. And strange. Rosie went on. I heard bits and pieces. Once I looked up and my eyes fixed on her round dimpled knees...and this feeling—this tearing nearly consumed me. With only a trace of self-pity I will tell you that keeping my hands off myself required the spiritual strength of a Buddhist priest (and that is just word of mouth).

> *Am I doing all right? I really don't know what I'm supposed to say. But my stomach feels a lot better. Do you want me to tell you about my childhood?...I read that's what causes all our problems. I was a beautiful child. Long blond curls down my back. I have a perfect back. Oh, I told you that. Anyway, I got ringworm, and Mama had to shave all my hair off, and I was so upset I wouldn't leave the house till it grew back. But it grew back red. Not this color...*

(She pats orange curls for the two hundred thirtieth time.)

> *...I touch up now—but a beautiful red-blond. People used to stop me on the street to look at my hair.*

She went on. I sat consumed with passion demons. Mercifully time passed. The hour was up. I had not ripped open my chic little fly and raped the Riveter. I, however, did not rise to see her out. This one knew about things like that. We made another appointment. She unscrewed herself from my couch, leaving a deep cheek-shaped dent in the cushion, and swung her middle-age ass out the door.

I remember sitting very quietly for several moments. Not fighting the incredible power of my need. I got harder. The pain was luscious. I sat still, straining toward the periphery of my control. Savoring every second of this long-ago Chevy-shiny sensation. And then I rose, unsteadily, and walked to the couch. And I sat right down in that deep, warm, buttocks-dented place—a little brown corduroy volcano. I inhaled sweet cheap perfume—buzzing through my brain.

My wall light flashed. A patient waited. Wait, patient. Have patience. This moment was not to be hurried...or wasted. It might have to last me another twenty years. I rose and undid my pants. As they dropped my cock soared, so big and blood-filled I did not recognize it: my dream organ. And I kneeled on the floor in all my panting, hurting pleasure and put my nose into the corduroy volcano hunting for pussy smells, head spinning in jasmine scents and heat, and I came. Oh god-Jesus-shit. I came. Egg-cream slather. Palsied explosion. Polaris speeds. Boom. A pure, a true sex spasm. Toe-curling. Mind-blowing. I came. The Chevy was gleaming, positively gleaming. Egg cream on thick pile. On brown cushions. On my resurrected prick. I lay still. My nose still pressed in the hole. Breathing in higher bursts of air. Whish. Wowee.

The phone rang. And that patient waiting. I rose. Cleaned myself, my floor, my sofa. Cleaned me off everything. Splashed cologne. Reentered my trousers. Combed my hairs. And last: hardest. Undented that fucking beautiful cushion. And moved to the door, with calculated but transparent indifference (oh yes—sorry to keep you waiting—tied up long-distance, please come on in, heh-heh) and my famous slight smile, contrived little supercilious half-grin—worked on in internship, perfected in residency before hundreds of hospital john mirrors. Hmmmmm...not really a lie though. I had been long-distance...off the wire...off the walls...outer space...out of control. Led by my sex, out of mind, and into a tunnel of ecstasy.

7

I am very hungry. I will put the microphone as close to the fridge as possible, but I most likely will sound somewhat muffled and distorted on playback. However, we all sound that way so much of the time I doubt whether it will bother the listener.

I think—salami...and herring...some cocktail rye...a little mustard. And a beer. And a diet soda for dessert. And, let's see, too early for the Oreos—let's do a Twinkie number. Got the plate. Cloth napkin, plastic knife and fork (dichotomy). Okay. Ready. It is now 10:23 a.m.

Now while I eat I think it's time to tell you a little about my personal life. Sort of a tension reliever before I return to Prick's Progress and all. It is probably terribly symbolic that I choose to tell you about my marriage while I am stuffing my face with herring and Twinkies. If you care about such things. I don't. Never did. Made Freudian therapy impossible for me. Made me want to grab certain patients by the throat and scream things like "IF YOUR AUNT FANNY WAS YOUR UNCLE HARRY YOU'D BE YOUR COUSIN MARTHA, YOU WHINING LITTLE CREEP!" Things like that. All of that motivation bullshit.

"I was dreaming that I was swimming in the ocean and a huge, horrifying wave rose before me, and I tried to stay on top of it but I couldn't and I was drowning, and when I woke up I was sure that that wave was my mother and I needed her protection. But I was unable to reach her—she would overpower me and I would be lost." They would explain: "Or then again—the wave could be part of my rage at my father and I am trying to control it because it can destroy me and as a child I was so frightened that it would—or then again..." I would sit: wanting to grab the Drowner by his waterlogged neck and shriek, "MAYBE YOU JUST ATE TOO MUCH PASTRAMI LAST NIGHT—MAYBE THE FACT

THAT YOU LIVE ON A BOAT HAS SOMETHING TO DO WITH IT, YOU JIVE TURKEY MOTHERFUCKING PEANUT HOLE!"

Anyway, I never did that. I suffered through. And specialized in the "new therapies." Emotional catharsis. And that was vicarious since I did not have any emotions left. And some of the time it was fun.

It was really interesting, for example, to have some really uptight broad, some primarily constipated lady, mince her way in here. Walking like she carried her car keys between her legs. And the face all puss-lipped and tense. And have her sit down and start her blah-blah-blah: "And then Doctor Vander Quack said that he felt I had reached the essence of my conflict and released my neurotic dependency needs and that possibly I might now benefit from a more emotional therapeutic experience. However, I am so in touch now I don't feel that is really indicated. I would, however, like to talk to you about my husband, who seems to have a rather deep-rooted conflict between his adult and child ego states—and blah-de-blah-blah-blah...," and I would let her go on for awhile. This one particular time I finally interrupted and suggested that she pretend that one of my wife's macrame pillows was her husband. I placed it on the floor in front of her tight little toes: "Oh-ho-ho, how ridiculous—I couldn't possibly talk to a pillow. I am a civilized graduate of psychoanalysis and blah-de-do..."

I gently suggested, admitting how above all this she was and everything, and how silly it was, that she just try. And within seconds her right leg shot out and flew that fucker like an NFL place-kicker. Leg shooting up so high I saw crotch hairs and the pillow hit my Tiffany lamp and nearly broke my pre-Columbian bud vase. Emotional field goal. Right between the posts, baby. All the way through the garbage gurgles to the truth. Kicked his fucking brains out. Those moments I liked.

Ah, a little snack does wonders. The beer is cold, the Twinkies are fresh. What more? Okay. My wife. My life:

I got married when I was in my last year of medical school. For the following reasons: I did not want to be distracted from my singular and consuming ambition and professional commitments by the need to go to the dry cleaners, shop for groceries, pay bills, work at a second job or chase pussy. I found a nice girl for that role. She was willing to work, run errands, tidy up and—more reluctantly, but spurred on by fantasies of being a Doctor's Wife—let me screw her without energy or passion but at least with not much resistance. So, as I threw myself totally into my work, I did not have to distract myself hardly at all with any of those life details. Period.

Of course we did not say that. We said, "We are in love." The perfect couple. She was attractive in that skinny, nose-bobbed Jewish

Princess style so touted in current fiction. She was selfish and superficial but harmless. Not venal. And lowmo way. She loved especially that I was a good catch, a good investment. She would have money and position and a Mexican maid and manicures and facials and a Mercedes and a fur coat and join a private backgammon club. And never come. Which was, of course, mostly my fault. But frankly I never cared enough to go through the hours of preop that would be necessary to bring her off. Maybe if I had tried, things would have been...there's that Aunt Fanny shit again. Anyway, neither of us did. She, when coerced—or if I had bestowed some especially nice bauble or bit of news on her—would consent to give me head. (Approaching the task, however, as if I had asked her to swallow flies.)

And then I graduated. And began my internship. From then on I was not home much. I began slipping into linen supply rooms with nurses. Me and the rest of the world. (God, what a derivative bore my life was.) She "conceived" (her word). Son born. And for the first five years of his life I was a white-coated flash swooping by his bed at odd hours. Later he told me that until he was seven years old he thought I was a ghost. I didn't tell him he was right.

The only other thing to add to this little "nosh" talk is a brief statement about football: There were then, and of course are now, Sundays when I am home and cannot legitimately (even sociopaths have their guilts) find a reason to absent myself. So, there is football. Its place in my life is incalculable. I sit. For hours, hypnotized. Nibbling continuously. Drinking beer or Campari and soda. Watching those beautiful fucking mountain men beat ass. I never think about it. Never, never analyze it. I just sit there. Being "with my family" (ha). A mindless blob in torn tennis shirts, unshaven and smelling of perspiration. I grant my presence. Holding court from my leather chair. Two feet away from my Raiders, my Rams, my Steelers, my Dolphins. Knees twist. Men fall. Tempers flare. Referees rule. Coaches pace. Crowds turn ugly. Or ecstatic. And they run and catch and pass and fall down and jump up and are cunning and quick and in love with themselves and in love with each other, and they hate the offense, and they play dirty. Spikes in the back, cleats in the head—human rocks mashing together, falling like frenzied lovers, holding each other. I sit. Oblivious to my wife's requests. Heedless of my son's questions (needless to say, he does not like football).

On Sunday the set went out. Blank and void. I stood before it in my football ensemble. Beer in hand. And prayed to it. I felt tears well in my head. And I was very frightened. Sunday could not be lived through without it. I felt that I was losing control. What will I do here with them, without football? A scream was caught somewhere in my throat. I needed my fix. My football hit. I left the house. Bought another set at a Sunday mart. I knew then, though I denied it, that I was an obsessive personality. I did not realize, however, that football was just the beginning.

One more slug of diet soda, and we will resume....

8

It is now 11 a.m. I am lighting a cigar. And I think, perhaps a touch of cognac...so...

There I was. I wandered through the rest of that fateful day like a home-movie Frankenstein. Unnerved. Numbed. Disconnected. I went home smelling like stale sperm. Paranoid flashes. They know. Everybody knows. Someone saw me come all over myself on my office floor. And told everybody in the whole city.

From years of practice, however, I was able to perform with my usual feigned involvement—and by bedtime I felt reassured that no one had noticed anything funny. I did not, however, sleep that night. I did not think about my poor incinerated parents, either. I though about Liebshitz: "What in the hell was that all about, Doctor?" I racked. I pondered. Nothing cleared. And I could not stop thinking about the way it had felt. Kneeling on that carpet fucking the air. And of course every time I thought about it my cock began to swell and pulse. Like a boy.

I left for the office very early the next morning. Made busywork. Checked my calendar. She would be back the following day. I pretended to throw off this information. I kidded no one. I wanted that cunt back on that couch—I wanted to find out what had happened to me.

I saw patients all day. Went to the hospital and made rounds. Met my wife and some friends for dinner. Came home. Watched the news. Told my wife (on the remote chance that she should want to fool around) that I was very tired. And lay there again all night, my cock going up and down like a big pink yo-yo. But I did not touch myself. I was enjoying the frustration.

I left again very early. Made phone calls. Went through my schedule. Hit golf balls into my putting cup. Read *Time* magazine. Kidded myself. My first patient arrived. I have no recollection of who it was or anything at all that they said. I was not even tuning it in. Patient left. Heart pounded. Light on. She was out there again.

She was wearing a blond wig cut like a duck's ass. Thick nylon eyelashes and purple eyeshadow. Brown tight polyester slacks and high-heeled black suede wedgies. A wide yellow belt squeezing her waist so tight her belly popped out below, and a beige fuzzy sweater with puffed sleeves. She swung her ass—fatter in her pants and a little looser—past me and settled herself primly on the cushion. She looked pale and vulnerable. Different. Scared. We began:

> Doctor, I have really not been feeling well at all. I missed my dance Saturday night. My tummy was too upset. I have insurance from Mama and Papa. I think maybe I should see you more often. I did feel better after we talked.

I reassured her that money was not important—that we could work something out. And then I crossed the invisible line. I told her that I though it important to dig out some of her early sexual fantasies (giggle—she did giggle and open her mouth and lick her teeth and snap her strap and pound her ass into the cushion). I asked if she minded being hypnotized and she said, "Oh no, my sister Louise does that to me all the time. I like it."

Goody-good-good.

I then, zombielike, asked her to lie down, take off her shoes (bare, slightly calloused, very white feet, rose and yellow bottoms) and relax. She went under like folded cream. Still squirming her ass around. I sat for a minute, just watching her wiggle and breathe. And it happened again. My prick rose. Stiff as steel. All right, Rose, my dear, tell me about your first sexual memory.... I will play part of that tape now:

> Aw, this is making me blush. Nobody ever asked me about those kinds of things before. Let me see. Well, I remember being in the grocery store—in the back room. The storeroom. I guess I was about three—oh, couldn't be—that kind of feeling doesn't start till much later. Well, anyway, I remember being in the back of the store and some old Mexican man was back there. I was getting him some canned fruit—oh, I remember, I was older, much older. Oh, I don't know if this is the first dirty memory. Is it okay if it's not the first?

Yes, yes... it doesn't matter. Just relax and tell me about it.

(I have unbuttoned my pants under my desk. My breathing, as you hear on the original tape, is deep and fast.)

> Okay, I was probably ten or eleven. Yes, must have been, because I was wearing that red dress of Louise's—she had developed too much and Mama gave it to me...oh, this is embarrassing...

Don't be scared. I'm right here, and it's going to help you feel better.

(I have now broken every code of ethics in my profession.)

> Okay, I'll try. Well, I stood up on this stepladder to reach the canned fruit and this old Mexican man took his finger and put it up inside my panties—you know, into my female place. And he was breathing real hard—and—oh, this is so awful. I knew I should stop him and call Papa but I didn't. I let him do that. He took his whole hand and was feeling me all over and up my belly and I was scared—but you know, I just like that—I like it. My nipples got all excited and—I hardly even had any titties then and I got all—you know—what happens...

Yes, but it's important that you tell me in your own words.

(My hand was stroking my cock so fast I could barely form my words—I was ready. Oh, baby, I am ready—tell me now.)

> Well, I got all slippery and then—it felt so good—I moved one of my legs up another step and pushed myself down on his whole hand and I just went crazy—like...I was a little girl. But I remember pushing on his hand and shaking myself around all over that dirty old hand and spreading my legs out and juice was dripping all down my thighs and I was making noises in my mouth and then I pressed down as hard as I could. It felt like his whole hand was all the way up to my belly and I— you know...

I know, but you must tell me yourself....

> Oh, I orgasmed. I kept grunting and pushing myself against him; seemed like forever. And his hand was all soaked with juices and blood. I was a young girl—a virgin—and I jumped down and ran out. Oh, I was so ashamed. I threw up for days.

(I am at this point in a state of suspended animation. I am not sane; I am ravished.)

> Tell me how it felt. Just once more, and then I'll let you sleep for a few moments.

> *Aw, that's hard. Well, you know, I mean you're a man even though you're a doctor. It felt nice. I couldn't even stop my body from moving around. I would have done anything he asked—anything—and when I, uh...*
>
> Say the words.
>
> *When I orgasmed all over his hand I just kept doing it. I didn't really know what it was. But my whole body was jerking and I was making terrible noises—and I could have hurt myself but I just kept pushing his hand harder and...*

I took my prick in both hands and pumped myself off. I came on her words. I splashed off like soft snow. I came like a woman, the juice and my hands making me ooze out and spasm again. And I did it all without moving a muscle or making a sound.

> *Oh, please, is that enough for now? I feel all funny. It's embarrassing.*
>
> Yes. You are going to close your eyes and sleep now. And when I tell you, you will wake up and feel very close to that experience. And very good about being here with me.

(She smiled. Her wig shifting on her head. And began to snore, in a sort of muffled ladylike way. I reached for my water pitcher and Kleenex. And repaired my sated prick. And woke her up. Scheduled her next appointment for the following day.)

9

I am opening a beer. To chase the brandy. And a touch more magic powder. I have rolled a ten-dollar bill into a suction tube and placed it in my left nostril—and the coke flies. I need it more now. I am tired.

So. She left. And I left. Put a note on my door telling my patients that I had been called away unexpectedly. Most expensive jerkoff of my life. Forfeit five hours at your ever popular fifty dollars per... I left. I went to a porno film. Something about a girl fucking a pig. The pig wanted a relationship, but she just wanted to get laid. (Coke joke.) I drove around. Took myself to a fancy restaurant for lunch. (sweetbreads, braised endive, a full bottle of Mouton Cadet '74, a tarte citron and espresso.) I went to the gym and sat in the sauna until my sweat ran wine-colored. And then I went home. And through all of this, for the first time I could remember, I did not think about anything. I was totally relaxed.

My wife's name, by the way, is Judy (ten points if you guessed)... we were invited that night to a dinner party. Good, I thought. The party was at the home of a colleague. A replica couple. A Xerox printout. Arthur and Judy and Frank and Ruth. We were all the same age, educational level. Wives had the same nose job. House had the same layout. One more wood floor and oriental rug—one more fern in a basket; one more couscous recipe. One more tennis story. Okay. You get the idea.

Well, this particular night: there were four "couples." Four salts and four peppers. Four sugars and creamers. Except, little did any of us know, one was a ringer. Arthur had his werewolf suit carefully hidden between his legs. But I did not know that quite yet. I knew that I felt special. Alive. Child-flushed. And unbearably superior. Even for me. We sat on the black leather "playpen" and drank decanted Burgundy.

And ate appropriately runny Brie. And chatted. The wives talked to the wives about diets and consciousness raising. The husbands talked to the husbands about cars and the bond market. Staying scrupulously clear of shoptalk (doctors cannot bear not being the only doctor in the room, and there were two of us so we had to watch the bullshit—and *two* lawyers; needless to say, the competitive catty/petty/bitchy territory that is really much more naturally the habitat of the male was palpable). Fact being, we put that number on the Ladies as a way of smoke screening their superiority and power over us. If they fight each other for Us they won't have time to see what a weak pinky-pricked bunch of why-me's make up the rest of the world. And it worked like a charm for round about five thousand years. Screw you, Betty Friedan. Started the proverbial ball roll—and did they! And are they!

Had a patient once, very passive-aggressive sort who told me that sometimes he had fantasies of swatting women's pussies with a great big flyswatter. You nasty things—make us all crazy trying to get into that dirty hairy little slit. Take that.

The women come in here—like my wife and Frank's wife and the other two cookie cutters yakking away—worrying and whining about their haircuts and their "saddlebags" and their stretch marks—like we were some sort of perfect sex gods all. So terrified of not being young enough, good enough, pretty enough, and basically we don't want you to be any of those things "enough"—and we really just want that little slot; never, never thought about her manicure when my cock perked. Spending all that time and money trying to look like the cover of *Cosmopolitan*—and drying up—wet and plain wins it every time, babies—and we know that; and for some reason we never tell them. Just keep swatting those invisible flies. And looking for the snapping slit. The wet and plain of our puberty—who keeps growing up and getting chic and stale.

Must be our fault. Responsibility should be publicly accepted by what is left of the functioning heterosexual community.

So. Where was I? See, I told you. The coke loosens the tongue. Oh. We conducted ourselves in the acceptable dinner-party-among-the-upper-middle-class manner. I drank quite a bit of decant. Everyone kept their cheeks clenched. We went in to dinner, where for some peculiar and tedious reason the following discussion began. (I will not identify the speakers since they are all the same, anyway. But the women started.)

"I think at the rate women are getting their consciousness raised that it's going to be harder and harder to find a man who can relate to us. We really should all be lesbians because we are leaving the men so far behind. Women have the guts and compassion and strength. Look how we're growing, and the men aren't changing at all...."

(Someone changes the subject slightly.)

"Does that idea turn women on—making it with another woman?..."

"Does making it with another man turn men on?..."

(Impasse—subject shifts again slightly.)

"Does the idea of watching two women make love turn women on?..."

"Yes. I have always thought that women making love to one another is very erotic. Does it turn men on?..."

"Yes. I guess all men have fantasies about watching two women make it...."

(The lawyers are blah-de-doing; the shrinks are holding dimes between their cheeks vertically.)

"What about watching two men do it? Does that turn women on?..."

"No. Not at all. Does it turn men on?..."

"No. Not at all..." (Finally we agree on something.) "...we don't want to WATCH men doing it—we want to BE DOING IT...Just let me put it in your ass...just for a minute, baby. 'No, it hurts,' the Sassoon-cuts scream. But HE'D LET ME. Mythical God..."

So. There we were. Eating Mongolian lamb or some such affluent Jewish peasant food. And getting a little piss-eyed. And having this retarded discourse on turn-ons. When we all knew that not one of us had really come THAT way in years. Or ever. Frustration and steamed rice. Sex and saki.

And suddenly my mind connected. And I surveyed this gathering of my peers. And I remembered Rose. And from the bottom of my little toes moving up my calves and into the marrow of my spineless spine I felt this enormous smile squeezing out of me, like a perfect shit watering my eyes, tingling my back, and I knew: I was no longer one of THEM. I had slipped through the knotted noose. Removed my head before the ax fell. Changed. I had a secret. A new dimension. A hobby, if you will. My dime fell to the floor. I sat...smiles exploding inside me. Escaped. Broke out with a pea pod clenched in my wolf teeth. I surveyed the scene. I had found something. A room of my own. Where I could lock the door. And play. Any game I wanted to. Free. I could be anything there. I could be a bad doctor and a bad boy. I could come in a fucking coffee cup if I wanted to. I could do anything. I had found a human Barbie doll to release my rage on. To do anything with. I knew that (I am now convinced) the moment I saw her. I could do anything I wanted to. And live in my lust, wallow in my sadism. And stop having to live as though I were not an animal. And not be judged. No one would know. She would never tell.

I had disappeared. Before the mandarin oranges. Munching on an almond cookie in my Marcel Breuer ripoff chair. Listening to my comrades...this smile squeezing...throbbing against my skin inside out. I knew what I was doing and embraced all of it. In the present—"put it in the present and tell me about it"—my own little riot in Cellblock 39—munch-munch—I made my getaway.

10

I am *not* Arnold Palmer (or Napoleon). Which of course will be a tremendous relief to sports fans. And immediately followed by your typical who-the-fuck-cares retort.

Well, I care. AND YOUR AUNT FANNY'S UNDERPANTS. (It is only fair to tell you that I snuck in another hit of big C—and the time is now 11:32 a.m.) Cared. All neurotics have bases of comparison. Mine was Arnie. The sportswriters told us (fifties on) that he was about perfect. Always kind—open—made eye contact with the gallery; shook hands, never introverted, never smug, never arrogant; strong, friendly, powerful, a winner, loved by fans and peers alike; good businessman, millionaire, humble, broad-shouldered, charismatic, fine fellow, loving husband and father; flew own plane, still going strong today (seventies) at forty-seven. And with his own army, "Arnie's Army" seventy-year old ladies with Coppertone bandy-legs sticking out of the grass-assed golf shoes; luscious young tour groupies; old pros from Utah—even when he ties for fucking fifteenth place in the Tennessee Ernie Open. They come. Loyal; drawn by his decent, open, all-American magnetism. Hasn't won a tournament in seven years; one hundred fifteenth on the tour. Still draws the biggest gallery. Ex-presidents invite him for dinner. No paunch. No scandal. Even owns a string of dry cleaning establishments. And smiles; and that eye contact with strangers, with creatures that talk during a thirty-thousand-dollar putt. Smiles. At them. He was one of my self-torturers. Made me feel shitty about my wonderful self. Gave up golf because of him. Tennis was safer. Because all the players were such obvious psychopaths that I was in no danger of exposure. Infantile maniacs! I would mutter to myself. Please, Himwho, keep Arnie out of tennis.

I am also not: Steve McQueen/Robert Redford/Paul Newman. Not tall, not blond, not brave. Dune buggies/motorcycles/race cars terrify me beyond reason. And besides fear, it takes me too long every morning to make it look like I still have my original portion of hair to have it all blown apart, leaving me open to ridicule by Bob/Paul/Stevie. "Huh—thought he was a MAN—but he's just a Cue Ball Coward—huh."

And I'm not Martin Luther King (naoooo!)/Bobby Kennedy/Ralph Nader or Adlai Stevenson.

I am not, again: Harry Reasoner / William Buckley / Norman Mailer / Ansel Adams / John Ford / Andrei Gromyko / Walt Disney / Vince Lombardi / Jack Benny / Fred Astaire / Harry Truman (it gets easier as more of the people on my lists die off)....

What is my point?

After all, in a society where nobody cares who you *are*, who is going to give a flying fuck about who you are not? Except for my fantasy of walking around an APA convention cocktail party introducing myself to all my fellow dime squeezers: "Hi there, I am not Martin Luther King, and this is my wife—who is not Ali McGraw....OOh hello there, you're Doctor Hutz Futz from Bellevue, wasn't it...yes, and I am still not John Wayne....

It is not (to digress on my digression) sexist either—I am also not: Golda Meir/Margaret Mead/Racquel Welch (yes, men too, ducky)/Anne Armstrong/Eleanor Roosevelt/Germaine Greer/Carla Hill/Pearl Bailey (that one still hurts)/Dinah Shore/Billie Jean King or Mary Leakey or Ethel Kennedy.

What I am (and this will all come clear shortly, I promise—knowing that I break promises)...what I have *been* is a Doctor.

Doctor, doctor, doctor...say it loud and you feel like singing. Say it soft and there's music ringing. DOCTOR...doctorrr.

It saved my insecure unathletic little ass. I had something more important than the world's acclaim. I had pleased Mommy. And they—THEY them—wished they could be what I was. Paul would trade one of his piercing blues to be what I was...a doctor. Instant awe. Hushed pause. Respect. Women fall. He's a ddd oooo cccc tttt oooo rrrr.

And since people are chronically crazy and only occasionally sick, being a Head Doctor was even more impressive. Power. I had real power. Ask any hostess. Ask any patient. Ask anyone. But Rose.

Ha! I kept a promise. The point being, Rose was not impressed. Rose was too cunt-brained to be impressed by that. I mean impressed with me as a Man, by that. She was becoming more and more dependent on me as a Doctor-Parent-Judge, but I needed her to be vulnerable to me as a MAN. And that way she was not the least bit impressed. Joe Namath ten years ago. That impressed the constipated crap out of her.

I have skipped around, left you out again. I am feeling some hostility toward you, whoever you are Okay:

After that night with the salts and peppers I dived: I saw Rosie three more times. And basically the same scenario unfolded. I hypnotized her—got her to tell me what was becoming a fucking cornucopia of "dirty memories," to quote the lady—and I whacked off in unbelievable gut-thromping ecstasy *and* I began to want more dimension. My taste whetted, my surrender acknowledged. God had not smitten me. So I wanted more. But I needed complete control over my damsel. And I didn't have it. Because the shriveled little bitch did not dig me THAT WAY. Something had to be done. And I could make her pay for judging me (yes, Werner, I let her) and rejecting me and reminding me of who I was not, later.

First I had to enslave her. Bend what little mind she had to my whims. The ol' prison camp number. A little Blue Cheer in the Brain. I had to move slowly. And carefully. Because she could still leave. And I did not want to even think about that. It has ceased to be a negotiable possibility for me. So first I had to make her stomach worse. (I had, by the way, diagnosed her "problem" a slightly spastic colon and a touch of your regular Why-me colitis. Dumb prick internist—he could have had her himself.) I spent the next Saturday afternoon at the library brushing up my pharmacology. And I found a perfect little prescription that would upset her stomach. And nothing else. I wrote out a diet guaranteed to put her on the bowl at least three times a night. Her sleep

Then I would suggest, oh, something simple. A little seventy-two-hour marathon. I would brain-clean her. And she would be mine.

11

I am having Oreo fantasies. Before lunch. You are hearing crackling, tearing sounds as I open the cellophane. I may as well digress a bit further...it will give me time to separate all my cookies. Then I will play the tape of my next session with Rose—show you how brilliantly I proceeded with my Plan. And I can eat my wafers—lick them clean, melt the cookies in my mouth in peace.

So...let me tell you about my book.

I have for some time been jotting down notes for my epic work, *Sex Without Intimacy*. Based entirely on personal experience. I have, you see, come close to perfecting it—intimacy being the American male's most feared situation.

One afternoon I reached the precipice, with a secretary from the free clinic where I—for tax purposes—donated several hours of my precious time to treating pubescent drug addicts and religious fanatics looking for Himwho in everything from brewer's yeast to sodomy. Monomaniacs of the first order.

Anyway, there was a secretary there. A twentyish ACLU type. Wet and plain. And (shudder) warm. Pretty and smart. I neutralized this overpowering threat to my snug little life-style by looking for flaws. I found: her thighs were too big, and her ass I presumed would be full of those little fat-creases. And she knew nothing about Modern Art, and her bottom teeth were crooked. Not much, but I could use it in a pinch. Enough for me to risk fucking her without fear of INTIMACY. I worked on her for weeks. And the time came. One rainy Thursday afternoon.

I had just finished a particularly unpleasant session with a pimple-chinned "Moonie" who had had a paranoid break and thought that the North Korean Army was coming to get him. (Maybe they were.) She was impressed at my calm amidst his screaming hysterical humanity. I played on that. We went to a motel where her overwide thighs and ass crinkles excited rather than neutralized me, and I knew that it was remotely possible that by accident I had chosen a real whole woman. And I was in jeopardy. I knew that any form of kissing/hugging/snuggling or conversation would be unadvisable.

Probably because she was somewhat in awe—Doctor, Doctor—I was able to manipulate her into the following sex routine: She gave me head. Then I asked her to sit up on my very stiff prick. She sat, thighs and thick black-tufted slit open and wet, purple-nipple tits bouncing around; and she fucked me off. I made excuses about my schedule and got out of there. Fast. I had done it. I had completed the sexual act without ever touching the woman. Not a pat. Not a word. God forbid a kiss. I had done it.

Later I began to think that since I had met that hurdle and survived I was qualified to instruct others in the art. Thus my book.

Kissing, by the way, is always the most deadly. Lips are so personal. So tactile. So private. Touching someone's lips or their tongue—*that* is intimacy. *That* is the first to go. I will devote at least three chapters to how you avoid kissing THEM. I plan to sell it mail-order. So no one will be publicly forced to admit they are interested. And we can go on talking about relationships and loving and touching and being open and vulnerable and all that pop psycho bleeding-heart blah-de-do—while learning how to avoid that seething hot pool, that perennial threat to our LIFE PLAN known as intimacy. Or love. Or passion or whatever.

Other chapters will cover:

HOW TO CHOOSE SAFE PARTNERS. Avoid those with wit or a sparkle in their eye or Self-Esteem. Self-Esteem is a no-no- for *sex without intimacy*. Women with Self-Esteem, that is—this, as you may have guessed, is exclusively for men. Women are veritable piranhas of intimacy. Craving it as much as we are terrified by it. Maybe it has something to do with menstruation—having blood pour out of your body every month. Must be scary as shit. How much more vulnerable can you be than sitting at a dinner party in a white dress and have this gush of red ooze out of you? Must build strength; character; an ability to cope with basic realities. Blood comes out of them. Kids come out of them. Tears gush out of them. Loss. Loss. Must make it easier.

They giggle. Scream. All out there. Ick. Strange creatures. Must help them with intimacy, though. Because they are usually good at it. Takes strength. (I have never met a weak woman, in case you are interested. Dumb, ignorant, neurotic, frightened, anxious, whining, hypocritical, superficial, greedy—all of those things—but never weak, not really. They always survive. Make do. Pioneer. But I'd never tell them that. That's in the book too—don't ever tell them anything good about themselves. Very treacherous.)

Oh, so... Self-Esteem: Unh-uh... they see through you. They sit up in bed just before your onanistic number and say things like "You cold unfeeling son of a bitch, you lousy lay, I'm a person, not a thing. Go whang off in the bathroom if that's all you can give." Stay away from them.

CHOOSE WOMEN WITH WHOM YOU HAVE NOTHING IN COMMON. Always a plus. Cocktail waitresses are good if you are an intellectual type. The greater the communication gap, the less chance of accidental intimacy. Teenage hitchhikers who chew gum are also good. Stay away from "peers." Or women who make you feel guilty. Nice Jewish girls are deadly for nice Jewish boys. Find a Catholic receptionist who still wears miniskirts. Safer. Much. So for me, for example, a dumb gum-chewing nineteen-year-old Polish typist with an inferiority complex would be ideal.

(I would also at some point like to start a computer *Sex Without Intimacy* Dating Service, cross-indexed to expand the scope of the written material.)

THE CALL GIRL. Of course this is the logical choice. I had a patient once, a fifty-five-year-old German jewelry salesman who had never married and never slept with a woman who interested him. He would wine them, dine them, pet with them. Send them home. And pick up his little book in the middle of the night and phone Rent-a-Broad or whatever. A girl would arrive, let herself in, suck him off and leave. Most of the time he would never even turn on the light or see her face.

The problem with this for middle-class overachieving insecure egotists like myself is that we would not be able to leave it at that. The fantasy would be: the Hooker, after hours of violent lovemaking, throws herself at our tufted little toes and says "I can't take your money, I should pay you! I've been with a thousand men and never, never had I felt anything till tonight. You are a miracle. Here, let *me* pay *you* for what you have given me."

You see the problem. However, for less egotistic but affluent sorts, this can be the perfect solution.

NEVER LET THEM SEE YOUR FLYSWATTER. Always be on top. "Ho-hum, another piece of pussy, yawn." The perfect posture is that you are doing them a favor. To deign to stick your golden rod into their ordinary tedious little hole. Such a favor that anything they can do for you that's special would be to their benefit. And never call them by name. Absolutely never. More intimate than neck rubbing or forehead kissing. Do not *ever* say their name when fucking. "Honey" or "oh baby" are okay. Fine really—but no names. I have so perfected this that I never even call my wife by name. And not just in bed. I have not said her name—can hardly say it now (Juuudddyyy)—in ten years. Call her "dear," "sweets" or some other pet slop. Never say her name.

SUCKING PUSSY is good also . Because you are totally in control and they are totally vulnerable. I mean, what could be more naked than having your legs spread with some Machiac gaping at your hairy little slot? Which is a work of nature but not necessarily of art. And getting hot. Thrashing around with someone's tongue in your privates. We are doing it to them. And that is one thing that they cannot do to themselves. No matter how many yoga classes they take. That is good. If you like that sort of thing. I often don't.

Well, you get the picture. My cookies are laid out in two long black and white parallel strips on my desk. A truly beautiful sight. So I will now resume.

12

Moving right along...I will now play my Baiting the Trap tape. Which takes us back to my smile. So there I was. I had investigated. I had a plan. And I was nervous. I needed all my manipulative skills, all my professional and personal technique to prime her. I had given her the prescription and the diet. She had not questioned me about them. It had been two unbearable days since I had seen her. And I was climbing my symbolic foreskin. The light went on. She was there.

She looked pale. Her left eyebrow was penciled in higher than her right one. Her orange bangs hung limp and overlacquered on her furrowed brow. She was pouting. Like a Betsy Wetsy doll. That was exactly what she looked like, I thought. Even to her pink puffy-sleeved blouse. A giant old Betsy Wetsy doll. Lips all rouged and poked out.

She wiggled in, less confident, and sat in HER cushion. My Oreos are waiting, so here is what followed:

How are you today, Rose? Is it all right if I call you Rose?

Oh, yes. Or better, call me Randi. That's what most men know me as.

All right, un, Randi. How's your stomach?

Terrible, Doctor. I've been taking the medicine and following that diet but I just keep getting worse. I was up all night. This morning I could just see lines in my face and I don't have any wrinkles; I have my mother's skin. I just don't know what to do. Maybe all that sex talk is bad for me.

No, no. You see, Ro—Randi, the therapeutic process is slow. It took years to develop these tensions and it takes time to relieve them. Therapy is not a straight line. Obviously, your conflicts are more deep-rooted than I first imagined. I have an idea, however, something very new, that I've had tremendous success with. I had one patient with exactly your symptoms, and after two weekends with this new treatment she was completely asymptomatic.

What does "asymptomatic" mean?

Symptom-free. Pain-free. You see, your stomach problems are caused by inner conflicts. Sexual repression of some sort. And we need to open up that hornet's nest, so to speak, and relieve the pressure. Now, what I propose is an entire weekend here in the office. We will not leave and we will try to get to the core of your conflicts. But it is essential that you trust me, believe that I am your friend. Because if you don't, if you resist, if you do not put yourself completely into my hands and follow my instructions without questions, it will not work. And I don't want to scare you, Ro—andi,—but if we do not get to the bottom of this, this stomach trouble could become very dangerous.

Oh, gosh! I don't want to hear that. That scares me. I told you, I'm very nervous. I can't stand any bad things. And my skin...I'm getting wrinkles and I'm losing weight. My breasts are one of my best features, even at my age, which you probably wouldn't believe how old I am—and they're starting to get puckered. I don't want to get worse!

Just relax, dear. You are not going to get worse. I am going to do everything I can to cure you. If you trust me, it will work. And ridding yourself of the tension will make you feel and look sixteen again. But to me you look as fresh and young as a teenager even now.

(I interrupt in the middle of a bite to note that this first personal reference has maximum effect. She blushed and ground her ass, patted her hair at her neck, looked surprised. I had scored. Inroad for Arthurla as MAN.)

Oh, you're just saying that to make me feel better, Dr. Freedman.

No, no. Not at all. You are a very beautiful and desirable woman. But of course many men have told you that. So, now...if you're willing we can get started on this right away. How about this weekend? I will make some changes in my schedule. I care very much about you. And I can help you.

Oh, well, I have my dance Saturday night. And the movie in my neighborhood—well, I go every Sunday—that's when the picture changes. I've never missed one. If I miss one, then you see, the next week it throws my schedule off...but, well, I guess—I mean this is more important. How long will I be here?

From Friday evening until Monday morning.

Oh, goodness, I can't do that! I couldn't wash my hair or do my facial—and my newspapers! I'd have all those newspapers piled up. Oh, I couldn't do that. I'd have lines from not sleeping and everything. I just couldn't.

Ro-andi. Do you want to die?

What? Oh gosh, no! My parents lived to eighty-six.

Then trust me. I have a bathroom, a bed, whatever you need right here. I even have peppermint ice cream. Don't be frightened. I wouldn't do anything to harm you. I am not only your doctor, I am your friend.

Where is the bathroom?

Right in the middle of that wall. The wall opens. I even have a tub.

Really?

Really.

Well then. I guess it's all right. Do you have a hair dryer?

Yes. A blow dryer.

No hood?

No, but it is perfectly adequate.

All right. I'll pack a suitcase. Does it get cold here at night?

Never. The room is climate-controlled.

Well, all right. What time?

Be here Friday evening at six.

Could we make it seven. I don't want to miss the six-o'clock news.

Seven it is. And keep taking the medicine. Even if it doesn't seem to help. And this weekend I will give you new medication that will relax you completely.

Okay. I will, Doctor.

Now there's my Ro-andi. That's my pretty little girl.

Oh, Dr. Freedman. You are so nice. Not like most men.

I'm so glad you feel that way. As I said, it is very important that you trust me.

I do, Doctor.

Good. Good-bye till Friday.

And that is how it crumbled, Oreowise. I am at this moment hoping that a group of very dedicated, very serious psychiatrists is going to be my audience—the sound of you falling off your leather chairs fills me with garrulous glee. I pride myself on that bit of work...should have been a used-car salesman. Do you have a hair dryer?...with a hood?...no?...Oh, guess I'll just have to die then! Unbelieveable. A wonder she was. One of a kind.

So, I was set. Countdown started. She left. And I, despite the idiocy and the tension of holding the line with Thumb Brain, was hard as holy hell. Probably because the commitment had been made, the ethics so totally smashed. I felt that I could experiment more fully, practice up for the weekend with my newfound amorality. And this is what I did:

I made an obscene phone call. To a former patient, an actress. A nymphomaniac who had been whizzing in and out of sanitariums like an NHL puck. I put a towel over the phone receiver, thoughtfully securing it with a rubber band so that my hands would be free, and called her number. She answered the phone. Breathless, sleep-postured voice. I said (knowing her soft spot):

"I want to eat your pussy."

And she moaned. And said, "Wait a minute, let me pick this up in the bedroom." (Animal crackers—a world full of animal crackers.) I held on, taking my pants completely off and bringing (very quickly, I might add) Rose's cushion over to my desk.

The phone reopened. "Tell me," she said. "I'm naked and I have my beautiful thighs all spread apart. Tell me, baby."

I told her the following:

"I am taking your cunt and your ass in my hands and tearing them open. Your clitoris is oozing it's so hot—it is dying for me to put my mouth on it. But I don't. I dig my hands deeper into your cheeks and spread you open. I take my teeth and put them around your nipple and suck till you scream and your cunt is bursting... Tell me what you want and I won't give it to you until you say the magic word."

She is crazy, moaning and grunting into the phone. "I want you to bite my clitoris—bite me—break me open—make me come and come and come; make me crazy... suck all my juice out of me, take it all... take all of it... now... now!"

I put the cushion over my erection and came with it. And hung up the phone. She didn't say the magic word. And I did not even feel guilty. She never comes anyway. That's the definition of a true I'll-pick-it up-in-the-bedroom—nympho—never gets it off. Besides, this way I could call her again and she would remember me—well.

My life was getting much more interesting.

13

I have just taken a Percodan. Percodan, if the listener is not of the "faith," is a pain-killer (apt). It is one of those drugs so lifting, so emotionally enthralling, so life-enhancing that many people look forward to being ill just so they can take some. And it makes your head light up with ideas. It makes you love yourself. Love. Love. Love. Love. You. You love your work, your life. Your family. The world. Mind spins. Ideas soar: "I will write a book, I will go to Uganda and save political prisoners. I will learn Russian." Everything seems possible. And easy...effortless...beautiful.

But it wears off every four hours and then the pain returns. It has something to do with "prices," if you're into that EST bullshit. Anyway, I have taken one. I feel all of that and am high enough to rattle off pieces of experience—gathered during my last seventeen years of watching strange things happening to people—that somehow contributed to my being here today.

Did you know that:

1. People die of rage. Within twenty-four hours if it cannot be stopped. One night during my internship a man was brought into emergency. "Brought in" is hardly the word—he was dragged by two orderlies who could easily play defensive end for the Vikings. In a straitjacket. He had been injected with a hundred milligrams of Thorazine—enough to put King Kong down for a winter's nap. And he was not contained. His face was a blood-hot mask of fury. His body twitched around in its canvas prison like popping corn. We interns stood over him, amazed and helpless. What could we do? Any more medication would be dangerous. And the screaming: long, piercing, gut-tightening howls. "Gag him!" some medical genius said. I was not very knowledgeable about this sort of thing. But instinct told me that if we sealed his last hole, muffled his only available emotional exit, he

would explode. We argued this point. I lost. To the senior resident, who made his pontifical appearance. "If we do not quiet him his body will not be able to stand the strain of the rage," he said. I said, "But people need to release their anger. If we stop him it could be just as dangerous." He said (smiling condescendingly), "This kind of rage is not normal. It does not run its course. The body turns on itself, anger coming possibly from a lifetime of repression—possibly from a form of schizophrenia—but if we cannot control it he will die."

While we discussed this, the man's body began to buckle—tense—like some contorted oarsman. The howling became deep animal grunting. His eyes rolled up in his head and shot down side to side and up and down. We were very nervous. Scared too. What we really wanted was for him to disappear. All of us projecting our own rage, seeing the possibilities. Finally—beyond being doctors—we were human. So the gag won. I will never forget the eyes of that poor sucker when we put that tape over his mouth. Like a horror movie when they bury the bad guy alive.

In the middle of the night he quieted. Somewhere near morning he started again but the gag stopped us from hearing. And before we were called, the power of his rage snapped him. He was dead. At twenty-five. On the death certificate it said: reason for death—uncontrollable rage. And people worry about being hit by a truck.

2. On the light side: you, listener, if you are not a group of my "peers," may find the following inside glimpse of a major American hospital interesting.

Being an intern is not one of life's better experiences. Here you have come, made it through college, fighting and competing and filled with bottomless performance anxiety, and then medical school—more of the same. For almost thirteen years of my life I never had a full night's sleep or a digested meal (why-me, why-me). Anyway, after medical school they give you your little M.D. pin and you take the Hypocritic Oaf and—cocky and snotty as any overachiever whoever drew breath—you put on your Doctor Whosis badge and your white coat and appear at whatever hospital has condescended to accept your indenture.

And you are right back at the bottom of the pickle vat. Even the coats rate you. Interns wear short white tunics. First-year residents wear white coats and ties. Senior residents wear long white coats. This is not a law, but the thought of an intern prancing around the corridors in a long white coat would send shivers of disbelief up the spine.

So you are low man on the medical-military-industrial stethoscope. You spend months opening invisible doors and hitting blasts of Santana Ego. Or hot air. Or, as my dear friend from the Panhandle—Doctor Eugene Dix (who had a paranoid break during his last year of residency and became a patient on his very own ward)—used to say, "So much bullshit the cows are ducking."

As interns, our particular personality disorder came from chronic cases of overdiagnosis. No one had a gas pain. It was a malignant duodenal ulcer. A headache was certainly a massive hemorrhage in the upper right quadrant of the cerebral cortex. Every mole was melanoma. Every silence was precatatonic schizophrenia. A cigar was never a cigar. So we had that—and also this great puff of finally being a doctor. And having no one at the hospital to impress, being freshmen all over again, we flaunted it at everyone else. Sometimes I wore my white jacket out to dinner. Not just sometimes. All the time. I would begin every phone conversation with "This is *"Doctor"* Arthur Freedman"—even when I was making social calls. And I wasn't kidding either. Anyway, that was that. But the staff. That was something else.

The chief of staff of my unit, Doctor Ed Merleman, was a paranoid schizophrenic. He ran the unit like the *Caine* before the Mutiny. Crazy people in the beds, crazy people standing over the beds. And bureaucrats filling all the cracks. Twenty-eight requisition forms to get Junket instead of Jello. You get the picture. Fight-fright-fight. And never enough time to really help. And this madman running it all.

Every year when the senior residents leave, they have a party, sort of a Dean Martin Roast of the staff. And we came up with this sophomorically riotous quiz show. The grand prize would be two weeks of therapy with Ed Merleman. Second prize would be *three* weeks of therapy with Ed Merleman.

You get the idea...everyone fell down...except Merleman. We were called into his office the night of the party and told (you could hear the steel balls rolling in his fat little fingers) that if we went through with this subversive, malicious plan to discredit him, we would not be allowed to leave the hospital with our release papers. And he is still there. And he is not, may I reassure you, the only one.

3. Back to the patients: There was Bones. Bones was a seven-foot Negro who weighed ninety-seven pounds and walked around the inpatient psychiatric unit eighteen hours a day, grinding his teeth in such a way that it made it sound like his joints were rusty—like the Tin Man—when he walked. Bones would not eat because he thought people were trying to poison him. Otherwise he was a most pleasant fellow. We used to practice—Dix especially—trying to learn how to squeak like that, but no one ever could.

4. In emergency I saw people stroll in with switchblade knives sticking out their backs. I admitted a twenty-two-year-old fashon model who, in a frenzy of self-hate triggered by terror of not being beautiful and rage at believing in all the delusive, twisted recesses of her propagandized

psyche that if she wasn't perfect no one would ever love her, had broken a plate glass window and mutilated herself with shards of glass. Slashed open her face to an oozing, unrepairable monstrosity.

5. I had an old Mexican schizophrenic respond to my perfectly civilized question of how she felt she was being cared for by dropping two very large, foul-smelling turds right on my loafers. All in a day's work.

6. I had a forty-five-year-old cocktail waitress who wanted me to show her how to be a lesbian because she was a nymphomaniac but didn't trust men. I thought about opening a clinic for all the women who hate men. Show them how to suck pussy (rub a clit perfectly, pick up girls—after all, we sure as hell know more about that sort of thing than women do). And vice versa.

7. And of course the suicide attempts. Once some asshole in Medical called up and said "Freedman, we have an unsuccessful suicide over here," as if there would be any point in my looking at a successful one.

8. Suicide: every conceivable way to pull the plug. Swallow the rubber ducky...anything. Drink bleach. Set yourself on fire. Wash a bottle of Scotch down with forty reds...heroin...razor slashes...shoot yourself in the tum-tum. Drive car over cliff. Give self-abortion—with knitting needles or butcher knives. Jump off roof. Or the cry-for-help attempt: take three aspirins and call everyone you know. Those kinds make me impatient. Hate all that manipulative bullshit. I mean, you get some baby that swallowed oven cleaner — she means it. Dear old suicide. When Kesey's book came out, people thought, "Oh, what symbolism, what poetry." Poetry—shit. It's all real. And if the patients ever sat in on one of the therapists' group sessions—the idea intrigues.

And my friend Dix. The only real male friend I ever had. The McMurphy of the other side. Cared too much, about the sick people. And the insanity of the bureaucrats. And the Merlemans. I saw his caring drive him mad...he was sort of my Kennedy figure. I used to talk to him. I had this marriage, and this baby. And I had not committed to any of that. Could not feel what they wanted me to. Everything went into my work. Wanting to be the most omniscient fucking shrink the world had ever seen. And Dix soothed me. Shared his overview. And then it got too much for him. He started trying to save the whole miserable frothing mass—daily. Worked twenty-four hours a day. Trying to plug up the whole leaking dike with his own hands—control the flood, save the marine life, clean out the closets, plan the menus—and he moved out of my reach.

One night he tried to kill Merleman with a restraining cord. Wrapped it around his neck—screaming, "If I can stop you, I can save everyone." I saw it. And I decided that caring like that was too risky. So I just turned that off. And graduated top of my class, in Doctor Dix's place.

Even the Percodan isn't making this cheerful. Anyway, I have to take a pee—and I will bring the microphone as close to the toilet as possible. I will, if nothing else, be the first psychiatrist to pee into a cassette recorder. But not, I hope, the last.

14

So far I have done booze and sweets. And toked, sniffed and popped. And I am feeling *very* straight. Too straight for my next discourse. Our first "Weekend Together." I think perhaps another snort to keep the Perc working...now where was I... Oh, yes.

I remember that Friday vividly. It was Valentine's Day (apt). And the day Sam the Swan died.

I had cleared my schedule. Made family arrangements. I had, after all, done many marathons before, just not on a one-to-one basis. So that part was easy. I could have been handling a truckload of Gestalt Groupies for all my wife knew. Or cared. Anyway, I had brought in supplies. Which I will describe in a moment. But first a word about Sam.

Swans (on the remote chance that you, brilliant audience that you will be, do not know already) often die of broken hearts. You see, they are not only beautiful (and dangerous) but loyal, totally monogamous creatures who mate for life and cut themselves off from their peers. No bridge parties, swan switching or the like. They live with and for their mates.

Well, that Friday I was sitting at my desk (naooo!) leafing through the paper, waiting for time to pass, and I saw a tiny little Reuters item from London about Sam the Swan. And being a swan buff, I clipped it.

Seems that Sam's old lady was beaten to death in Hyde Park the day after Christmas. Well, the other swans turn off to that kind of number —lest it remind them of what may lie in store. So Sam was left, true to his lady love's memory and without the company of his kind. No bird nookey. No tossing a few with the boys after a hard day's gliding. Nothing. And he pined away. People tried to feed him. He would have none of it. Finally they took him away to a swan convalescent hospital where he died shortly after. And hopefully is now floating around with what's her name in Ol' Himwho's animal division.

Well, I disliked that story a lot. I thought, Sam, Sam, you pansy-assed turkey turd—none of them are worth a heart hole. Didn't anyone ever wise you up about women? No odds in it, Sam. Should have talked to me. Just went ahead and committed to the bitch. Lost your friends, pride, everything. Let her really get to you. Dealt yourself out. For what? A nice neck and a few feathers? What a waste. I, smug rug well vacuumed and centered beneath me, awaiting my "fly," felt vastly superior. Totally in control.

(I am putting on some music, so if my voice sounds faraway don't worry. I am not passing out or anything like that. The Junk is agreeing with me completely. Ah, Itzach Perlman, my crippled beauty. A little Dying Swan fiddle music, if you please. There.)

Okay. I pondered Sam's fate. Feeling unbelievably strong and energized. Excited really. Charged. The scene was set. I had carefully researched the project and decided on the following plan of action:

Rose was, you see, a hysteric. One of legions of aging baby-women. Her most palpable fear was of getting old and ugly. Seeing her perfect YWCA back bend. So, if I programmed her to believe that she would remain young and beautiful (remain—ha) with me—that I was the stud who could do that for her—I could capture her. Work on her fear of being old and wrinkled and unloved—and then convince her that I could keep her young and lushy. How?

Like this—class.

First, I would tranquilize her to lower inhibitions and anxiety. Then I would hypnotize her and suggest this aging idea. I would also tell her that she would not be able to sleep or eat or use the bathroom without my permission. And then, in this highly suggestible exhausted state, I would give her a little purple juice—a small vial of the always useful, most maligned mind-bender, lysergic A. (Shit, it worked for Mr. Manson—had a whole fucking harem doing anything he said, from slicing open pregnant starlets to buggery and the like).

Perfect. And then later maybe I would tell her she had imagined it all. Doctor Freedman had never put one carefully manicured forefinger on her. All in the mind. Fantásy. And that would really scare her. Sooo—more treatment. More stomach. Good props. Maybe I could even move her in—take another office down the hall...(the possibilities were endless). Pimp her out to my colleagues:

"Got a broad in a room you can do anything with."

"Anything?"

"Yeah."

"Really? Anything? Ummm-hmmm. How much?"

"Free. Consider it a professional courtesy."

Nice thought. And I could watch. Strip them all of their dog suits. See the real dehumanized protoplasm behind the carefully constructed facades. The Pervert behind the Publican. The Atheist buried in the Anglican. You get the picture.

And of course I would tape every single one. Maybe I did. You'll have to wait and see, ducks.

So, at last, I was ready.

She was due at seven. At exactly three I left the office to do some shopping. I returned at five-thirty with the following purchases:

A shocking-pink battery-powered vibrator.
A flesh-colored dildo complete with rubber balls.
A black lace garter belt.
Black net stockings with seams.
Red silk bikini pants with a hole for the cunt to stick through.
A red lace bra with holes for the nipples to stick through.
Two gold ankle bracelets.
A black satin sheet (queen-size).
An electric hand vibrator.
A riding crop.
A circus animal whip.
An authentic pair of police handcuffs.
Three spools of heavy twine.
A large jar of petroleum jelly.
A lime green battery-operated vibrator.
A blindfold.
A short very small black skirt.
A pair of white thonged sandals.
Copies of: *Hustler, Oui, Penthouse, Playgirl*; several underground porno sheets with titles like *Suck; The Story of O* and all the Alex Comfort books.
A collection of photographs of fat women doing each other.
A porno film entitled *The Lady Eats a Piece of Baloney.*
An untitled film with three men and three tired-looking teenage girls doing each other on a water bed in someone's garage.
A recording of people coming.
A recording of sado-masochism. Screams and sobs and the like.
A film of a farm boy fucking a sheep. Entitled *Farm Life.*
Twelve vials of amyl nitrate.
A seventy-five-dollar lid of Colombian.
A Thai stick.
A handful of Quaaludes.

Peppermint ice cream (*and* chocolate sauce).
A fifth of very rare Hungarian brandy.
Cold cuts.
Water bagels (two Jews alone on a Sunday morning).
Some magic powder.
A baby-blue battery-operated vibrator.
A hand mirror.
A two-pound jar of unfiltered clover honey.
Fifty dollars' worth of color film for my Polaroid.
And of course my tapes.
A Japanese finger vibrator.
A large bottle of heavyweight mineral oil.
A watermelon.
A wide black leather belt.
A very small low-cut white sweater.
A pair of very high open-toe red leather pumps.
A 45-rpm recording of "Disco Lady."
Same—"Won't You Be My Rocking Chair."
A Robert Goulet album.
A Bartók concerto for strings and percussion.
A 45-rpm recording of "Little Surfer Girl."
A double bag of Laura Scudder's Potato Chips.
A quart bottle of Gallo ruby port.
Three boxes of Scotties.

And...my master stroke: I hired a lesbian prostitute for two hours on Saturday night at fifty dollars per hour. A risk. But I could always pay her off and send her away if things were not working out. I had, I felt, covered all the bases.

By six-fifteen I had everything ready. I took a shower and changed into jeans and a polo shirt. And sat down at my desk to relax for a while.

That was my first mistake. Sitting there in that sepulchral, twilight place. All alone with this scheme. This warped erector set. This period piece of pretense. This windmill tilt. This emotional sand castle. Mordancy posing as Liberty. Delusion posturing as Fantasy. Misanthropy as Knight Errantry. I sat. And this north wind of doubt blew over me. Judgment. Terror. My plank walk into the Dead Sea. All of it. Elements of my princely plan whizzed around in my possessed, feverish mind. Shatterpated. I had not counted on this intrusion from the Other Side of the Coin. And I did not like it at all. This odorous party pooper was not on the guest list. No visit from Tiny Tim tonight, babycake.

I got up and paced. Waves of fear. Warm currents of panic pulling me down. And I: struggling toward a surface of unknown elements. A surface, possibly—probably—more deadly than the sucking, down-drowning feelings tossing me so carelessly about, but the only place to go now. A surface in the night sea. A Swiftian rescue. A siren song. Homeric Island. I pushed against this gate-crasher of reality. Brought in my brain bouncer. And surfaced to find nothing. No chair shadows. No mermaids. No mythic monsters. Just the Good Doctor. With sweat pouring down his face. In the dark. With his light kit. And a glass of brandy in his demented, white-knuckled fist.

I put my wet suit in the closet. Stood on my riptide and surfed it to shore. Fuck you, reality. Suck ass, anxiety. I'm going to have my party. I've waited a long time. Bought the paper hats. Everything. So bug off. Let me go back to where I was an hour ago. Don't tell me not to. I want to. I need to. I have to.

I drank my brandy in a single swallow. Rinsed my mouth with Listerine. Hated it, but used it. Last time I would do that with anything, I promised silently. Smoothed my hairs. And walked to the door.

II

15

I opened the door and casually sauntered out. There she was. Small pink naugahide overnight case on the chair. The late edition of the *National Enquirer* in her hand. A fuzzy nylon wuzzy coat.

And two strangers.

One middle-aged woman stranger who looked rather like a dress extra from the Addams Family. And a huge male stranger in a mix-and-match lime-green polyester leisure suit. I conceal my paralyzing shock.

"Well, hello, Ran-Rose."

"Hello, Dr. Freedman. I'd like you to meet my sister Louise and my brother Morley. They were a little bit worried about me—coming here all alone for a whole weekend—being sick and everything, and they wanted to meet you, too. I've been telling them how smart you are and everything, so they came with me."

(Goody.) "WELL, HOW NICE." (I smile, wondering how I can slide on out the door and run screaming into the night). "Won't you come in? I'll be glad to answer any question."

"Thank you, Doctor." (Green Polyester beams down at me—looking like a hulking middle-aged Moonie. He clasps—yes, clasps—his hands together, and for a moment I think he is going to kneel before me and ask the Lord to forgive another sinner in his smarmy kingdom).

"Doctor, it would be so very, very kind of you—if you would allow Louise and I to speak to you privately for a moment. I have great respect for your profession—all the good you do—comforting the sick, the flocks of God's creatures who cannot find peace, who do not trust the working of the Lord, who have confusion in their heads and their souls—like poor Rose. And I do not know the rules of your work, but Rose is still very much a child, and some things I feel would be better discussed outside of her presence."

I am searching for my dematerializer. Mr. Spock, someone, remove me from this spinning mass.

"Well, if it's all right with Ra-ose. My first responsibility is to my patient. I have no secrets from Rose."

"Oh, it's okay with me, Doctor. You know how I get upset with anything bad—and well, maybe he can help you by telling you things about me—or whatever—but I might be embarrassed. And it would give me time to read my paper. Betty Hutton is on the cover—she's been a drug addict for years and she's trying to make a comeback. I always loved her—I'll just wait here."

"Okay, then, won't you come in?"

Louise sighs loudly. I hate sighing. She is holding a sweaty wrinkled hankie in her very white hands. I hate wrinkled hankies in white hands. She pats her dyed black hair (family habit) and eases her flabby white body into Rose's cushion. Sighing all the while.

The Frog God stands over me (I have beat my retreat and positioned myself behind my desk, fantasizing fighting my way out by dangling a crucifix in front of them or hurling twin pink and blue vibrators at their heart cavities). His eyes fill with glowing watery schizophrenic euphoria. He just stands there. Beaming at me. Louise sighs aggressively. I decide to play. At least until I recover from this zig in my meticulously planned zag.

The Lime-Green Morley stranger leans in toward me until his face is close enough to mine for me to see broken blood vessels on the bridge of his nose and get a blast of perfectly obscene breath. He continues to gleam at me, and for a moment I think that he will unfurl his hooked frog tongue and pop me into his mouth.

"I cannot tell you, Doctor, what an honor this is. You, a man of science, a healer of minds, and myself—a simple man—not educated—a man of the Talmud. A man of faith. Coming together to help one of God's lost souls. My poor sister. Who has sinned. Who has not accepted the Lord. Moses made us his Chosen People—and we were deaf—blind. We betrayed him—we broke not only the commandments from the mountain but the entire book, the hundreds of God's commandments that were spoken to Moses. Rose has broken many of God's commandments. She is guilty of sins of the flesh. I have not been able to help her. She will not enter the temple of her God—God of Israel, God of Abraham, Isaac and Jacob—she will not atone; she blasphemes the Lord. She lusts after her neighbor. She commits sins of the flesh with gentiles. I have no hate in my heart—for any of God's creatures; I simply grieve for my sister—for she is being punished for her sins. Her body is in turmoil. She has broken commandments—and a sickness has entered her body. We must help her; it is our duty to try and save her soul."

God has become a giant hebe schizo with polyester pants and rancid mouth odors—who can see through my closet door—whose watery beady x-ray eyes are surveying my handcuffs and red panties with the cunt slot. I am in a lot of trouble here.

"Oh, Morley, please stop that. You're boring the doctor—and I've got a headache." (Boring?) Saturday night at their house must be neat. Vampira from Five to Seven rises and comes slowly toward me, holding a yellowed newspaper clipping in her hand.

"What sign are you, Doctor? Wait, don't answer. I am feeling energy around you. You are a Scorpio with Sagittarius rising, aren't you?"

"No, I'm an Aries with Pisces rising." (I lie.) And I am now in *deep* trouble—not even that kid in the fucking *Exorcist* had to take on the Voice of the Lord and Jean Dixon at the same time. All I wanted to do was play a little. Just have some good clean S-and-M yoks. Cast a few seeds on the water. Recapture my boyhood passion. A little reality therapy. Can't anyone take a joke? Every man's fantasy. A willing, breathing, moving, passive, dependent, mindless, submissive, horny piece of permanent ass. We don't have androids yet. I'll be your very best friend. I'll trade you a cat's-eye for it. All my Bazooka and a Hershey Almonds. I need this fuck. Oh, God of Meeny, Miney and Mo-Ol' Himwho—come on. Turn the other cheek or something—get these messengers from beyond out of here—I had everything all planned. My surprise party. Shit.

She sighs and stares at me. Actually she is not a bad-looking old broad. Some of the same hula-hula of dear forgotten Rose.

"You have beautiful eyes—your eyes are not Aries—your eyes are the Scorpion. Have you ever been sketched in profile? Have you ever been sculpted in the nude? I do lovely nude soap sculptures. Late at night. After I hypnotize myself. I would like to paint you sometime. You have a wonderful mystic quality about you. I see your face on black velvet— with wild animals leaping around your head. There is a very strong aura coming from you. Have you studied phenomena? Many psychiatrists are turning to it now, you know. Have you read this?"

Bleepy-de-woo-woo—I am lost in here. I am feeling, for the first time in forever, a loss of positioning. I am malleable. I am not in charge. I am not controlling this situation. And that is not permissible. And not possible. And I must do something about it immediately. I receive the yellowed newspaper clipping from her hand. It is one of those panic-wonder stories that hysterics nourish themselves with. One of those CANCER-CURE-FOUND-IN-RUMANIA pieces, this one centered on a tumor-shrinking formula made from Himalayan rat blood or something. I feign interest to buy some time—to regain my balance—to experience this unwelcome new bit of information about my precious self. That I am more anal and compulsive than suits my image. And as flexible as an ice cube.

"I saw a vision of this before that article appeared. I saw the laboratory and the formula being written out on a blackboard. We must get this for Rose; it is her only hope."

"But, Louise—may I call you Louise? Louise, Rose doesn't have cancer. Her stomach problem is psychosomatic. That's why she's here."

Louise is shaking her witch head back and forth so fast specks of dandruff fly out of her hair and hang in space.

"No, no, no. Forgive me, Doctor—it is not your fault—you cannot help what you don't know. Powers that are not yet yours. I see the tumor —in her. Even if all the doctors and their machines do not see it, I know that it is coming—it will be born—and you cannot save her without this medicine—or without phenomena."

The Frog Prince leans in closer—I spot a blackhead on his ear.

"Excuse my sister—she gets carried away. She does not accept the Lord, either. But she seeks spiritual connection. She is not yet lost. You must try to understand us. We are simple people. But we are outsiders to this society. We are not accepted. This is a world of people who have lost God—have lost decency—have turned away from the teachings of the Talmud. A world of adulterers and murderers. Liars and thieves. A world of sinners. Sodomists. Perverts. That is why Rose is sick. God is punishing her. Louise does not understand that."

"I do understand. I see the sickness sooner than you can. I see salvation for her. She is not an old soul. She has many incarnations to serve before she sees—"

"It is God's will. We see only what He reveals to us. It is dangerous to look beyond."

I have had it. I have stabilized enough to be afraid of this little passion play. Here I am, with a cast of characters Edgar Allan Poe would have scratched, and I am seriously dealing with these looneytunes—ON MY OWN TIME...and why? Glad you asked. So that I can do nasty little shameful things to a fifty-year-old floozy? Me? Gary God? Insane. Watch it, Doctor—got to be careful how you throw that word around.

So, okay. I'll worry about that later. Right now in my "Present Moment" (thank you, Dr. Dyer) I want to get these remnants out of here. And I want a crack at Rose. Even if I just fuck her. I don't want to stop, and I don't want to get caught. So what do I do? I say:

"Please, both of you, sit down." (I rise slowly from my desk, first making sure that they are seated—Power Play No. 1.) They are sitting side by side on my brown corduroy—scene of the original sin. I slowly walk toward them—getting into the mood of it.

"Morley?" I say his name questioningly, eyeballing him intensely. "Louise?" I take her sweaty white hand. "You two have been extremely helpful. And now I am going to tell you something that may surprise you.

I know. I am a student of the Talmud, Morley (my man), and I have also experienced phenomena. I have, you know, worked extensively with hypnosis and the healing powers of the mind. I, too, see the tumor that is coming. I can work as a doctor to bring Rose back to God—help her repent and change—before it is too late. But I must work without interruption. You must trust me. I can help Rose, bring her to God. And save her. You needn't be afraid. But you must let her stay with me as long as necessary. You must trust me."

I rise, benevolent and grand, and return to my desk. Louise has her eyes closed; just a hint of saliva grazes her lips—made her come, I would swear it. Toad Tongue lifts his mass of flesh, leaving my beautiful cushions choking for air, and rushes toward me, grinning widely.

"You are a good person. You care about your fellowman. You are wise. Bless you."

I am seriously afraid that he is going to lick me. And for a moment I feel sorry for him. Something chokes up in my throat. I swallow it away. Mrs. Munster floats behind him and shyly touches my arm.

"I saw it in your eyes. I will work with you—I will send vibrations here—I will meditate all weekend. Tell Rose to picture the tumor—let it take a form—and then we can destroy it—together. Working together, we won't need the serum."

The three of us stand in the middle of my office. Sighing and panting. A *Mad Magazine* Trinity. I have won.

And, the moment came. We were alone. I am going to do something here. I am going to sniff a little more C and do some splicing. I want to play; I want to orchestrate this scene carefully—insert my monologue at will. So we are alone. And I offer our beginning:

You have a very nice family.

Oh, thank you. They mean well. We don't agree on things, but they really have good hearts. You know, Louise used to be really gorgeous. She had hundreds of guys after her. But she married a nobody—he had curly hair and she was getting a little older—but he got bald. And she had my nephew—did I tell you I was an aunt? Nobody believes I'm old enough. Anyway that almost killed her. She wasn't built for having kids. She was never the same after that. And her husband, Norman, he works nights and she sleeps all day—so they don't spend much time together. My nephew's real cute—but I've heard that he's kind of funny. He likes to hit girls—tie them up—things like that.

No!

(Maybe he could give me some pointers—I ponder.)

Well, I shouldn't say—I don't really know for sure (tongue over lips—my cock throbs). *I mean he never did it to me.* (Giggle.)

That giggle. The lewdest, sleaziest sound I have ever heard. God bless that giggle.

You know, Dr. Freedman...

Call me Arthur.

(She blushes from her neck to her ears.)

Oh, that sounds so funny. Like you were a regular man. You know.

I am your doctor—but I am also a man. You were saying?

Oh, yeah. Well, I'm real nervous about this. I've never spent a night away from home before. And I'm kind of scared. About what's going to happen, and being all alone with a strange—well, you know—I mean you could do anything—oh—please don't take that personally—you know—it's funny. But, I have been very sick—I had eight poo-poos last night—I couldn't even eat my ice cream, and the pain has been so bad. Morley thinks that it's because God is punishing me for (double blush) *you know, my "dirty memories" and all. I always thought that was silly—I mean I don't hurt anyone or anything—but sometimes I wonder...*

I want you to forget all of that. I am going to give you some new medicine right now that will make you feel better—and then we'll relax a little and talk.

(I prepare a little dose of twenty-milligram Valium and brandy water.)

Here Ro-Randi—shall we be Randi and Artie for tonight?

(I have never been Artie, not even as a mere sprout.) Cascades of giggle-blush hair-pat gurgle-swish. She is beginning to flirt with me (unappealing as I still am to her—huh—should have squeezed in a few tango lessons). She swallows willingly.

Can I unpack now? Slip into something more comfortable? (Pant.) I didn't mean that the way it sounded.

It sounded just delightful.

(Heh-heh-heh—this may be easier than I imagined.) I am loosening up. I have lost all doubt. All fear. I have no reality except this room. No rules except the ones I choose. No observer on my shoulder or in my feverish little head. No map. No guide. No one has ever charted this course before. Sir Francis Drake and the Straits of Magellan.

Please—you can put your things in the bathroom.

She curtsies. Yes. That's what I said. And wiggles into my wall. I hear little squeals of girlish glee. ("Oh, a Water Pik—oh, what a nice tub—what a cute toilet cover.") I pour myself a large Scotch and toot a line. She emerges from the bathroom. Wearing gold slip-ins with Arabian Night toes curling into the air. Inset with rhinestones and pieces of purple and red glass. My eyes force themselves off these incredible shoes and move up over purple and pink and red and green swirls of nylon. It would be called in department-store lingo "At Home Wear"—but they never describe the sort of home. Around the neck—which to my joy zips down the front—are chicken feathers or duster feathers posing as ostrich—dyed in matching shades of the nylon. She has also added a small green velvet bow to her freshly teased orange head. A sight to contend with.

You look lovely, Randi.

(Blushy-blush-blush.)

Thank you. These are all my best colors.

Her lids start to drop. The medicine is working.

I feel real sleepy—but nice. So relaxed. Like when you hypnotize me, only better.

Good. Now why don't you lie down on the couch and we'll start. Do you trust me?

(I take her arm—feeling warm soft skin and inhaling cheap flower scents—swooning inside—my prick is virtually swooning—mouthing syllables—boola boola—my dream coming true.)

Yes, doctor.

Yes, Artie.

Yes, Artie.

Are you comfortable?

Um-hum.

Is there anything you want before we start?

Well, maybe one thing, if it isn't too much trouble.

Anything.

My panda.

What?

My stuffed panda. I won it in a swing contest. I can't sleep without it. It's in my suitcase. It has a pink bow around its neck.

Of course.

(I slip stealthily into the bath module and fetch the pink-necked panda from her clutter of possessions. It smells of talcum and jasmine. I have not snickered once. I am beginning to think that sleeping with a panda bear is cute.)

Here you are, Randi. Don't open your eyes—I'll put her next to you.

Him.

What?

Him. It's not a her, it's a him. (Giggle.) I only sleep with boy bears.

(Ha-ha.) That's adorable, dear. Now I'm going...

Guess what his name is.

I don't have any idea.

Just guess.

(I loathe guessing games.)

Murgatroyde.

(Giggle...gig-gig.) No, silly. Guess again.

(I hate this.)

This is fun, Randi. Uh, Earl.

No, not even close. Give up?

I give up.

His name is Victor Mature. After my favorite actor.

Oh, that's nice. What good taste you have.

(My heart sinks—not even on an acid trip could I pass for El Greaseball.)

Okay, Randi, now—we have work to do. I am going to hypnotize you. I want you to think of something very peaceful. Concentrate on it—very hard. Relax completely.

(I put her under with no trouble. The pills, the brandy and the hypnosis. She is out. From where I sit with my glasses off, she could be an acid rainbow—sweeps of color rising and falling, stabs of orange appearing over the sofa edge. Chinese New Year's. Writhing dragon worms dancing down dark alleys. I rise and move to the end of the couch, talking to her all the while. I slip her golden slippers off and put my nose to her yellowed soles. My cock brightens, glows, grows.)

Now, Randi. I am going to share some secrets with you. Only you and I will ever know this. You will listen and you will believe everything I tell you. It is the only truth. You will never forget it—unless I tell you to. I am the handsomest, most wonderful man in the world. I am your dream man. You love me. You will do anything I say. You will never say no, never resist—you will let me do all the dirty, lovely things I want. If you do, you *will never grow old. I have the power to keep you young and desirable forever. You will never be sick again. You will be free of pain. You will never sag or wrinkle. You will always be the Most Perfect Back. But only with me. Only if you obey me. Worship me. Listen to me. If you resist you will get sicker. You will get old and ugly. Your breasts will shrivel. And you will be all alone. No one will want you. Even your panda will go away. And then you will die. You are only safe with me. I am your savior. You will only feel desire for me. You will burn with lust for me. I am the handsomest, most wonderful man you have ever known; with me you will never grow old—and nothing will ever scare you again.*

(Not bad. Not bad at all. I chanted on and on. And she twitched—once she almost screamed—her head snapped back and forth—somewhere she knew—somewhere this baby-lady knew the game—the danger, the threat to her will. Like children do. Survivors. Children are. Sometimes it appears to me, listening to my pain people, that growing up is merely a process of breaking down our ability to survive. Well, her child was fighting—but the delusion was more attractive than the reality. I knew her fantasy. I Orwelled the shit out of her. Promise her anything, but give her razzmatazz. She chanted with me—we repeated each image over and over.)

I am the handsomest sexiest man you have ever seen. You worship me.

You are the handsomest sexiest man I have ever seen. I worship you.

You get the picture. Should have tried this game out years ago. On my wife. On my son. Could have improved the quality of my home life appreciably. We worked for an hour and a half. And now, I felt—it was time for a test.

I touch her arm. She murmurs.

Randi.

Um.

Who do you love?

You, Artie.

What will you do for me?

Anything.

Unzip your robe.

Her little pink hand reaches up and pulls the zipper all the way down. Her lips are parted in gypsy girl smile. She wiggles that obscene fat ass into her (blessed) cushion. Pink nipples pop out sideways. They are firm little titties. Like I thought they would be. And so white. Creamy. She sighs and lies still. I am throbbing. But I must control myself. Each step is a wire walk. I must be sure she is ready.

What would you like to do?

I want you to do dirty things on me.

How much do you want me to?

Very much.

Beg me.

(Giggle—pant.) Please, please.

Please. Please what?

Do things to me.

No.

Why?

Because you haven't been a good girl. You didn't finish your medicine.

She is beginning to move. Her hips rotate slowly. Her hands fondle her nipples and move down to her round, soft belly.

I'll do anything. I'll take my medicine. I'll be a good girl. I want you to play with me.

All right. Just wait a minute. You need me. You will be sick if I don't touch you. But you must wait.

(A little lysergic A. Perfect mood now. Trusting and hot. I prepare the potion. She is moaning, open and ready. And so am I. All of my years of discipline—every time I didn't jump up and stick my fingers in some why-me's raisin eyes—all of that control is working for me now. I sail across the room. Merlin at Midnight.

> *I want you to drink this all up. It will help you see how strong I am. You will see how beautiful and young you are with me—you will see how I can love you beyond your wildest dreams. And then, for a moment, you will see how horrible things will be if you don't obey me. You will see yourself—shriveled and ugly. And then I will appear and save you. I will save you by entering you. My cock will save you.*

(She swallowed. I repaint the picture. Her eyelids are twitching. She responds like a human movie screen. She begins to sing softly under her breath. Her eyes open and focus on me.)

> *Uwwwwwwwww. Uwwwww. You make me so happy. I feel so good. Do you want to see my back? It's perfect.*

She rises, remarkably steady considering, and lets her robe drop. My head pounds with desire. Beyond anything I have ever felt. Hammers on marble—beating into my head. She stands. Green bow falling over her cheek. Round firm shoulders. And those titties. And that little fat tummy. Tight little waist. Round thick thighs. Strong calves. And she turns around. Rose and her back. And her wonderful ass. I am on contact high. My prick is kicking against my jeans.

Then, suddenly, she screams—her hands cover her face—she falls onto the carpet rolling—thrashing around—cunt opens—legs sprawl—she is wailing—clawing at her head—

> *No, no, take away that mirror. It's not true. I am beautiful. I am young. No, no. That's not me. NNNNNOOOOO. Save me. Artie, save me. I'm not a witch—she's a witch—help me.*

Her body is rubbed red with rug burns. She lies on her back. Knees bent. Legs spread. Eyes staring in private terror, open and focused on her own tidy package of fear. Long, moaning cries replace the screaming. She quiets. I am ready. I stand and walk to her.

> *Can you hear me, Randi?*

> *Yes! Yes! Save me! Save me! Make it go away. I'm ugly! I'm horrible! My back is all wrinkled! My spine is bent! OH, OH!*

I drop my pants and rip my shirt off. My eyes are filled with water.

Steaming tears of lust. My prick is steel. I am Zeus. I am all power. All control.

I want you to look at my cock, Randi. I am going to save you with it now. All bad pictures will go away. The more I do to you and you to me, the younger and prettier and safer you will be. Are you ready?

Yes, yes. I am. I am.

All right. I want you to get on your hands and knees and crawl over to the couch and lie down with your knees up in the air like a puppy.

She has quieted. Her face softens. Her lips open. Saliva runs from her mouth. Perfect acid trip. She is meeting me in tomorrow land. Her breathing is deep. She crawls. Ass swaying. She climbs up on the couch and rolls over. (Would have been a wonderful spaniel.)

I am here now. When I touch you, your head will fill with beautiful thoughts. And you will desire me—until I tell you to relax.

Yes, yes.

I move to her and bring my hands toward her breasts. I realize as the heat of her body grazes my palms that I have never touched her—that if I stopped now, little harm would have been done. My hands stiffen over her body for a moment. And then the heat—a gravity force of heat and mania pulls them down. Contact. And I am moon-bound. My hands rip into her flesh. My mouth takes her nipple, tasting-biting-sucking. Starving boy-baby. She shrieks in joy. My lips and tongue move like well-trained animals down her body—swallowing her belly—digging into her thighs.

Now. Kneel, my dear, put your head against the back of the couch and spread your body out—as far as it can spread.

(Giggles. Delight. My baby, bunky doll.)
She turns backwards. Yellowed heels pointing out. I push her head down violently, forcing her into a human U. A Rold Gold pretzel woman. And I enter her. Mingling screams of ecstasy. Hers. Mine. Frothing. Strokes. I fuck to kill. To break. To take. A weapon I bring. To this fuck I bring: thirty-nine years of hostility toward women. I bring my nakedness. Blood and cartilage. Raw meat. Heart. I bring every scream I have ever swallowed. Every tear I have never shed. Every feeling I have suffocated.

Every patient I have lied to. Every women I have not raped. I bring to this. THE FUCK OF A LIFETIME. A new game show. I whirl her around on my cock like a pig on a spit. I ram her. I jam her. I probe and play. She is a blur. A soft pink blur. A wet rubber ducky. Anything. Her body vibrates under me. Meets my every thrust. A good dancer, she is. Done this step before. I cry out.

TURN OVER NOW! OPEN YOUR MOUTH. NOW!

And I come. Down her throat. Down beyond that lamb-chop tongue. Purple lipstick on my balls. Bees in my bonnet. Bang. And it is done.

Well, my friends. Called your bluff? It *was* done. And it was worth it. We both slept. When I woke up she was still sprawled out half on the couch, half on the floor, with "Victor Mature" under her arm.

Skipping around now, I am going to play our Samba Sequence. Just to prove that the party really rolled. You will hear male laughter. It is me. It may sound a bit strange, because you have never heard me laugh. To be honest, when I first replayed this tape, I didn't recognize myself. And I realized that I had probably not actually ho-ho-hoed in years. A tight smile, a chuckle, a well-placed smirk. But not a HA-HA-HAR-HAR. Anyway, it is I.

This section took place very late into the night.

Rose is mine. More hypnosis, twitters of acid and lots of vino. Me too. And coked on out. I even give Rose a snort or two, and she is flying. I believe at this point she is wearing the garter and heels combo, but we may have been into the tight black skirt and red bra with the nipple holes (I'll call the fashion press later). We have eaten our first meal together (bologna, bagels, watermelon and ruby port). Sitting on the sofa leafing through porno magazines. I have fucked her silly. She has sucked me dry. I have bruised and bitten every inch of her bouncy little body. Hickey Heaven. She is a total mess. A human dump. And so "suggested" that she thinks she's Helen of Troy. Her orange waves have hit the breakwater. Her makeup is sweat-smeared—and her skin a mass of blotches and black-and-blue marks. I am happy with my work. I have peed in her mouth. I have slapped her chunky little cheeks. I have ass-fucked her three times. (First filling her crack with clover honey. Good advertising gimmick—"And now, homemakers, still another use for natural sweeteners!") The coke keeps me arousable and awake. So, we are re-

laxed and I am flying on the Big C and, maybe not the best judgment—
but I think—why not? And I let her toot another line. Playback:

*Oh, Artie, I feel wonderful... I am so happy. I haven't felt this happy
since I won the Samba contest at my club. That was—that was Christmastime, 1958. I danced with Frederic Chateau. I told you about him. He was
an actor, producer, financier, a professional ballroom dancer and a
bullfighter. And he chose me as his partner. I wore a pink sheath. With
slits all the way up the sides. Both sides. And I made a pink tulle skirt to go
over it—so you couldn't see anything when we dipped. And I had pink
sequins on my eyelids. Boy, could he dance. And everything else. (Giggle
—tongue lip.) Not like you—but I didn't know you then. That was when
I was still working. At the studios. I was head manicurist. All the stars
wanted me to do their nails. I even gave pedicures. I met Rita Hayworth
once. She was my idol. Everyone said I looked like her. Mama and Papa
didn't like it. They thought only bad girls worked in the studios. "A bunch
of shiksas and goyim running around with paint on their face." That's
what Mama said. Oh, so I wore this pink ensemble. And Frederic wore
a white satin tuxedo with a pink rose in his lapel. And the announcer—
they hired a professional announcer and famous judges. The star judge
was Errol Flynn's illegitimate son. Well, we were on this ramp. I even had
a pink rose in my teeth. And the announcer said, "And now, ladies and
gentlemen—in the Samba Competition—a beautiful redhead, one of our
regulars, Miss Randi Laine—with her handsome partner, actor and outerpronure, Fred Chateau." He got a little upset about that—them calling
him Fred—but no one laughed or anything—and then the music started—
Baa-ba-ba-ba-de-ba—they had a quartet and someone using those cute
little maraca things on sticks—and anyway, we came down the stairs—
I had matching pink satin heels with straps like the chorus girls wear—
and we were smiling—and we didn't miss a step, and we never looked at
our feet or anything. Like Vernon and Irene Castle—remember? We
smiled at each other—looked into each other's eyes—and when we were
through people shouted, "Encore, encore" and clapped real loud. And
we won. First prize. I have the trophy. I'll bring it in sometime. It's goldplated. And there's two little people in dress-up clothes on top. And it has
my name engraved on it. Randi Laine. First Prize. Samba Competition.
Coconut Club. 1958. Here, stand up. I'll show you the routine we did.
Come on.*

Me. (Ho-ho.) No, I don't do exhibition dancing.

*Oh, come on. Don't be a spoilsport. I'll teach you. The samba is the
sexiest dance in the world. And I'm good. I can teach you the shimmy, too.*

Come on.

Okay.

(I said okay—that is not a tape defect.)

Oh, good. Okay—now. Oh. You can't do it dressed like that.

Dressed like what? I'm naked.

That's what I mean. You have to look elegant.

I'll put a tie on.

(Giggles, giggles—we both get the giggles.)

Okay. Okay—Randi. You close your eyes and I'll change. It'll be a surprise.

Okay. But hurry. Turn on some music.

(Sergio Mendez, my Latin lovely. I push him into the tape deck.)

Who's that?

Brazil '66.

Don't you have Prez Prado?

No.

Oh.

I madly rummage through my closet. Looking for suitable attire. I emerge wearing: the red underpants with my cock pushed through the pussy hole. My LaCoste golf shirt with my Pancho Segura sweatband around my forehead. And Gucci loafers. A truly creative and eclectic choice.

Ahhhhhh. Oh, you look so cute. You are so perfect.

(I beam.) Randi has added her gold mosque mules and a tight white sleeveless sweater. What a team.

Okay now. Just follow me. We go forward and then back. We'll start real simple. Then we'll add the hips—you know, it's all in the hips. I—it's so funny, me showing you—I've never been in love with anyone who wasn't a Latin dance expert before. It's always been my weak spot.

(My pride is pricked. I grab her and twirl her around with such force her skirt splits all the way up the rear.)

And who said I wasn't a "Latin dance expert?" I have been teasing you—I am the Gene Kelly of the medical profession. I will dance you to death. Turn your feet to bloody pulps.

I grab her perfect back and take off. Doing steps never dared in a public place. Steps never attempted anywhere before. (Or ever again.) We whirl and twirl. I lead her up over chairs—a bit of adagio on the couch, mad hip rotating against the wall—I dip her to the plush pile and throw her backwards into my hairy hands. Day-day-ee-day-hay-o—So Dance...So Dance Samba—we dance on. I spin her away—SOLO. She writhes, she wiggles—her hips pulsate against her shredded skirt. I begin a brilliant conga solo on my frightened desk. Booga-booga, ole...

Watch this, watch this, Artie...look, look...

She has taken to cartwheeling. A small backbend into the splits. A wonder she is. Honey from her ass sticks to the carpet as she rolls out of the splits and into a knee-level shimmy.
Yahoo...conga, conga...I samba alone to the fridge...crack open a bottle of beer—grabbing for a pen without losing the rhythm—ballpoint on beer glass...cha-cha-cha...wahoo.
Randi/Rose has shimmied along the floor to me—she squats, tits flying around like pinwheels—arms thrust out, belly quivering—she shimmies before me—African tribal rite—booga-booga. I grab her—bending her backwards—pouring beer like lamb's blood over her head—into her purple-smeared lips—ceremony before the sacrifice—my offering to the Gods, the Friday Night Used Virgin Sacrifice. My hands move to her hips—I shake her sideways faster and faster—wooo—hoo—
A knock. A loud bang on the door. Whooooo. Who?

What's that, Artie? Burglars?

(She wipes beer off her neck and throws her bruised little arms around me.)

No, no, my dear. Not burglars. Remember—you are safe forever with me—I will take care of it. I want you to lie down on the couch and think beautiful thoughts—think of my cock—think of the samba. Do not be afraid.

I am terrified. I move to the door, forgetting my "ensemble."
"Yes?"
"Open the goddamn door, will ya. I've been banging for twenty minutes."
"Who is it? This is a private party."
"Well, I was invited by a Doctor Freeman or someone, Charlie—and I'm here on schedule. And if you don't open the door there's gonna be trouble."
My god. It must be the prostitute. Time had stopped. It was Saturday? What to do. I open the door a crack and move into the waiting room. A tall blond leans against the wall. She is wearing a black leather jacket and black leather pants tucked into black leather boots (saving all worry about color coordination). Her hair is clipped short and greased back. Huge gold circles dangle from her ears. Her mouth—outlined in brown, filled in with pink—is grinding a wad of gum to death. A small brown cigar rests between her thumb and pinkie. A Scars Catalogue Lesbian Prostitute—order now. I am intimidated.
"Yes, hello. I am terribly sorry. I had no idea it was that late."
She is looking me over. Very slowly. A smirk forms at the corners of her pink and brown mouth.
"Must've been quite a party. You should've told me it was a masquerade ball."
I remember. My hand moves down and pushes my cock back into the panty slit. It pops out again. I pull my golf shirt down, trying to cover it. She extends her hand.
"No names, okay, Doctor? Just call me Lady."
I take her hand. My shirt flies up and my cock pokes out. Damned nuisance sometimes.
"Okay, uh, Lady. Uh, maybe I'd better explain things."
(Smirk-snicker) "Yeah. I think maybe you better. I like to check out the crew before the cruise, if you can dig it. Nothing painful. Got it, Doctor?"
Her eyes raze me. Black cobweb lashes covering memories. Bitter miss. A "lady" who maintains her composure before a coked-out drunken middle-aged psychiatrist with his prick hanging out of red panties. "Oh, hello there." A life like that. I start to judge. To manipulate for control. And this voice in my ear—these hot wet invisible lips against my ear—whispers, "Who you kidding, buddy-boy? Look to ye'self." I have lost

my game book.

"Well. I have a patient in there. This is part of her therapy, you see. Very experimental, very confidential. I want you to become part of her fantasy. I thought—well, I will prepare her first, and then—and then I want you to come in, strip off her clothes—make her lie on the floor facing me and perform oral coitus."

"What?"

"I want you to strip..."

"Yeah, yeah, I got that, Jack—what's the other number? Oral what?"

"Orax sex."

"You want me to suck her cunt, Doctor?" (Smirky-smirk-smirk.) I stand tall. My hand in front of my straggly little enemy.

"Yes. And I will take pictures."

"No pictures."

"I am paying for..."

"No pictures." (The face is iron.)

"All right. No pictures. But no bonus either."

"Boo-hoo."

"There's no need to be hostile. We are both professionals. I am trying to save a patient's life."

"Oh, gee. That's great, Dr. Kildare. One hundred dollars in advance. And let's hurry it up. If I'm the angel of mercy—we'd better get started. I have another gig in two hours."

"Okay. You wait here. I'll get the money—and then I have to talk to my patient. And I would appreciate it if you would try to curtail your sarcasm in front of her. She's a very gentle woman."

"I'll be fine with *her*. It's men I hate. I try, but I just can't cover it up, Doctor. Hurts my work, too." (She moves very close to me—I am waiting for her to grab my shriveled little tool and twirl me over her head like a lariat.) "I hate you. I hate all of you. I can hardly look at you without throwing up. I despise every wormy-ass one of you. I look at you and I see a prick head. I see snake eyes. You all make me sick. Nothing personal. I've been that way for years. And in my work, I don't meet you in your best light. So I have never had a reason to upgrade my opinion. So let's just not get into it. I do my job good. And I won't hurt the poor gentle dear. But don't expect me to be nice to you, thread-head, because I hate you."

(Well, how refreshing. An honest opinion.) For some reason I grinned at her. I think I may have simply lost control of my facial muscles. I backed out of the room. Raced to the closet—put on my pants. Opened my desk and pulled out the envelope (planning) with her "fee." (To be billed on my income tax as "consultation.") Jogged back out—handed her the money and asked her to wait. I tiptoed back to Rose—who was out cold. Broke open an amyl nitrate capsule under her nose—broke one under mine—and up we went again. I resuggested her—told her that someone was coming to make her feel good—that she was to do it for me—that it would be very exciting and would please me—and I would watch her—and if she was a good girl, I would give her peppermint ice cream with chocolate sauce later. She smiled. What a good baby. I trotted back to the door and invited our guest in.

She paused in the doorway—black webs clicking over the place like a retinal Nikkon. Click on Rose. Click on tape deck. Click on honey in carpet. Click on state of couch disarray. Clicky-click—click.

Okay, Doctor. Want to make the introductions?

Rose, open your eyes. (Eyelids flutter, eyeballs roll around.) *I want you to meet, uh, Teresa. She's a wonderful dancer. She's a friend. She is going to do lovely dirty things to you. And I am going to watch. Okay?*

Okay, Artie darling. Shall I show her my back?

No, my dear—that isn't necessary. Just slide down onto the floor and don't worry about anything.

Okay.

Good girl.

(What a dream girl.)

Nice ass, for an old broad.

Lady flicked the zipper of her jacket with Amazonian power. And hurled (yes, hurled) it against my Morris Louis lithograph.

I imagine you want me nude.

Yes. Thank you, that would be fine.

(Dignity—I regain a speck.)

She rips down her boot zippers—causing the hair in my ears to itch. Rip, rip. Boots crash against my desk. Snap, snap. Leather pants hit the lamp. She stands over Rose. Huge siliconed breasts like double boubles. Purple-black nipples. Long tight torso. Long strong legs. Tense one, this is. Throw her down and she'd spring right back up—without bending. A human wishbone. Crackle, snap. Not so much a body as a flesh-covered wall against rage. Climb me and I'll kill. Nick me and BOOM. On her right buttock is a small tattoo that reads... "For Women Only." On her left buttock is a larger tattoo showing a mouth biting off a cock. It reads... "Power is a dead dong." Unconsciously I cross my legs. How refreshing, I reiterate. A little up-front anger. I swallow hard.

Got any coke, lover?

Yes. Yes, I do.

I prance to my desk and return with two very well-sliced lines. (Anything to please. Perfect host, always.)
Her nostrils flare. Two long snorts. A bull sniffer, this one.

Beautiful. Okay, baby-doll. Mama's gonna make you feel real good.

(The coke has improved her spirits immensely. Mine do likewise.) The amyl and all has hit my trigger again. She kneels over Rose—spread and still wet and white and baby-blue bruises—and I perk. I jaunt over to my desk. Sit. And quietly undo my zipper. No dead dong in this joint.

Stand up, honey.

Lady helps Rose to her feet. Rose stands, dazed and woozy, a sort of Beetle Bailey recruit. Lady begins tearing off her outfit. Rip—slash—pieces of clothing fly through the air. She stands, weaving with each removal. Lady seems to be enjoying herself.

Sexy old broad you got here. Not bad a'tall.

(The coke is a big hit.)
Rose is bare. Standing at attention. Beer still glistening on her neck. Lady moves toward her slowly. They are standing face to face. A big blonde dyke and a little red Rose. I am mesmerized. Lady looks her over slowly. And then she grabs her, pulling her forward in a passionate embrace. Face to face. She pulls her head back and kisses her. Moving her groin against Rose's tummy. (This was not in the script. I feel a flash of... jealousy?) Lady likes her too. I am pumping away. Virgil Voyeur. I have never seen anything like this. Rose is murmuring. I think she thinks it's me. (So much for ego trips.)

Okay, honey-bunny. (Honey-bunny?) *Lie down and spread those beautiful legs.*

Lady commands. Rose plops down. Raggedy Ann in wonderland. She lowers her head slowly and spreads her legs. (Wowee.)
Lady is grunting in her throat.

You're a sweet little number. I'm gonna give you my super deluxe job.

Lady squats between Rose's legs. She reaches down and bends Rose's bruised little knees.

You have pretty hair.

(Rose touches her bleached thatch.)

Thanks, doll.

Lady smiles and wets her lips. The room is still. Totally quiet. And then her head lowers between those wide white portals (it was poetic—you should have been there). I am huffing and puffing. Rose is huffing and puffing. The big bad wolf is getting off. Rose is licking her battered little lips and murmuring low (obviously all tongues are alike in the dark—no gender tag on two lips and a tongue-o). Lady rolls Rose over and buries her face in her ass. (That was a nice touch.) Rose is going off.

Ohhhhh. Ohhh. Uwwww. That feels so good. Do it more. More.

Lady raises her head.

Give me a vibrator, jerkoff.

I reach in my drawer with my free hand and throw her one. (The green one.) Whizzing sounds. She runs it up under Rose's belly to her nipples. Two lovelies on all fours—shaking and have a jolly ol'. Then she moves it down to her own big black slot. (That was also not in the script. But I am in no mood to haggle.) She flips Rose over effortlessly and turns backwards, ass to head, and goes at her again. One hand holding the little green machine on herself, the other pressing on Rose's pretty red pubis. A crescendo of sounds. (I will play them into this tape now as background.)

Ummmmm. Uwwwwwww. Uhhhhhhhh.

Grunts. Passion pants. We all go off. Snap. Crackle. Pop. Louie,

Louieee. I quickly recover. Grab the Kleenex and clean up. Pulling my pants back under the desk (in case Lady didn't know what I was doing, ha). The Blonde Bomber gives Rose a big noisy mouth kiss and straightens up, raising her arms above her head and stretching her body.

Nice stuff, honey. Anytime.

I am sitting nonchalantly—do-de-do, nice day, isn't it?—at my desk. She looks at me. Steadily. For what seems like months. And snickers. I am afraid she might bite me. And shakes her head slowly from side to side. (Memories, I have just become one of her memories—"Did I ever tell you about the shrink and the old broad with the honey in her ass?" Trade talk.) She moves arrogantly around the room gathering up her leather goods. Zippers rezip. Snap. Rip. Zzzzz. She ignores me. Rose sleeps. A slack-jawed smile on her lips. So Dance Samba.

Okay, Ben Casey. That's a wrap. Call me again sometime. Nice pussy. (She stares at me with total and lavish contempt.) *You got good taste, for a man.*

Lady, I assure you—this is a professional situation, not what you think...

Oh yeah, yeah, I forgot—Tinkerbell. Forgive me.

(I resist an urge to tee off with her left tit—sticks and stones.) But of course, she is quite correct. So I do nothing. I stand up. She sways toward the door.

Thank you, uh, Lady. I trust this will remain completely confidential.

You can sell tickets on that, Doc. I have my reputation to think of.

(Smirk, snigger—I fight my tongue which is trying to blast out of my mouth—nah-nah-naaa.) She opens the door.

So long, lover-boy... don't take any wooden vibrators. (Snicker. Slam.)

We are alone again. I am hungry. I fix a snack and open the window. It is dark. Saturday night. Everybody loves it. Rose is snoring. I rummage in the fridge. Nibbling. Turn on some Beachboys. My little surfer girl. I light a joint and pour some brandy. I feel good. I wait. She sleeps. I make noises. She sleeps. I want her to wake up. I want to play. I feel funny. I chop another line. And move to her. I prop her up. Put the straw in her nose and make her inhale. And she is back with me. I have company.

Never got to the dildo and the whip. Or the electric vibrators, or even the sheep-fuck movie. I kept her loaded and hypnotized. (I even told her that she had read her newspapers and done her facials.)

Sunday she slept on and off. I would bring her to to have her suck me off. A couple of times I screwed her in her sleep. The necrophiliac in me adored it. I once had a patient whose husband made her play dead every time they "made love." One night she had a bad cold and just as he was coming, she sneezed. He yelled at her, "You Bitch!" and broke her nose. Or so she said. I only hear one half of every story, you know. Lots of pieces don't fit. Rose and I, however, fit. I never slept. I had left the realm of reason, thereby not needing reasonable things. Like sleep. Like food. I had turned into some drug-hazed sex machine. My feats. My staying power. My energy. Were amazing.

By Sunday night her bruises had settled down. And I was about ready to try some rough stuff (as I said, a lot of merchandise hadn't been tried on yet). We were lying on the couch watching *Kojak* ("Uww—he's so ugly—I don't know what anyone sees in him") when the phone rang.

I jumped. As if shot. The intrusion was stupefying.

"Hello?"

"Doctor?"

"Yes."

"This is Rose's brother, Morley."

(Heh-heh-heh.) "Oh, yes. Hello." (I reach for my doctor voice.)

"Louise and I wanted to know what time to come for her in the morning. I pray from five to six, so if we could come for her at seven o'clock that would be very helpful."

Come for her...I had forgotten. They had brought her. My eyes shoot over to my sweat-stained disheveled darling. Oh god.

"Yes. Seven would be fine. I must tell you, Rose has been through a lot. I don't want you to be upset by the way she, uh, looks."

"I only see the inner beauty. The body has no meaning to God."

(Good.) "Yes, of course. I think we have moved dear Rose closer to her spiritual center, and the pain has stopped for now. So please don't worry."

"Bless you."

(Gesundheit.) Moses hangs up.

I panic. Not even Toad Tongue could be inward-looking enough not to notice that his immaculate lacquered little sis looks like revenge of the vampires.

Randi, dear. We are going to play a game.

Oh, good. How 'bout Name That Tune, that's my favorite.

No, not that kind. We are going to pretend that you have a big fancy party to go to and I am going to get you ready. Do your hair—(What do I know about hair? Have had only strands for years.)—make you up, give you a bath. Won't that be fun?

Oh, that's silly. Men can't do things like that.

I can. Remember, I can do anything. I will take care of you.

I remember. Well, okay, I'll do anything you want, but don't you want to play with me first? I can't help it. When I look at you I want to do things.

(Lip and tongue and a wiggle-wiggle.) My cock hardens. Amazing. Absolutely amazing.

Okay, my sweet, let's do it in the bathtub.

(Two birds—one pebble.)

(Gibble) Oh, that sounds wonderful. Ummmmm. Let's do it now.

I help her up and lead her in. She sits unsteadily on the john smiling at me and humming (hmmm—hmmm). I turn the water on and begin rummaging through her cache of lotions and notions. Something to alter every corpuscle on the female frame.
"Rose, do you have shampoo? I can't find any shampoo."
Rose is stoned. Rose is now splashing in the tub singing "The Man That Got Away."
"I don't use shampoo. I have hair professionally done.... Ever since the world begannnnn...There is nothing sadder ttthhaan'"
I find a bar of Tangerine Jelly Soap. (It was that or douche powder.) I move to the tub.
"All right now, I want you to lay your head back. I'm going to wash your pretty little head."
She grabs my penis and sticks it between her tits.
"Play with me."
"After I wash your hair we'll play." My cock hardens. Even turmoil and absurdity cannot reach Superman.

"You're no fun."

She lies back in the tub with her legs spread and begins shimmying around underwater.

"Sing with me...Da-da-da-da-da-da-da. Some day he'll come along, the man I love..."

I grab her head and push it backward under the water. A hammerlock on her neck, and scrub away with abandon. The soap slips, I slip, I reach for it and lose my balance, landing on top of Rosie-baby in the tub.

"Oh, Artie. You're so cute."

She grabs me and begins bumping around under the water. I decide that her hair is clean enough.

And so it went. I washed her. I dried her. I set her hair with bobby pins (a task not to be underestimated by anyone who has never tried to pin-curl a hypnotized drunken woman who is sucking one's cock when one is working against the clock and full of enough booze, grass, lust and cocaine to impress the vice squad).

I blow her dry, I make her up. Choosing from an assortment of glosses and glues not seen outside a Woolworth's cosmetic counter. I find her clothes. I dress her. I cover all bruises in view with pancake makeup. I comb her out. (Even tease and spray.) I clean the bathroom. I tidy the office. Puff the pillows. And put on the clothes. I make coffee. I lay her down for posthypnotic suggestion. I tell her what to remember (all the good stuff) and what to forget (the rest). I tell her not to tell anybody in the whole world, or she will lose me. I tell her that she is to come Wednesday for her regular appointment. I bring her out. It is 6:45 a.m. All in a night's work.

The Addams family comes. They beam at me. I beam at them.

"How do you feel, dear?" Louise moves in for a close-up.

"Wonderful. Like a new person. Artie is a wonderful doctor." (Whoops—I forgot to tell her "Artie" is only for special occasions.)

Morley peers down at me—a new blackhead has surfaced on his other ear.

"I prayed all weekend. Louise said that she could see you—could hear your thoughts."

(I swallow.) "Well, I felt those vibrations and so did Rose."

"I knew it. I just knew it. It's all in the eyes. Scorpio. I saw your tail shoot over your head and sting. Kill the poison."

(Not actually far from the truth.) "Yes, well, Rose has worked very hard. I think she should go home and right to bed."

Louise reaches for my left hand. Morley clasps my right hand. Both of them swoon into me. (Eye contact is their strong suit.)

"God be with you, Doctor." (Morley's halitosis hangs in the air.)

"Thank you."

"Bye-bye, Artie."
"Good-bye, Rose."
Louise sighs loudly. Unwilling to release my hand. (I ponder the possibilities.)
"I really would like you to pose for me. I do see you on black velvet. With yellow centers to your eyes—and maybe a centaur—perhaps mounting a centaur—a scorpion around your neck. Someday. I must paint you."
She sighs in falsetto. I smile warmly and ease myself out of her clammy grasp.
"Of course, dear, someday."
We all beam again. Morley comments on how nice Rose's hair looks. (I almost say thank you.) We agree to talk soon. I have made new friends, it seems.
And then she picks up her little pink plastic suitcase and she's gone.

And I went home. My wife was taking a tennis lesson. My son was at school. And I was suddenly very tired. "Drained" would be the dramatic description. Emptied. And lost. It seemed that I had been away from here for years. That this was the lie. That the weekend was the truth. That this was not my life. I could barely remember what they looked like, my family. I wandered around. Trying to replace my self. And when I couldn't, I went upstairs, slid into my monogrammed silk pajamas (that is who you are, Doctor, a man who wears monogrammed pajamas and lives the good life). And I slept. I slept all day. And all night. I heard sounds under my sleep, stirrings, comings and goings—I tried to fight my way toward them—break the twilight—connect with my life. "I'm home, dear." I kept trying to say that in my sleep—"I am here"—but I couldn't. I sank deeper. Dreams of toads and witches, whips and water. Flames and loss. Mother. Father. Screams and sighs. Somewhere an old man sat with his head in his hands. Sobbing. Hands reaching toward him—trying to hold him. Reaching. Missing. Sobbing old man. "I'm home, dear." "What's for dinner, love?" "Can't anyone hear me? wake me up—help me up—I want to come back now...can't you hear me?"...
Nobody came. I slept all day. And all night. At five o'clock that Tuesday morning, I pushed away sleep and sat up. My wife lay serenely beside me. I wanted to wake her.
I wanted to tell her.
I got up and went downstairs and sat in the kitchen until the sun came up. I thought about the weekend. And I realized that I had had

fun. In fact, it was the best weekend I had ever had. And that thought filled me with such a piercing blast of self-pity that I put my head down on the polished pine breakfast counter and cried like a baby. First time in memory. Me and my Yuban...and this dripping loss. This steaming cup of fear.

16

It is now 2 p.m. I took a nap and scanned the paper, in case you are interested. I am not, after all, a machine. Machinelike, but not complete. I have the saved paper to scan periodically. Any one will do. I only buy one per week. The news, the news from the human cesspool, never changes. Floating the Pound, Tax Cuts; movable pieces and the rest—the backbone of the news, the rapes, murders, car crashes, fires, robberies, mutilations, deaths and maimings. All the same. And I can't change any of it. Probably wouldn't if I could—believing as I do in the eternal sameness of human nature. So I solve all of the problems of society by not reading about them. Simple. Should be a class in it. Or a how-to book. Maybe I can do a sequel to my sex book. *How to Be a Happy Person in a Pig-Ass World*. It would be a very short work:

1. Stop reading newspapers.
2. Abandon *Time* magazine and *Newsweek*.
3. Stop going to parties and talking to people.
4. Stop earning a living.
5. Give up dry cleaners, car washes and trips to the post office.
6. Give up believing that if you're a good girl/boy you will get everything you want.
7. Bury Prince Charming.
8. Same Princess Charming.
9. Give up Christmas, Thanksgiving, Mother's/Father's Days, the Easter Bunny, the Tooth Fairy and Santa Claus.
10. Keep Halloween.
11. Stop taking good care of yourself.
12. Forget that nothing is fair.
13. Accept that there is no such thing as a happy ending.

14. Only do what you want no matter whom it hurts.
15. Fire-bomb your car.
16. Cancel your insurance. And flip the bird to the IRS.
17. Be snake mean.
18. Be obscene.
19. Stop looking for Mr./Ms. Right.
20. Stop reading how-to books.

I could go on. But this little ramble is, needless to say, not on course. And then again, it is. Because the course is whatever I say it is. No surveyor on this road. But me. And I am feeling snarly. And dead. I think I will perk myself up. A little glass of Scotch should do it. Maybe what I should do is create a new specialty. I could see only new patients—which is all I have left now anyway. I hear one new historia—and before the characters in their bogus little bubbles become unbearably boring, I refer them to one of my peers who is more suited to their particular needs. Sort of a middleman: yes, Dr. Modus for impotence; of course, Dr. Operandi for phobias; Dr. Quid for behaviorial mod; and Dr. Pro Quo for psychoanalysis. In and out. I like that. Every time could be the First Time. Always a sense of hope; of romance; of expectation. And out. Before they face facts. (See no Santa Claus, no Prince Charming section.) Before they realize—horror of horrors, shock of shocks—that I don't make them well. They have to do that themselves. And that's hard. People mostly want to "go to a therapist," they don't want to have to change. Going to the therapist gets them off the hook. "Well I'm going to a therapist—so there!" They can go forever. As long as the money holds out (or the therapist holds out). Doesn't help a yin yang. Going becomes another in the long list of self-delusions, copout bullshit. Going is nothing. Going to the opera doesn't make you Robert Merrill, does it? Well, Going to a Psychiatrist doesn't make you Mary Tyler Moore, either. It sounds so simple. It's amazing how few sad souls understand that. *They* have to do *the work*. *They* have to give back the marbles and the gumdrops—even the poison ones—that they clutch to their stubborn-neurotic little chests. "No, no, no. I don't want to let go of *anything*. I just want to feel great, have a perfect life and not change one teeny-tiny." Hmmm. Well. Happens over and over. I used to get mad. And try to make them hear me. After all, how was I going to be a good doctor if I didn't have good patients? But nothing worked. And then I just accepted it. And saw it all as entirely their problem. And my practice took off. Give the folks what they want, my friends. Like a charm, works like a lucky charm.

I am lighting some Thai stick super-grass. And you are listening. And you are believing me? Why? I may be a psycho in a furnished room. I said I was a killer. I said that this "spool" is my confession. You are trusting me. Waiting for me. It may all be a lie. Or if it is true...you do not know me. My name may be false. I have not once (check it if you want) mentioned a city-state-phone-exchange-anything that would pin me down. This may just be one big bullshit. But I know *one* thing. You, whoever you are, don't want it to be that. You would rather I killed my Rose, hated my fellowman, lived the life of de Sade—anything. Than to find out that I am a liar. We can forgive almost anything but being lied to. It's in the genes. Have I planted doubt? I hope so.

I am sure you are familiar with the great man theory? Unless you happen to be a chief of Detectives at some police station. Well, the Great Man theory asserts in essence, that without Einstein there would have been no theory of relativity; sans Freud no opening of the unconscious; no Hitler, no Nazis, etc. The man led the events. The person formed history. Every egomaniac in the world licks his lips. To have an effect. To leave a mark. To matter. To last. I wanted to matter. When I was still a kid in med school, I read a little ditty from Max Planck. He said: "New scientific truth does not triumph by convincing its opponents and making them see the light, but rather because its opponents eventually die." Hmmm. Sort of turned me off research. And depressed the crap out of me. Can't make a fucking imprint. Jung waiting for Siggy to fold. Even the Great Men.

Just before I finished my residency, my parents came to visit me. We went to the country, and it had snowed. I hated them. I remember being very defensive and angry at them that trip. I was walking ahead of them—and I had this feeling, this thought—I was afraid to look backward, because I thought that I wasn't making any footprints. I was leaving no mark in the snow. I was terrified. I shouted over my shoulder to my mother—"Are you following my footprints?" She said, "No." I turned and ran back, tracking them, seeing them. My parents saw me rabbiting around in my own footmarks. I told them I felt I was leaving no footprints. They exchanged a strange look. A "loon" look. I wanted, you see, to make marks. And there has been, always, this paranoiac floating, this disconnection—this lack of place in my own life. I never went walking in the snow again. Some day, I might turn around and find my fear confirmed. My feet skimming the snow. Not connecting. The risk is too great.

Now before I continue, I want to explain something. You may be wondering why Rose was so easy "to love." Why she followed my every wish, lusted and thrusted without more exhaustive manipulation on my part. I shall explain. First, you see, I am extremely devious and skilled. A lot of what I transmitted to Rose during our earlier sessions

I have not bored you with. I conveyed to her that seeing me was a privilege. That I only saw the most beautiful, glamorous women in the world. She was, as I said before, a hysteric. With a Lucite self-image. Randi as pinup queen. Hysterics are highly suggestible. She was also a passive-dependent personality. Also highly suggestible. I gave her permission to love me. Daddy will take care of you. Not to repeat myself, but we were a fit. She wanted to believe me. She was a born truster. She was also, by the way, not a neurotic. She was easy because she had few conflicting layers of information. She had rumbaed around for fifty-odd years taking everyone at their word. Not judging herself. Not judging them. One-stepping along. Everything is exactly what it seems to be. Whatever you say is true. Whatever I do is fine. Wonderful defense mechanisms. She had rituals. Routines. She was literally and completely without goals. Without ambition. (Which, any doctor will tell you, is the key to a long and happy life.) She had no games to run. No axes to grind. No hostility and no anger (worth mentioning). She was, of course, delusive. But, you know. Who decides? She was the closest thing to the currently touted "natural child" that I have ever run into from EST to Essalen. She giggled, she came, she lived her little life just fine. She was satisfied. She was not competitive, frustrated or lonely. She had painted her little picture and put it on her scrubbed little wall. She just was. And after all, I was doing nice things to her. The only bad thing in her life was her tummy trouble, and I was curing her. I did not need to use that device anymore because she was so willing to trust me. So passive. I existed now in her world. How I got there or why she was seeing me no longer mattered. My bet was she would never say, "But my tummy is fine now, Artie—why am I still coming here?" She loved me now. She saw me as she saw herself. I was a tall, curly-headed twinkle-toes and she was Rita Hayworth. Fine. I'll drink to that. (Have been for hours, by the way.) This was not a usual case, I may add. Somehow—I knew I could have her or I would not have responded so violently to her. I knew it was possible to take her. My body knew it before my head. Immediately. And also, she had no reason to resist me now. I made her feel good. She trusted me. And, I might add, I have always been a highly effective hypnotherapist. So Rose and I were *Zeitgeist*. I got what I needed when I needed it. Also the dear soul was a sucker for flattery. Most people are. So that, too. So, I had done it. We were an item. The immediate problem was how to incorporate this Devil's Dance into my daily life. I did, after all, have one. A form. People that existed outside my innerspace. There was air and light and motion beyond the walls of my professional cave. How to juggle. It is one thing, you see, to disguise form as content in one's work and in one's marriage, because we, or rather I, had had so much time to work it out. But now there was this new wrinkle. A new dimension to contend with. New thoughts in my cabeza. How could I incorporate without strain? Without some change in my demeanor? A change in my computerlike behavior might elicit new responses from my family and friends. People might ask me for new things. See the glimmer of difference as hope, as a new possibility for contact. Or just sense something, be curious. Ask me what's wrong. (Or what's right.) And I certainly did not want that. And also, though I am loath to admit it, I had crossed over a line. I had broken my Oaf. Peed on my Creed. It is, you see, one thing to stagger along as an arrogant, not committed or truly responsible practitioner. Well trained, but not well motivated. But still, a doctor. People bring their bloody little lives in here. That's why I never considered surgery or the like. The botch would be unbearable. The slip would show. Better fuck up a head than a heart valve. Anyway, I had my limitations. But I was not a quack. My Great Machine was in operating condition. And I functioned in the form. I had never had a suicide. I had even helped people. And I had not betrayed my oath. Not in the Biblical sense. I was at least a member of the take-two-aspirin-and-call-me-in-the-morning school of medicine. I had been that. And now I was something else. I had this secret. I knew where the body was buried. Figuratively speaking, of course. I was doing something bad. And it felt good. And it felt strange. I had changed disguises. I was, rather, between disguises. And that made me vulnerable. And that was dangerous. And I knew that if Rose and I were to continue this tango, I would have to slip into a new costume—without anyone noticing that I had changed clothes.

17

I got through Tuesday. I thought I was doing fine. My fly seemed well zipped, et al. I even went to dinner with my wife and son and talked about getting a new car. And school. And tennis lessons. Like a regular family. Meanwhile my mind whirled on, looking for something, a backup to explain any changes in my appearance, attitude or hours. I threw around several. And tried to stay loose.

On Wednesday, right on time, Rose came. Alone. She looked delicious. All powdered and recovered. She was wearing: a bright red miniskirt, black stockings and high black suede pumps (the stockings were seamed and crooked, bless her frozen little soul), a gold waist cincher and a tight yellow blouse with puffy sleeves. Before I could even begin to hypnotize her, she was all over me. Kissing my feet, my hands, rubbing against my startled joint.

> *Oh, Artie, Artie, I missed you so much. Even Victor couldn't comfort me. Let's play—I want you to play with me. I'll be a good girl. Look how beautiful I am. I sent my photo in to a talent search contest in Photoplay. You've made me so happy. I love you. You're so handsome. Ummm. Do dirty things to me. Pretty please with cream on top?*

And that's what she got. With double cream. I resuggested her afterward. But all, I realized, that the hypnosis, drugs, etc., had done was speed up the transference. She would have been mine anyway. She just needed the big bad doctor to give her permission. While we romped I forgot about a patient, who sat outside for forty minutes waiting for me. Things were being affected.

> *Can I come tomorrow? Please? I have some records we can dance to. And maybe you could take some pictures, wouldn't that be fun, Artie? Pleasy-please?*

I said yes. Meaning that I had to cancel two other appointments—and reschedule my oil change.

The next morning, I heard my wife crying in the bathroom. I dared not ask what was wrong. I pretended not to hear.

My son threw up at the breakfast table and had to stay home from school. I gave him a mild sedative.

Rose arrived on schedule with a stack of Prez Prado, Bob Crosby and the Modernaires. I brought out the Quaaludes and some port. And all the vibrators.

We danced naked. I poured port all over her horny little ass and licked it off (she loved it). I requested that she play with herself, with the pretty pink vibrator (she did). She came with her little yellow feet flying in the air. (It was adorable.) Then we went to work with the Polaroid. Avedon would be green. I shot up between her legs and her armpits. Shot her face going down on me and me going down on her. Pussy pictures. Tits and ass. Posed with whips and chained to the door. She even got me coming off into the camera with my own brawny hand. Now I will play a little conversation from that tape:

Artie?

(We are lying on the couch—in spaceland.)

Yes, Randi, dear?

If I tell you something I never told anybody before, will you promise never, ever to repeat it, ever?

Of course.

Well, remember I told you I was married once, for a little while?

Yes.

And I left because I didn't want any babies—because of my shape. Well, I didn't just leave for that. I left because I missed my dressing table.

What, my dear?

You see, at Mama and Papa's I had this beautiful dressing table. With a lace skirt around it and a three-sided mirror and a little satin-covered seat. And I had room for all my makeup and a special Kleenex box and a silver cup for my lipsticks and brushes. And he hated it. He made me leave it there. And I missed it so much. I decided that if I had to choose —I wanted my table.

Sound thinking.

Well, now, though, I think that if it was between you and my table, it would be you.

That's very sweet, my angel. Because you know that I can take care of you and your table can't.

Yes, I guess so. You say such smart things. Oh, something else. I never told anyone, never ever.

What?

This is hard. It's one of my, you know—dirty memories.

Yes, yes. Nothing is hard, with me here. Tell Artie.

Well, you know Morley, my brother?

Yes.

Well, Before he got all religious and became like God or someone, I mean when he was young, he was kind of funny. I mean he wanted to be an actor—and that didn't work out and he used to cry and have fits and sometimes he would crawl under the kitchen sink and eat sugar and butter and things with his hands. Well, one day he was outside in the shed where we made the pickles. And I went to find him and he was in there in the dark licking butter off his hands—and he asked me to sit down—I guess we were almost teenagers—or he was. And well, pretty soon he took my panties off and put butter on me and then he made me put it on him and he was—and he put his thingie in me. He said if I told anyone he would cut my hair off. I had this long pretty red hair. But I never did. But with your brother—that's not supposed to be good, is it? I mean it felt real good. And especially—because it was a secret—you know. Has anyone else ever done that? I mean they'd tell you, wouldn't they?

(Well, well—Frog Face falls from grace—oleo and away they go.)

> *Happens all the time. Forget all about it. After all—it just happened because your brother liked to play with you so much.*
>
> *Everyone likes to play with you. You're very popular.*
>
> *Oh, Artie—you make me feel so good. You can do that to me—with the butter or anything. Any time you want. Just let me know so I can stop at the market first.*
>
> *I will, I promise.*
>
> *Oh, Artie?*
>
> *Yes, Randi-cake?*
>
> *One more thing. I would like it, if you could sometime, to go to my dance with me. Maybe we could enter a contest together?*
>
> *Well, we'll see. I am a very busy man, you know.*
>
> *Oh, I know. I guess that's why I never meet any of your friends.*
>
> *(Uh-oh.) Being alone with you is all I want. I'm too jealous to share you.*
>
> *(Giggle, wiggle.) Oh, you're so cute. Let me kiss your cute little thingie. Mmmm. Mmmm. We could do our samba. If he's still alive I could probably borrow Frederic's tuxedo.*
>
> *Maybe someday. Let's not talk about it now, my dove. Just close your eyes and pretend my little thingie is a great big bowl of peppermint ice cream.*

A pattern began to form. Rose was coming on Tuesdays, Thursdays and Saturdays. And staying for hours. Which naturally interfered with my practice. I was scheduling my patients around my nookie hours. So I was (seemingly) working 15-hour days. Which was confusing to my wife—because I kept telling her that we were broke. We were. Patients were deserting. I was referring away. My colleagues were pleasantly puzzled. I had decided that if and when my family or friends (all of whom seemed long ago and faraway) questioned me, I would claim male menopause. Gotcha. I would even go so far as to say I was involved in a highly experimental new therapy module that I could not talk about yet. Which was true in a way.

But I was still most definitely possessed. I was consumed with my playmate. Our playpen. Insatiable. Male nymphomania. Whatever. And only for her. The thought of touching my wife was repugnant. Not even the most luscious and wondrous sex goddess could move me an inch (let alone seven, har). But just the thought of Rosie made me flood with desire—wolf noises growled in my cashmere-covered throat. Rrrrrrr. And I did not care about anything else. I stopped reading and playing tennis. I stopped playing chess and watching educational television. I was almost on the verge of giving up Sunday football. So you can see this was serious.

I had this whole private substratum. This other life. "I was an undercover agent for the Sexual Obsessives of America." I was losing weight. I was losing friends. I was losing patients. I was losing control. And I was ecstatic. A walking, talking nerve end. A prick with a man attached. When I was away from Rose I fantasized about what I would do with her when I was with her. And when I was with her—I did it. And thought of nothing. Mindless, spontaneous. I was just in it.

We went on like this for a month. My new friends, Morley (my man) and Louise (baby), sent me sweet little letters and newspaper clippings. From Louise I got a detailed account of everyday life in Herculaneum in A.D. 79. (She had had a vision of me dressed in Roman bath clothes waving to Alexander the Great across the Bay of Naples.) From Morley I got a copy of the New Testament and his personal list of over five-hundred lost commandments from God to Moses (I was advised to check and see which ones Rose had broken). I thought of having a small private party just the four of us (and a pound of Parkay)—but decided against it.

My wife was red-eyed most of the time. She was taking sleeping pills. And larger and larger quantities of white wine were being delivered. We had still not spoken of it.

She was being rolfed. She was being ESTed. She was being Acupressured. And playing backgammon. She was toying with the idea of having her eyelids done. (Over my shrieks of poverty.)

My son was quiet. He had a bad cold and stayed in bed for a week. He sprained his wrist and stayed in bed for three days. He got the flu and was home for ten days. The school was concerned. He also appeared red-eyed in the mornings. What a cheery little trio over the soft-boileds. Two sullen swollen-eyed victims—and one manic madman. And no one talking about it. Swallowing the yolks whole. Slimy gulps of anxiety and rage. A little salt and pepper and we can choke it down for another day. I felt political. I Led Three Lives. "I will tell all on a need-to-know basis, my own family unit." They chose not to need to know. So I left earlier and earlier and came home later and later. Bad little boy. Waiting for Mommy to spank my hands. Testing. Stretching. And no one was stopping me. The red eyes and the sleeping pills and the sprained wrists were much too subtle. Feeling no guilt—I was immune to the Attack of the Martyrs. (Never have played into that hand much, anyway.) So I kept going. With only an occasional glance over my shoulder to see if anyone was shadowing. No one was. Except, perhaps, American Express and my accountant.

When my property tax bill came at the end of that month, I did not have money to pay it. I sold a Kashmir rug from my parents' estate. (I had planned to give it to my wife for Christmas. She had even ordered new upholstery for our matching eight-foot sofas to complement it. I didn't tell her.)

I had all of my clothes taken in two sizes and turned down an offer to teach an abnormal psych class at the university for the next quarter. (I *was* an abnormal psych class.) Entering my office, my palace, my shady little shrine—all of the tension would melt from me. Release would flood my bloodstream. Deep breaths would push forth from my slender diaphragm. Home. Lust and laziness. I cared nothing for anything outside of my Den. (Other doctors in the building had begun to cast their eyes sideways after greeting me.) I took no heed. Jealous. All jealous. What they would give to have what I had. A new waistline—a stiff rod—a boy's saber. A willing slave. An undemanding, receiving, responding, malleable bitch. I was conqueror. Odysseus. Attila. Sitting Bull. King Solomon. No more cocktail party touchy-feely. No more dinner party double entendre. No more fuck-the-hostess fantasies. Eat your wizened wiener hearts out, gentlemen. I am getting it on. And off. And without risk. No clinging teenyboppers calling your wife up in the middle of the night. No false promises, no "marry me, marry me"—no performance. No "you're the best, baby" bullshit. No plotting and planning. No remorse. And no promises. No Tiffany baubles and suicide threats. I had it all. Fantasy of the week. Rose.

And then something happened. It was a Tuesday afternoon. Rose had just left (for a touch-up). I was lying on dear ol' brown, as I had come to call my corduroy playground, dozing off. Just me, a joint and my svelte bare ass. When there was a knock at the door. I jumped, heart racing—grabbed for my pants, yelling "just a moment" in a most undoctorly manner. I stuffed the joint in my coffee cup and crept to the door.

My son was sitting in my waiting room. His books lay beside him, his hands were clasped in his lap. It was getting dark and the light cast shadows on his small bony face, reflecting up on his glasses (yes, we looked disconcertingly alike). The effect was sobering. A baby and an ancient man. Frowning into space. He had never come to my office before. Never.

I could feel my throat close. I was, it seemed, about to reach the bottom of my slide.

He stood up and faced me. We made small talk—"aren't you supposed to be at school" talk. "Nice office, Dad" talk. And I brought him inside. He stood. I sat, trying to remember how old he was. Who he was. Twelve? Was that possible? Yes. My twelve-year-old son, who had never been to my office. Who had, for that matter, never been anywhere alone with me in the entire, short, lonely course of his life. Stood over me, firm and to himself. A whole person. A smaller version of me. I felt very frightened. Unprepared. I moved into role. Plugged in my doctor suit. (And turned on my recorder.)

Well, son, it's nice to have you here. I won't tell your mother about school. I imagine you came because you wanted to talk about something.

(He nods. Our glasses meet—not going to make this easy for his old pop.)

Why don't you sit down and tell me what's going on with you?

I'd rather stand, thank you.

(They always say that—another martyr trick—not an inch of territory will be relinquished here.)

Okay.

(There is a long moment of silence. Currents of tension—ray gun above us. I swallow hard. He swallows hard.)

What is it, son?

I came here to ask you a question.

Okay.

What are you doing all the time you're away from home?

You know what I'm doing, I'm working—I'm teaching...

Mother thinks you've got a girlfriend.

She told you that?

I heard her telling someone. And I asked her. And she said yes, she thought so. And if we're going to have a divorce—well, I think I have a right to know about it. I'm the one she talks to—with you gone all of the time—I have to listen, and she's sad all the time—and crying—she's crying in the morning and when I come home—I can't even bring friends home—and everything's crummy. And I want to know what's going on.

Well, son, I understand how you . . .

David.

What?

My name is DAVID. (His hands clench and tears fill his eyes) *DAVID. My name is DAVID FREEDMAN. I'm thirteen years old. I'm not "son"—I'm DAVID. I'm a person. You're my father. You're supposed to care about us. You don't care about anything. Mother is getting worse and worse—and I am too. I get sick—I feel bad—I don't want to come home anymore. Other dads take their kids places—or talk to them—once in awhile anyway—but not you . . . you ignore us—all the time. Like we don't exist. And you never hardly ever are home, and if you hate us so much, why don't you just tell us—why don't you just go away with your girlfriend—just get divorced—and go away—and get it over with . . . so we're not always waiting for you . . . It's so awful, all that waiting and you don't come—and when you come you don't even look at us—you just pretend—everything you do is pretending—you treat us like things—and we're not. I'm not. You don't even care. You never ask me anything about myself. I could be anyone. And Mother treats me like a grown-up and a baby at the same time—and she tells me all of this stuff—and I can't do anything about it. You're the grown-up, you're the big man—why don't you do something? She says we don't have any money and I can't take scuba lessons—and yet—you're always working, working, working. . . . None of it makes sense—you just lie and pretend and never tell anyone what's going on . . . like we don't exist . . . like we don't matter at all. . . . It hurts our feelings . . . and I can't stand it anymore. . . . I'd go away if I could—but there's no place to go. You're the head of the house—you make all the decisions—big-shot psychiatrist. Well, you'd better decide something about us . . . because if you don't—if you don't . . . something's going to happen, something awful is going to happen. . . .*

(His glasses slip down his wet face and onto the floor. His skinny-boy body shakes with fury and tears—fists still clenched.)

I am rigid. Packed in dry ice. I cannot move. I cannot breathe. My mouth is wired out. I battle this paralysis of the heart. I must move. I must hold him. I must not let this go on. He is not he. He is me, too. My selfishness moves to the point of monstrosity. I must move to save both of us. Resurrect myself at twelve—no, thirteen. He is thirteen, he is right, he is suffering—if I can move, maybe he can be saved—we can be saved. And I cannot move. Not a finger. My tongue seems to spread in my throat. My head bloats with pressure. The Tin Man. I sit. Watching my son, this David Freedman, choke on his pain.

During the last days of my residency, when I thought I had seen everything—handled every sort of trouble, separated myself from my work enough to face the Big Time—I got a call from the county burn unit. A young burn patient was behaving strangely. The surgeons and intensive care nurses thought he was becoming irrational. Would I come over and consult? Of course. I went. They wrapped me up in layers of sterilized material. Turned me into a padded monkey man, covered my face and head and led me into this room. A thirteen-year-old boy had been in a boating accident. Off for a jolly summer cruise with his mom and dad, his two cousins and his baby sister. Sunshine, Kool-Aid, fishing and water-skiing. Wonderful summer weekend. There was an explosion on the boat. His parents, his baby sister and his cousins were killed instantly.

And he, the survivor, lay there. His nose and ears were burned away. His penis and testes were gone. His body was curdle. Seventy percent of it screeching in scorched, mutilated, unregenerative agony. The child in the bed was screaming, "KILL ME...KILL ME...KILL ME..." And everyone bustled about him: "Now, now, drink this—just try to relax, you'll be better in the morning..." "KILL ME!" They wanted me to consult. Yes, son. You have a bad attitude—there are worse things in life than being burned into freakhood and neutered. And losing all sources of structure, family and comfort. Much worse. Keep a good thought. The Lord works in strange ways. Yeah.

I stood by that bed and became that boy. I lost all ability to separate. To practice. I stood, watching the wet cement seal me up and prevent me from moving. Gradually, he did become psychotic. Shouting filth and obscenities—growling like an animal—as if he was trying to make everyone hate him enough to kill him. It didn't work. He lived. The staff thought they had done a terrific job.

The night I first saw him I went out to dinner with my wife and some old college friends. I remember being extremely animated—ordering a lot of expensive wine, laughing too loud—and right in the middle of having this great carefree old time I saw that face, I heard that scream. "KILL ME." And I vomited all over the table. And I never discussed it or thought about it again. I never forgot it, either. It became a little cartridge in the brain plate.

And now I was frozen exactly the same way. My son sobbed until his fists unclenched. He wiped at his helpless face with the sides of his parka sleeves. He never reached for me or accused me or shrieked at me for not comforting him. Maybe in some way, as if he were my patient, it was better that I didn't—because the gesture was not honest. The gesture held odors of gauze and cement and the terror of exposure. Letting go and dying. He was letting go. I thanked God for that—all alone, he was letting it out—and maybe that would be enough to save him. I had passed the point of that kind of surrender. Never to know it again. And I had nothing left to give him. And he was me there. And so there was this swelling truth about it.

Finally he stopped. He bent down on the carpet and picked up his glasses. I tried my arm. It moved. I raised it and handed him a Kleenex across my desk. He took it.

I'm sorry, David.

No, you're not.

I am. But I understand how you feel. I want to help you and I can't. I can't seem to even move from this seat. And I can't explain anything to you.

You can, you don't want to.

I can't. And I don't want to.

(His face squeezes together—squeezing small—strangling out the tears. Spasms of hurt. Of endings. He has been brave. He has come. He has offered himself. His need. His love. His hate. All that he has. And it cannot help us. It isn't enough.)

David. I promise you this. I will never leave you and your mother. I am not a very good man. I am very selfish, very empty. I am trying to reach something. Maybe if I can—follow this course—which would seem insane to you—it may help me. It may help me feel more. And then maybe I can be a better father to you. I don't want to lie to you. And I can't tell you any more without in some ways lying to you. That means you are going to have to be very strong. I think you are very strong. Coming here took courage. Crying and telling me what you think—getting angry—that is very healthy. It will help you. You have helped yourself. And basically—that is the only real help we ever get, anyway. I don't want to lie, so I won't tell you anything else. And I doubt if things are going to change much, for now. They may—probably will—get worse. And I'm sorry. You are going to have to deal with a lot. You have a strange father. So did I. Most people grow up with pretty unpleasant families. Some of us get through it fine. Some of us don't. I think you will. You can come and talk to me again, whenever you want. And I will try... I am trying to change. I am doing something that may help me. I don't know. And that's the best I can do for you.

We stare at one another for a long while. I am impressed, moved, by the courage of his stare. I see my boy/baby—remember holding him, helping him walk. Tears I wiped so easily—and feel the weight of my metal arms. This iron lung over my heart. He blows his nose. It doesn't help. His face is flushed with raw hurt. He nods. And without a word, he turns his back and walks out the door.

Well, class? Threw you a ringer, didn't I? Not exactly what you were expecting this term.
You all know, of course, that the genesis of psychology was philosophy. We sort of grew out of it. I did very well in the subject. And I would like to take this opportunity, while I drink some café and clear my banging little brain, to offer some. Philosophy, that is. Some that may surprise you.
It may surprise because it is coming from me. Who—after my most recent confession—you must now loathe with new depths of loathing. I want to say this: *I* do believe that inside every wormy little one of us there is a Godhead. A touch of the big brush. There is this small—let us call it a waning ember—in there. It is totally different for every single one of us. It holds our own truth. Our own path. It holds happiness. And peace. The trick, class, is to find it. And it don't matter a shit how you find it. Rebirth. Psychoanalysis. If you can find that puny little ember. Yours. You will have a good life. If you don't. You won't.
Now, outside of Baby Jesus, just about none of us are born knowing where in the fuck this slippery little kernel is. That's why we spend so much time working against ourselves. Choosing the wrong professions, the wrong relationships, the wrong floor wax. Can't find the frigging little Godhead. So our lives never click. Had a friend once who called it the "hole inside." Walking around all our lives with this hole we can never fill. Try to. Pour booze into it. Big Macs. Sex. Have babies. Buy power boats. See shrinks.
"Got this funny feeling inside, Doc."
"Really? Describe the feeling, my good man."

"Well, like a hole."
"A hole?"
"Yeah."
"A big hole?"
"No. Yes. Well, I don't know—exactly—but nothing seems to fill it. Not even love."
"Hmm. Sounds serious."

It is serious. I watch, you see. I have been watching lives being lived between the clicks for years. I can sometimes hear the gears grinding. See the holes growing. If you find the click you win. Pop psychocorn calls it "doing your own thing"—all of that jazz—but what it is—is finding the Godhead. Before you die. Finding that little sparkling in the ashes—that is you. That is yours alone. That allows you to accept the hole. The hole, you see, is not fillable. It can be accepted at best. And that is peace. And freedom. Click. And it ain't easy, Trixie. Even people that work very, very hard. Therapy. Retreats. Prayer. And, horror of horrors, change. Surrender. Faith. Revelation. Even for those rare dudes who are willing enough, brave enough (and/or desperate enough) to pay the price. Even then, it's fucking hard work. And lonely. And you may not like your puny little ember a'tall. May not fit your image. Some folks get theirs in their hot little hands—and are so appalled at who they really are that they snuff it out and spend the rest of their frightened little lives stuffing Mallomars in their caverns. Or something.

It takes hard work and guts to find it. And total surrender to accept it. If you can. And do. You will be one of those rare and lucky sots who, in the words of my favorite Greek poet, "Escape the nets of the world. Who live neither in the pack of wolves nor in the flock of sheep." One of those. Who know something. Who were, accidentally maybe, stoking around in the dying flames—and hit their spark. And what have we here? Usually, finding it involves so much loss, so much rage, grief, pain, loneliness and grit that we make some sort of soggy settlement with our hole early on and forget it. But the only ones who "get out of it alive" are the ones who keep stoking.

I have seen it happen. It made me very, very jealous. And scared. Because I knew that I had blown it. (I even know when.) And I knew that basically—short of a miracle—I would spend the rest of my life popping caviar and Jack Daniels into my hole. Covering it with silk shirts and tickets to the Super Bowl—et cetera.

I can see a potential Clicker at forty paces. Not all of them know it—not all of them ever find it. But I know who has a shot at it.

When I was in college I had an affair of sorts with a Clicker. She had not gotten it yet. And I was too young and too busy stuffing my hole to have a clue about it. But she told me something once (when she dumped me, to be exact), and I never forgot it. I never forgot it—firstly because she was the only girl who had ever stirred the cockles of my decomposing heart—and also because when I began forming this Allegory of the Clicks, I thought of her as the first person of Godhead-finding potential I had ever known. She said to me, "I am leaving you Arthur, because—I have the potential for having a good life—I may not—I may blow it—but I feel inside me—that I am one of those very special people who can have it all. Can have everything good out of life. And I don't want to compromise that. And you would. Because you don't know about that." She was, in her fashion, being kind; what she saw in me was (young and feisty though I appeared—to myself, at any rate) I was formed. I was, most probably, through. The mold set. And she wasn't. Bad vibes, man.

I wonder about her often now. Once I tried to track her down. I wonder if she was right. Or if she blew it. Or if she's still poking around. Little lost ember, come out, come out.

Anyway, I thought that might make you all feel better. I think—maybe I'm just trying to make *myself* feel better—but I think my son is one of those. Funny, right under my nose for twelve, thirteen years—and I never spotted it. I think he is a Clicker. And I will write him a note one day and tell him that. That may be the best part of his legacy—right up there with the graphite racket and the keys to the Mercedes.

18

Well, for some reason I am feeling bright as a button. The coffee and confession—must be good for the soul. So, let us get back to my slide.

After my son's visit, I, being demented but not dumb, knew that the party was about to be crashed. That is, I knew—but chose to ignore—the information. Meaning, I did not stop. I did what every classic tester in the world does—I became more blatant. My son retreated for the moment, knowing that whatever it was that he could do he had done—and was probably, in many ways, relieved to have left his pile on *my* floor. My wife had her eyelids done. (Small price, I felt.) And apparently unspoken between us, as was our wont, we had struck another bargain. So, I picked up my stitches.

Now, as I was saying, a pattern had begun to form. Sometimes I would plan a sequence—even to diagramming positions I wished Rosie to take. Sometimes I tied her up. Sometimes I cursed her. We explored every sexual elevation recorded in print or film. We dressed up. We played games. Sometimes we just plain fucked. Missionary position. Good clean fun. I was drinking a lot. Toking a lot. Everything. And my prick was as sensitized as a radar screen. I walked around with a perpetual half-on (if you know what I mean). Women were beginning to sniff after me in unlikely places. Sometimes, even in the market, I would find a pair of lovely eyes scanning my groin. Takes one to know one. All us dogs in heat know where the bitch is.

And then it was Rose's birthday. Louise had called and asked if they might come by before her appointment with a little cake. I had jovially agreed. I had bought her a pair of purple satin panties with two deep circles cut out where her ass would nicely flop over. I had amyl nitrate capsules ready to pop and new handcuffs ready to lock.

At exactly noon on Rosie's birthday (the date escapes me) my buzzer buzzed, and I, wearing a smoking jacket and ascot—in perfect host fashion, coked up to suitable birthday spirit—breezed to the door. There stood Louise and Morley and Rosie *and* a stranger. A homely young man with a large black mole on his cheek and greasy hair. He was wearing cowboy clothes. And a sneer. I invited them in.

"I hope you won't mind, Doctor"—Louise sashays about setting up some white-frosted cake and little plastic forks and plates—"I've been wanting you to meet my son, Lawrence—I named him after Lawrence of Arabia—for so long. And Rose did so want her nephew to be at her party."

"Of course not, it's a pleasure to meet you." (I extend my polished hand toward this smirky greaseball.)

His nails are grimy, his palm is grisly, his eyes are boring into me like little black ball bearings.

Morley lumbers around after Louise opening a can of Hawaiian Punch.

"It is so good—to share joy with one's family. To break bread in peace and love."

Rose sits on the arm of the couch—very much the birthday girl. Her brittle orange waves are swept into lacquered perfection. Her eyebrows are penciled at perfect right angles. She is wearing a lime-green taffeta dress with a black velvet bow tied neatly at her little throat.

"Oh, Morley, you're so poetic. But we're not breaking bread—we're breaking cake." (Giggle, giggle.) "Artie, isn't he poetic?"

I freeze. "Artie." Lawrence's black metal eyes whirl right through me. Oh, yes, I remember now, this is the one who likes to tie ladies to chairs and stuff and such.

I change the subject. "Well, Lawrence, what sort of work do you do?"

He folds his dirty hairy arms in front of his chest and crosses his booted legs at the ankle. Suave.

"I'm a cowboy."

(A Jewish cowboy.) "A cowboy? How nice. Must be hard to make a go of it in the city."

"Not if you're good. I have a little ranch. And I put together Wild West shows—Miss Hillbilly America contest—that's one of mine. All those sweet little broads from Okie country. Nice gig. Probably a lot like yours, huh, Doc?"

(I smile) "I'm afraid I miss your point." (I put on my most serious, most officious man...healing mask.)

"I mean, lots of dumb broads looking for Santa Claus—'Make me happy, make me a beauty queen'—same gig."

Louise thrusts a piece of thawing white cake in my hands. "Please, Doctor, try this. I made it myself."

"Wait, wait, everyone." (Morley is standing on one of my Breuer side chairs.) "First, before we partake—I think a prayer is in order."

Rose giggles. Louise sighs. Lawrence snickers. I cough.

"Oh Lord, God of Abraham, Isaac and Jacob, bless this food that we are about to eat. Bless this house, and your daughter Rose, help her to find the path to righteousness, forgive her her sins. Bless Dr. Freedman—who is helping to lead her out of the wilderness. Baruch Atah Adonai Elohenu, Melech Haolam Borei Prihagofen. Amen."

Amen. Amen. Amen. Amen.

We take our little plates of starch and make yummy noises. I turn away from Lawrence. Lawrence is dangerous. I must be very, very careful with Nephew Lawrence. Louise dashes out of the room and returns with gaily wrapped packages.

"All right, everybody. It's time for Rose to open her presents. The doctor has work to do."

Everyone is smiling. The feeling is very strong that this is a big event for my new friends.

Morley gives Rose a little white prayer book with "Rose Liebshitz" engraved in gold foil on the front. Louise gives Rose a pack of tarot cards and a nude soap sculpture of Burt Reynolds that she has been working on for weeks (she announces). Lawrence gives Rose a bottle of Jungle Gardenia (interesting). I—needless to say—keep my presents out of it.

Rose is merry. "This is the nicest birthday I've ever had."

"Yes, thanks to Dr. Freedman." (Morley swoops down on me, placing his huge foul-smelling armpit next to my ear.) "You have helped Rose so much. Not only her body. But her soul. She has not consorted with gentiles. She has been home. A Rachel. Our Rose is becoming a Rachel. And we thank you. Now, come Louise, come Lawrence—the good doctor has work to do with our sister."

Well, yes, we do have some very delicate work to do here.

(Rose blushes—bad sign.) "Thank you all for coming. Uh, Lawrence, it was a pleasure to meet you." (I force my hand forward.)

Lawrence looks at it. Then those beady black balls snap up at me. He hits my palm—the hipster salute.

"Yeah, I'll be talking to you, Doctor." (Smirk—almost a perfect smirk too)

I see them out.

Lawrence is last. (You walk slower when you swagger.) And I know. That Lawrence knows.

Rose loved her panties. She wasn't quite so fond of the handcuffs, until I reminded her that her own nephew was a cowboy of some repute and used them all the time. I also pumped her a bit under hypnosis about Cowboy Joe. She giggled a lot. Once, apparently, at a family gathering where (horror of horrors) Uncle Morley broke out the Manischewitz, Lawrence stuck his hand up her ass. (Yes, that's what the lady said—"He, well—we were in the kitchen and I guess we were both a little tipsy and I leaned over to pick up a plate and he put his finger right up into my tushy.") I was growing more and more curious about this Lawrence. As I said, I was in spite of everything still not crazy. I knew in the true clarity of my paranoia that the powers that be—the outside—could bring down the House of Arthur like any other card number—one deep breath could do it. So, I thought, I must be very careful. And check this Lawrence out. Get the goods on him—as they say. Because he was there in that room. I saw that moley beaner face every time I spread those pretty purple-lined cheeks. Trouble in paradise. First my son and now this. And of course there were other things. Like losing my patients. And friends. Things like that. And my behavior. But still, I *knew* I was in charge—just acting out my fantasies as a way of reconnecting possibly with life. I could stop anytime I wanted. Rosie would be "cured," given some Di-gel and sent home. I knew what I could handle. A pro like me. And besides. It was still so nice. I mean so nice. The thing about Rose is, or was. That she was good company. I wasn't used to that. My wife was a deadhead. No sense of fun. Boring. Dry. Rosie was outrageous. Even the way she looked. Because it was all so bright. Powder and color and light. It was fun. She was fun. Because she too, in some way, had escaped those nets. She had shot those baby blues around the room long ago and seen what the world was and said: "Yick—let's dance." Nothing bothered her. Boy, may I tell you, that was a nice treat. Well, I shouldn't say nothing—if her hair didn't look right or she found a new "wrinkly," *that* bothered her—but even then her powers of delusion were so sophisticated that a warm word took her narrowed little mind right off it. She never analyzed. And she disliked no one. And I, who had started with such a magnificent, museum-caliber contempt for this common, this sack-brained oddity—this spindle shanks of humanity, this dumb cunt—I now preferred her company to all others. Pollyanna and Pop at home. We laughed. She shimmied naked over my open mouth. She rubbed my back and brought me lox and bagels. And she extracted from me a crater of erotic longing, a frothing, bubbling stream of juice, that thrilled and amazed me. I had never had this before. And I felt, for some obvious first-year-psychology-essay reason, safe here. I realized this one afternoon after a long and particularly groaning orgasm, as Rosie hummed little tunes in the tub and I lay with a cold beer and a joint—just lying—not needing to move or do anything. Not thinking or planning or watchdogging my life. My LIFE. My serious, important, studied for, worked out according to plan—on the upward swing, dated and controlled till I leave my incredible little cranium to

MIT. *My life.* Watched and thought about every moment of every day. Cradle to grave, I thought it all out endlessly, every day. I realized, lying there, that I felt absolutely comfortable in my own skin. And safe. And I tried to remember the last time I had felt that way. Felt totally centered. In myself. Secure. And funnily enough it did not take long. I found that I had not felt safe since the moment I had realized that I was a grown-up. Not when I left home, because first of all none of us really think we can't go back, put on our beanies and resume childhood as long as Mom and Pop are somewhere on the earth's face. So it wasn't then. And it wasn't when my parents died. It was maybe when I got married. I'm not sure. But at some moment a little birdie blew that tune in my tender little ear (hello there, Arthur, welcome to being a grown-up). And I had not felt safe one moment since. Had been looking over my shoulder waiting for the boogey man ever since. "If I study harder—make more money—play tennis better—learn Chinese cooking—I'll be safe out here with the grown-ups." Elementary. Sophomoric. And true.

But somehow, here in my sanctum with my fifty-year-old totsie—and no birdie on my shoulder—I felt safe. Tucked in my nice warm bed—in my jammies, with Granny making soup in the kitch. Don't ask me why. I only do that sort of probing for pay. But it was true. And I was drawn to it like the abalone to the rock.

By this time, I was spending nearly all of my waking hours (and many of my sleeping ones as well) in my officina. The game at home was, basically, how fast I could move before I found myself trapped by a piercing look from my son or a newly firm-lidded (but still red-rimmed) stare from my wife? I had finally told her that I was in a very experimental workshop—and that I knew my behavior was stranger than usual—but to trust me. She still had not confronted me about my "girlfriend," and I had moments of fantasy about divorce hearings and private detectives and the like. But I chose, Artful Dodger that I was, to dispel such thoughts.

About a week after Rose's party the phone rang in my office. I was puttering around—reading my old college yearbook, to be exact. (It was not a Rose day.) I assumed that it was she, calling to tell me she adored me. (My incoming calls were dwindling to that point. I had also taken out a second mortgage on our house.) I will play for you the tape of that conversation. (As automatic as saying hello had become my finger on the tape button—inroads into immortality. Watergate left its imprint and changed my life.) Anyway, I said hello and automatically pushed the button. The voice on the other end was deep. It seemed to be coming from faraway. It hinted of the South, and something in it made me snap forward, my mouth suddenly dry and my heart pounding.

Hello, Arthur, my man.

Hello, Dix.

(There is silence on the tape. It has been fourteen years.)

Well, now that we've got all the formalities out of the way—I am deeply gratified to know that you are still alive. You are still alive, aren't you, Arthur, my friend?

Haven't been. Not so sure now. I have been feeling certain stirrings of late.

(My throat is thick—I feel like crying.)

Where are you, Dix? Are you practicing, what? Are you okay?

One question at a time, my boy. Didn't they teach you that? Never overload the patient. Now, in answer to your third question, I am hunky-do. In answer to your second question, no. In answer to your first question, I am in my room.

Are you in town? Can I see you? I can't believe I'm talking to you. After you, well, later I tried to find you—and no one seemed to know where in hell you were. And you never called—you son of a bitch. It's been fourteen years—and zip—not even a Christmas card.

Arthur, Arthur, you are doing it again. Overloading me. In answer to your second question, I don't know yet. In answer to your first question, no.

Dix, I don't want to play games with you. Where are you?

I told you, I'm in my room.

What room? Where?

In a very nice little place with flowers on the ground and gaily painted bars on the windows. In the executive wing—so to speak—affording me certain privileges, like my own phone with which to call up long-lost friends and leave obscene messages at the APA.

(I will cry.) *You're in a hospital?*

No, no, dear boy. Don't be so crass. I am in a very elite sanitarium. Discreet and genteel. You forget, we Texans know how to take care of our own.

Have you been there long?

I have been here always.

Are you serious?

Never more.

I don't understand.

What is there not to understand?

Why you never got well.

But I did.

I don't understand.

My dear Arthur. For a bright fellow, you sure don't understand much.

Come on, Dix. Stop it. I'm not enjoying this.

Were you supposed to?

You tell me.

But I did. I cracked open like a porcelain egg. Happens to a lot of perfectionist, overachieving American boys. And as you may remember, I was a patient on my own ward—rather humbling experience, I may add. And then my family decided that it wouldn't do to have me amongst the herd and moved me on, and once my nerve endings healed and all the marvelous head men had had at me—well, I was better. In fact I was better than I had ever been. In fact I was never better. I saw very, very clearly. Do you know what I saw?

No.

I saw myself becoming you—nothing personal. I saw a life without peace. I saw a life of stress and compromise and bullshit. I saw all of those "cows ducking" into infinity. I saw the right wife, the nice little kiddies, the good life. I saw my compulsion to save the world—and knew that I would get right back on the merry-go-round because I still did care. And I decided against it. I decided to stay right here. And live quiet. And it's worked out rather nicely. I run groups here, get a little action from the nurses—once in awhile we even have some crazy rich nympho in to dry out for a couple of months. I leave the world alone and the world leaves me alone. Matter of fact, calling you is one of my first forays outside in a very long time.

Why did you? Call me now, I mean?

I'm not sure.

Horseshit.

Okay, Arthur. Good. You're catching up. For some reason lately—maybe it's looking forty in its fat face—I wanted to see if I was right. If my choice was any crazier than your choice.

I didn't have a choice.

True. You were hurled into destiny with the speed of laser. Never saw anyone so sure of his course. God is in my corner. Life is a shingle and a foreign sports cou-pe. Who was right?

It's just not that fucking easy. There is no right—and all of that stuff. You know about all of that stuff, Doctor?

Bravo, Arthur. You're not going to make this easy for ol' Dix, are you?

Why should I? First, you're asking an absurd question. And second, you sound even colder and harder than I do. And so now even I'm confused. You see, I would have said—you were. Though, as I said, the question is preposterous—maybe neither one of us had choices. You protected yourself from what you saw as reality one way—I did it another way. Prices are being paid all around, old buddy. But I do, also, feel certain anger. (The tears are forming again.) You were my friend. I needed you. You cracked and got out. I saw that—and turned off. I didn't want that to happen to me. I turned my caring apparatus off. But the equipment rusts. The model is out of date now. But it doesn't sound like your gears are in any better shape. So you tell me.

Touché, my friend.

I'm not working for points, Dix.

I know. You must forgive me. I haven't been communicating with the outside—let alone my past—for a very long spell.

You don't have to be in a little barred room for that. I happen to be a veritable genius on the subject.

I see.

You know, Dix—it is astonishingly coincidental that you should phone me at this particular moment in my life. I would like to tell you why. But I think I'll save it for later. Do you want to know what I was doing when you called? I was leafing through my college yearbook. Reminiscing. And who should phone—like God was watching me—but my most poignant memory. Dr. Eugene Dix. My former idol.

I see. I have just become a member of the "former" club. Sorry if this is disturbing your illusion. Maybe I'm just putting you on. I may be sitting in some huge private hospital in the Midwest that I own and operate—I could be a pillar of the community, have a loving, perfect marriage and six precocious youngsters. Give blood and donate all my free time to helping teenage drug addicts. I may be having a little jest.

Maybe. But even so, somehow all of that doesn't sound much better.

(We laugh then. We laugh a long time. We are friends again—the laughter filling in all the creases of time and change.)

It seems, Dix, that you and I, in different ways maybe, were so busy trying to fight the enemies—keep the coping mechanisms from splattering —that we forgot how to live. Our work was trying to help people learn how to live—in the world—in spite of the madness— and we were first off the block—running away from that open space so fast our sneakers had road burns. Only you had courage. You had empathy. And I envied that. We all live in little trick rooms. I'm an expert, I told you. But I've been running a little game out here—I have found a little spot of safety for myself. And this safety valve may very well end me right next door to you—maybe we could get a suite. But I think you know now—even when you tried to kill Merleman I think you must have known—that it's fucking pebbles in the stream. You have to find a way not to be afraid if you want to live.

You mean we can't drag good old Cassandra out, dust her off and hear some truth?

Not a chance. Besides, you wouldn't like what the old broad told you anyway.

I imagine you have a point. I retract my question. Let me ask you another.

Please.

What do you regret most?

Dying.

That bad, the prices you paid out there?

I am recently beginning to think yes. That bad.

I see. Any chance of a transplant?

Are you asking for me or for yourself, Doctor?

Oh, Arthur, Arthur, that was pricking of you.

You found the mine, Doctor. I just brought the pan.

Wit, fistular wit at that. I think the question should not be answered.

I think the question has been answered.

(There is a long pause. I think we are both trying not to cry. We want to stop performing for one another. We don't.)

Dix, I would like to see you. Will you think about it?

I will give it my undivided attention. That—and what I am having for dinner tonight—will play equal importance in my mind. I do have, you *see, a simplified life-style.*

Ah yes. Well, you know where to find me. I won't ask you to tell me where to find you. Just know that I'm here, anytime. And maybe next time we can stop trying to be so cute and really talk a little.

I was really talking a little. Don't start having expectations now, my boy. It will ruin your image.

Wouldn't want that.

I should hope not. Well, Arthur, my friend. I will call again. This may be the start of a trend.

Let's hope so. I do think we could use one another right now. Intimacy without proximity. Might serve both our purposes.

Good point. Bye, Arthur.

Bye, Dix.

19

The day after Dix called I fucked Rose for four and one-half hours straight. And never came. Then we looked at pictures in movie magazines. Then we danced a little. Then we looked at pictures in *House and Carport* or something. Then we sent out for Chinese food. Then we watched *Edward My Son* with Deborah Kerr and Spencer Tracy. Then I sucked Rose's pussy until blood ran from my lips. Then we had a little "chat."

Artie?

Yes, my dove?

Can I ask you a personal question?

No.

Oh, Artie, you're so mean.

You know better than that. Do you want your tummy to start hurting again?

No.

Then you must obey the doctor.

But if we're in love—we should know things about each other. I mean you know everything about me, but I don't know anything about you. What if we wanted to get married or something—you're like a stranger. In many ways.

Randi, Randi—I don't like this. You are making me unhappy. Do you or do you not trust me?

Yes. Yes. I do.

Then you must stop this. I think maybe we should do a little work tonight. I don't want to see you get sick. What's that?

What's what?

Oh, nothing. It must have been the light.

What, tell me—what did you see?

Nothing, my sweet. Just the way the light cast shadows on your face, I thought I saw a little wrinkle—on the side of your mouth.

Oh, no. Where?

Randi, Randi—relax. I told you it was just the light. Now, what were you saying?

Nothing. Never mind. Just forget it. Do you want me to play with your thingie? I haven't done it all day.

If it will make you happy. Of course.

She played with my "thingie." And I sent her on home. And my mood darkened. I lay down on the couch to think. Swoops and shapes tumbled before me—freeing the half-conscious—letting my guard down—I entered a twilight state. I saw Dix sail by—riding a big black horse. Close on his tail came Nephew Lawrence—twirling a lariat of black hair growing from his mole. Then came my son—galloping beside on a kangaroo. My wife peeked out of its pouch. Everything was going much too fast. I blinked my eyes to bring them down, control their gait. I could not. I tried again. I conjured up walls and guns. They galloped on. Rose pranced in, riding a bright red stallion and waving. I put my fist in front of her. She kissed it and cantered on.

I sat up, dripping with icy sweat. This was, after all, my game. No one could do anything without my permission. So what was going on here? Whatever it was, I did not like it. For the first time in weeks I went home before midnight.

My wife was sitting in a chair with her feet on the bed. She was drinking wine. Red wine, which was out of character. Her face was still and sealed.

I said good evening—told her I had done some "heavy work in the group"—and proceeded to bullshit my way toward the bathroom. I never saw her move a muscle and I know that she never lowered her legs, but with keen aim and vicious force the wineglass suddenly whizzed into the wall inches from my face. Splattering Burgundy and bits of glass on my hair and collar. I did not ask why she had done it. (Even I have my limits.) We looked at one another. For the first time in years. I found my mouth opening. She raised her fist. Closed. Much out of character. I shut my mouth. I continued on into the bathroom. When I came out she was sitting in exactly the same place, but with a fresh glass of wine in her hand. I flinched. A trace of a sneer appeared at the lower edges of her mouth. I said goodnight and got into bed. (Fortified by two Nembutol.) I fell instantly asleep. I awoke at 6:30 a.m. from a nighttime version of my horse story. Dripping wet and shaking. She was still sitting in exactly the same position with a freshly filled glass of wine. I said good morning, rose, showered and left before seven.

I stopped for breakfast (two eggs over easy, lightly toasted English muffin, small tomato juice, coffee and crisp bacon). When I got to the office my phone was ringing. It was my son. He was quite calm.

Dad.

Yes... David.

Mom cut her wrists. I called the ambulance. They just left. If you're not too busy, maybe you'd like to stop by the hospital. They need some information.

The slide was getting longer—turning into a great big frigging roller-coaster-style slide. Nothin' from Nothin' Leaves Nothin'—name of a rock song or something.

I called my service and left a message for Ms. Liebshitz. And cancelled my only patient of the day. And went to the hospital.

III

20

My wife is your basic passive-aggressive utility model traditional prefeminism mate personality.
  Sitting in the hospital waiting room, trying to look involved, I remembered something. I, young Super Shrink, was doing "couple counseling" (which I now view as something of a contradiction in terms). Anyway, I was doing it. I had this couple who were having chronic sexual problems. They came twice a week. He was always very quiet. I had quickly diagnosed him as the passive-dependent-manipulative partner in the relationship—which gave him great ability to control. I happen to hate passive aggression with the closest thing to fervor that I am capable of. She was very vocal and very desperate. We began sex therapy. Every vibrating device known to man was tried. Sexual surrogates were used. And nothing seemed to help. He was impotent or premature. She was frustrated and frigid. And communication seemed impossible. And my ego was at stake. We went on this way for one year. Then, one sunny morn, Mr. Passive-Aggressive (whom I was continually furious at for not hardening up and letting me bask in glory)—one fine day as I was about to suggest another new module—some "fishbowl" therapy, some displacement and the like—the man spoke. He stood up and walked to my desk and turned away from his wife, addressing himself loudly to me. He said: "Listen, I am sick and fucking tired of coming here week after week—wasting my time, squandering my money and having to listen to all this useless self-indulgent bullshit. The simple truth is, Doctor, that every time I take her tit in my mouth I want to vomit."
  Concise. To the point. The man had spent all of that time and money and had accepted the blame and ridicule because he did not want to tell his wife that. Anything but the truth. I learned a great lesson from it.
  And here I was. Sitting in a hospital waiting room. Waiting for my med school buddy, Dr. Reg Wheeler, hotshot surgeon, killer with a

tennis racket—drives a Maserati with each foot—to come out and talk to me about my wife's suicide attempt. And what was I to do? Say that the Cement Man does not wish to discuss it. "Tape her up and shut her up and I'll put her into group therapy and send flowers and buy her a mink coat—anything—just don't make me have to talk about it. Don't make me have to cry or carry on or feel remorse or stroke her helpless, bloodless little brow. (Don't make me have to kiss her tit.) Please."

She had lost all connection to me. As a human being. Maybe she never had any. I can't remember ever holding her in my arms. Caressing her tenderly. But that must be impossible. But it is not impossible that I never loved her. I never did. And now it had passed even the point of compassion. She, my wife, mother of my lost child, this Judy Freedman Person, this being who lived in my house, had affected me only by her break from form... only by how her actions were affecting the tensile web of my private party. This wineglass throwing. This wrist slicing. No. No. No. Wife Judy Person was not to do such things. Trying to force me to relate to ya, eh? Want to ram that nauseating tit down me throat, eh? Something must be done. Because I knew that I was not capable of dealing with this now. Not now. Now I couldn't even mouth it to the record. And I guess it was then that I began to let myself really see—that Rose was not a toy. Not a light switch or a TV show. Not a dial I could turn. I needed to hit that switch. But the lights stayed on, baby. The program wouldn't end. I sat there with my son, waiting for "news."

And it was even worse than I could have imagined. Reg was smug. (Never let a wife of mine get to that state—what's a matter, Arthur? Can't get it up for the missus?) It shone from his overgroomed, overtan little face. Reg, who walked forward on his toes; little Reg, who would visibly puff himself up when he made rounds—sort of a human bicycle pump—to create the illusion of tallness. Who now, always, had an airplane ticket sticking out of his pocket (once after a tennis game, when he was naked, I sauntered around behind him to see if he had one sticking out of his ass), always the illusion of about to fly off—dash to someone and something much more important than you—whoever you were—not a bad technique—worked pretty good with the nurses (see *Sex without Intimacy* tape). Reg, who once interpreted the receipt of a box of gift-wrapped shit from a former patient as a sign of the patient's deep appreciation for his help! "You're the shrink, Arthur—wouldn't you agree? He was sending me his most cherished possession, an actual part of his body." Whatever you say, Reg.

And, of course, she was fine (but wouldn't have made it without him). The air was filled with shame and fear (my son's). And raging anxiety (mine). The claustrophobia of performance. Did I know why? What should "we" do? Is she in therapy? Did you see it coming? And worst, "She needs you, Arthur. The boy needs you. Maybe you should cut down a little. Forget the Mercedes number for awhile—ya know what I mean, you're the shrink, Arthur—you know that's a cry for help." On and on. And then *they* came. Her friends. HER PARENTS. (My son had been a busy boy. Paid me back in grand style. A good potential Clicker—I was becoming convinced.) And everyone eyed me like The Thing That Fell to Earth. I had done it to her. Me. Bad Arthur. Dirty Arthur. Wolf in a Sulka shirt. It got as bad as it could get. HER PARENTS took my son with them. Poor kid. They were even worse than I am. (At least *I* leave him alone.) She did not want to see me. I was told. I rose to leave. Feeling as if I had swallowed ten raw stalks of mescaline and been forced to climb the side of the World Trade Center with King Kong on my back.

Her best friend was coming out of Wife Person's room as I passed. The look she directed at me is not describable in human terms. Water beetles on the bathroom floor at three in the morning have gotten kinder looks from insomniacs. And I took it all. I deserved it. I had it coming, as they say.

I once had a patient who loved her mastectomy. Everyone kept swooning around her—commenting on her bravery, her courage, her wonderful outlook on life. Horseshit. She told me later—it was a joyride. ("I thought I deserved to die. If all I had to pay was one boob—it seemed like a bargain—now maybe God would leave me alone.") Guilt. God love it. So this was the least I deserved. Or was it just the beginning?

I went home and packed a small bag. And moved into my office.

It is now, in case you have become so engrossed in my story that time has escaped you, 5:53 p.m. I am about to take another Percodan.

There is something about sitting around a hospital all day that really screws up your mood. Sometimes it seems hard for me to believe that I spent literally years of my life in one.

Ah, yes. Hospitals. Patients I have known and loved.... There was the old wino who thought he was Marilyn Monroe. We even had to list it as his name because there was no other ID. He vamped around the halls asking the interns to feel his breasts and calling, "Porter, porter—my bags please. Take my bags to my suite and I'll let you look at my legs." (They weren't too bad either.)

There was the lady who couldn't close her mouth. Damndest thing you ever saw. She would be fine, chatting away, and then, on some trigger word, her mouth would freeze absolutely wide open and would stay that way for days. Never did find out what in the hell was wrong with her.

There was a very nice manic-depressive Jewish lady who went on cleaning sprees. The first time she was brought in, she had picked up every cigarette butt on the sidewalks of the entire central city. "I just want to make things neat and clean for people, boobalaa." And she would pat my knee.

There was the little hooker who looked like an albino elf, picked up walking around town at night with just a towel on. She told me she was a Royal Princess and was wearing the towel because the Royal Robes had not arrived yet. Her breasts were tatooed. One was Tommy. One was Oscar.

And there was a man, thirty-four years old. He had been admitted by his mother with a raging skin infection covering the entire surface of his body. Opinion was that it was psychosomatic. Enter young Arthur. I asked him several questions, which were answered with relative ease. I then asked him to sign a release form for some tests. He refused. I asked why. He replied, "Mommy never taught me to write." Mommy had not taught him a lot of things. To read. To cut his food. Or to go out. Here was this mid-thirties grownup telling me that he had never been outside before and it was not as bad as Mommy had told him. He had been kept in a room for thirty-four years. Later, in therapy, I asked him what would happen to him when his mommy died. He looked me straight in the eyes without flinching and said, "Well, I'll die too."

Extreme? Yes. But...I have rarely had a patient who wasn't in every conceivable way working like a son of a bitch trying to find a way back into that all-holy Womb Room.

(What did she do to us in there, anyway? Put Hershey Kisses in the placenta? God only knows.) But letting go of the Mommy myth—the "someone there who will always love you and take care of you and forgive you and accept you and save you" and et cetera—We seek on. We marry them, we surrogate them, we have all sorts of anxiety attacks and break-downs when they are bad for us and we must let go of them. NO! NO! NOT THAT! NOT MOMMY! Breaking through that is the therapist's hair shirt. (And it still never comes back from the cleaners quite the same.) I even had a patient who was allergic to her mother. Broke out in hives and boils—eyes swelled shut—the moment she entered the same room with her. Incredible. Still wouldn't stop seeing her. (What *did* they do to us in there?) Primal screaming—all that shit. One doctor I know of puts scuba gear on patients and makes them lie in a tub of water to "relive the womb experience—recreate your own birth without trauma" or some such manure.

Anyway, the power of the Big M marches on. This guy's mother broke the mold. And see, he liked it there. No conflict. Whatever Mama said, went. (She must have had a fucking kiddieland in hers, maybe even peanut butter and banana sandwiches—someone should start investigating womb interiors more closely.)

Well, so much for old sea stories. I must admit, however (screechingly difficult though it may be), that the day when I packed my little bag and went to the office, I wanted my Mommy. In the worst way. Or anybody's Mommy. Rent-a-Mommy.

A professional service. For grown-ups in need. A nice plump, smelling-of-chicken-fat Mommy. A little old waspy, bandy-legged, talcum-and-sugar-cookie Mommy. A Mammy-Mommy.

"Yes, sir. Good evening. Rent-a-Mommy. What can we do for you tonight?"

"I'm having bad dreams—I'm scared my heart is going to attack me. And I'm all alone."

"Oh, you poor, bunky boy. What kind of Mommy would you like?"

"Um, I'd like one who smells good and has big bosoms and warm hands—and she will let me sit on her lap all night and make me oatmeal with raisins and cream and brown sugar and tell me she loves me and will never leave me and that my little heart is perfectly fine."

"Well, I have just the one for you. Do you mind if she smokes?"

"Not if she shares."

"Good. Her name is Mommy Marie. I think you had her once before, during your divorce."

"That will be the standard rate—payable in cash—when Mommy Marie puts you to sleep."

"Good. Tell her to wear something soft and snuggly."

Wonderful idea. It may be the Percodan, but I think I have hit on a winner. If we could just supply perfect Mommy models—who would need a shrink? And they'd never die and leave you or get drunk or harp and nag and whine and feed you full of neurotic fears and sexual guilt and all of it—and of course—Daddies too. Same thing for daddies.

And I am living proof. I wanted mine that night. And I hated mine. That's how scared we sophisticated types can get.

21

Enough sidetracking. It is hard, you know, for middle-aged men to give up the idea of being the Hero. To bury it forever. Publicly. (Whine, whine.)

So. I went to my office. It was dark and empty. And for the first time in a long while, it didn't feel so cozy. I piddled. I listened to a tape of Rose and me in Eros City. Put on some music, fixed myself a drink. And called my answering service. There were three calls from Rose. One call from Dix (with no number) and a call from someone named Lawrence. Lawrence? I knew no Lawrence. But it stuck with me. And then I remembered. Nephew Lawrence. I poured myself another drink. The phone rang. It was Rose.

Hello?

Oh, Artie, Artie—where have you been? I've been so worried.

Now, now, my dear—I had an emergency—I am a doctor, you know—things do come up. A very beautiful actress—very famous—patient of mine—needed my help. I could hardly refuse.

Oh. Yes. I understand. It's just that I was all ready to come over—you know how I get when I know we're going to be together. I bought a new dress. And I was so scared. I just sat here all day and cried and cried. Louise was very concerned.

Louise? Did you tell her why you were crying?

No, no. I wouldn't do that. I wouldn't break our oath.

That's my girl.

But when can I see you? Can I come tonight?

No... not tonight. Let me call you in the morning.

Okay. I'll be right here, right by the phone—I won't move.

Good girl. Good night, now. Oh, Randi, dear—by the way—I've been so preoccupied—I forgot to ask how your wonderful family was—

They're fine.

And your nephew, Lawrence? Have you seen him lately?

Uh-huh—as a matter of fact, he's stopped in to see me twice this week. Actually it's kind of funny—I mean he's never visited me before. Only on family occasions.

I see. Did he want something special?

Unh-unh. He just wanted to talk, he said. He's interested in psychiatry—for some show he's doing. Sort of like a Wild West show. He wanted to know about the way you work—he thought it might help him with the actors and stuff. Something like that. I guess I didn't pay that much attention.

I see. Well, we can talk about it tomorrow. Sleep tonight.

Not without you, Artie. I can't sleep at all unless I'm with you.

Well, take some of those little pills I gave you and try.

Okay.

Nighty-night, dear.

First my son. Then my wife. And Lawrence makes three?
I decided not to panic. After all—it might just be my paranoiac projection. He could want anything. Maybe he wanted to be my patient. Maybe he wanted to sell me a horse. Could be anything. Please, Him who—let it be "anything." I needed time to think. The wad in my mouth seemed to be expanding. And I didn't like that. At all. Somehow—the tables were turning. I had nailed them all to the floor with my own de-

mented little hands—and they were fucking turning anyway.
   That wife lying there pale and bandaged. The thought of those wrists—forever—forever—I would have to look at those neat little scars—cunty clever of her, I'll say that. Pills—you just throw up—pump all the damage away—but wrists. Stay. Marked for life. Every time she reaches for a cigarette, I'll see Arthur—torturer—driver of nice women to suicide. Now we would not just have sulks and red rims—now we would have wrists. Evidence. Memories. Things that cannot be taken back. Can't sweep anything under a magic carpet, can you? And my son. What would he do next? Run away? Flunk out of school? Rape a ten-year-old? Fingers pointing. Accusations pounding on my bare little head. Shit. Not to mention the bills. Mounting in my desk. Brought me right back to the old question. Is the fucking you get worth... you've heard it. And then came rage. Fury. Lashing, vicious rage. NO! I DON'T WANT TO STOP! I LIKE IT HERE! I'M NOT THROUGH YET! But the handwriting was on the wall. And there was still Nephew Lawrence. Poor dear Randi-ro. Poor little Arthurla. It wasn't fair. I REFUSE TO MEET YOUR DEMANDS—KILL THE PRISONERS—I WILL NOT BEND! I WILL GET LOADED AND SCREW MY VIRGIN SLAVE UNTIL MY COCK FALLS OFF! GO AWAY! DO WHAT YOU WILL! I CARE NOT! Except that I was no longer very sure who was leading the attack. And I was a coward. A true—better Red than dead—eat your spinach—and say your prayers—mainline coward. Like most sadists. (masochists seem more courageous—their aptitude for pain.) And I had not planned on any of this. And I had some serious thinking to do. I needed some help. I needed a shoulder. Dix—let Dix call back, Himwho. An outside opinion. An objective listener. (Someone who would tell me what I wanted to hear—ha.) And then this sinking—those wrists. No matter what I did—was it too late?
   I walked the floor. Pondering my own question. I had another drink. I had another 'nother drink. Finally I slept. Or rather I battled my way toward unconsciousness. The phone woke me. I stumbled to my desk and switched on the light. It was 6 a.m. I hit the tape button.

   Hello?

   Good morning, Doctor. This is Lawrence, Rose's nephew—we met at her little birthday party.

   Yes, yes—of course. I would have returned your call—but you didn't leave a number. Is something wrong?

Well, I'm not quite sure, Doc. But I have something on my mind that I sure would like to discuss with you.

Does it concern your aunt?

You might say that.

Can't we talk about it on the phone?

I don't think that would be such a good idea.

It sounds awfully mysterious. I really don't like this sort of intrigue.

Well, I'm sorry to hear that Doc. Because I love it. And I think that you really should see me. In the interest of your patient–whose welfare, I know, you care about sincerely. I think it would really be worth your while.

All right. Be at my office at eight o'clock.

A.m. or p.m.?

A.m.

I'll look forward to it.

I showered, shaved and changed. I put on a suit, a vest and a tie. Contemporary armor. I drank two pots of coffee. I swallowed a handful of vitamins (especially heavy on the B-stress formula). And I took a tranquilizer. And I locked the closet. And the drawer with our dirty Polaroids in it. I sat down at my desk. I took out my most impressive heavyweight medical book and opened it to create the image of midnight oils and intense dedication to my work. I chain-smoked little French cigarettes. I even called the hospital to see how Wife Person was doing. I chanted:

I am Dr. Arthur Freedman. I am a superior human being. I make fifty thousand dollars minimum per year. I am not impotent. I am a family man. A player of tennis and chess. A gourmet cook, a payer of life and car insurance premiums. I am one of the chosen few (not to mention the Chosen People). I live the good life—nothing can touch me here!

Blackmail? Ridiculous. A B movie. And then came the sinister whisperer (the critic-judge-parent—the enemy within). Oh yes, but what about incinerated parents? What about slashed wrists? Looks like a little gilding is flaking off the golden life, Doctor. NO!

> I am Dr. Arthur Freedman. I move in a world above all of that. I cannot be touched. I feel nothing that I do not choose to feel. I am a trained manipulator. I am cunning. I am clawed and swift. I will make mincemeat of my enemies. Ride on, Sir Lawrence. King Arthur awaits.

Sir Lawrence was late. (Couldn't find a hitching post for his palamino.) He swaggered in. Ol' slickum head. Greasy and seedy. My distaste was palpable. And he knew it. And he loved it. He sat down without invitation and put his dirty booted legs up on my desk. The King should not have to put up with such insolence. Sleazy knave—off with his oily head. I moved with crisp elegance, one hand thrust casually in my pocket. (A gesture greedily stolen from Fred Astaire.) And sat down. My finger slid nonchalantly toward my tape button. Just like in the movies. All I needed was a Luger pistol in the drawer and Peter Lorre in the bathroom.

I eased into my most officious, adroitly patronizing, ingenuously intimidating professional voice:

> *Well now, Lawrence. What seems to be the trouble?*

> *That doesn't sound like the way to start. Aren't you supposed to make me lay down and ask me about my childhood? My first wet dream—that kind of stuff?*

> *I was not under the impression that you were here to see me as a patient. Though—for your edification—I would still begin with basically the same question.*

> *Right on, Doc. You're a very classy type, aren't you? Got a quick retort for everything. Not a bit of Gary Cooper or John Wayne in your whole act. Okay. You're right. I am not here as a patient. Though that might not be such a bad idea. You've met my mother. Imagine having that leering over your crib. It's a wonder I'm not a complete nutcake. What I am, Doc, is a concerned relative. I am deeply concerned about the well-being of my favorite aunt. Rose is a nice piece of tail, ya know. Not too smart, but a nice old broad. And I am concerned about her.*

> *Well, if you are here to examine my credentials, I think I can supply you with enough information to put your mind at ease.*

Oh, that won't be necessary. I checked you out pretty good. Let me tell you a little bit about myself. Maybe that will make this easier to understand. You see, Doc, I am a very hungry guy. I grew up with a bunch of freak-brains. I was the only kid. So everyone practiced on me. I have as a result some strange ideas about the world, maybe. And I don't kid myself. I'm a slob. And I don't have an education—and a way with the words like you do. I hustle my ass. I am also basically lazy. So I play the angles. And I have a certain rat instinct. I smell opportunity. And you are the fuckingest, smelliest piece of opportunity that I have come across yet. For a small-time Western dude like me, anyway. Now I know—and I don't want to go through a lot of jive cowshit with you—I know that you are screwing my dear old aunt. And probably doing a lot of other kink-o numbers. I know. And of course you are going to deny it. And then you may square dance around about calling the police—or asking me to prove it. And I can't really prove it, except that I can. I have a couple of edges. And believe me, Doc, I don't care what voodoo shit you're doing to her—I know Rose—and I know voodoo shit—and I can turn her around anyway I want. And I can spook the cattle—so to speak—and cause a lot of embarrassment for your little wife and kiddie. And maybe even get you in trouble with your fellow headshrinkers. Do they still call them that? Anyway. It is obvious what I want. I want pesos, Doc. I want twenty thousand dollars in cash. And I want it quick. And if I don't get it—I will yodel my brains out. And don't do any of that victim shit about "how do I know that will be the end of it"—because you don't—you just have to trust me. I told you—I'm lazy and I'm on the take—but I ain't stupid. I'm a cowboy, remember. I like wide open space. Don't fence me in and all that jive. So I wouldn't be likely to push my luck. That's not the way small-timers like me operate anyway. Get in and get out. So you can trust me. I won't keep popping up—like in the movies. You won't have to take me out or nothing dramatic. But I do want the twenty—and I will make your life a living hell unless I get it. Do we understand each other?

Not quite. I don't have twenty thousand dollars. I am not sure I even have two thousand dollars. And believe me—that is not a ploy. As I told you on the phone, I am not interested in mystery. I will not even defend myself against your ridiculous accusation. Let me just say that—for personal reasons—if I could pay you to leave me alone, I would. But I can't. I am deeply in debt. My practice is not doing well. My house is mortgaged. My wife is in the hospital. I do not have the money.

Sell one of your suits.

I am not playing games with you, I am telling you the truth.

Truth doesn't interest me. Money interests me. Get some. Borrow it from Sigmund Freud. You can do it, Doc. And do it fast.

How fast?

One week.

Two. I must have two.

All right, Doc. I am not unreasonable. Two weeks from today. At 8 a.m. Same time. Same place. And no changes. I don't like surprises. Well, it's been swell, Doc. Give my love to Aunt Rose. Tell her not to do anything I wouldn't do. We always had that one thing in common. Loved it down and dirty. Same way you like it, huh, Doc?

I would like you to leave my office. I don't wish to continue this.

Now don't get touchy. It's bad for the image. I'll be seeing you.

Swagger-swag-swag. Buffalo Bill was gone. I got up and compulsively sprayed the chair with Lysol. My hands were shaking. My knees were shaking. This was too much. I paced. I needed to talk to someone. I needed to talk to Dix. I sat. How? He was literally invisible. A vanished man. It could take weeks. I called a detective agency. And made arrangements for a search. Two hundred dollars a day. Plus expenses. I needed his help. (And I needed twenty thousand dollars.) And last—and most frightening—I needed to get rid of Rose. I must undo what I had done. And fast. I looked at my watch. Ten o'clock. Rose was coming at eleven. I started to draft a plan. But even as I worked—making notes—hypnotic sketchbook—another weekend—I knew—that I didn't have the strength. And I didn't have the time.

She was early. A fresh, perfume-infused orangeade. Gurgling and gushing with joy. Kissing my hands, my prick—rubbing her fat little tummy against me.

Oh Artie—it seems like forever. I cried into Victor Bear's neck all night. And my tummy hurt. Make me feel better. Pretty please.

Rose, my dear. Something has come up. I want to discuss something with you seriously for a moment...

She was naked—little panties and stockings flying through the air. A brazen baby-doll. I had created her. And I was stuck with her. I steeled myself. For a full thirty seconds. And it started again. Like the first time. This seething lust. My prick throbbed against my fly. I felt drool forming on my lips. A Dracula. A frenzied madman. I grabbed her. I pinned her to the floor—spreading her legs so wide the bones cracked. And she loved it. She adored it. I bit her nipples—I sat on her belly grinding my cock against her stomach—pressing on her creamy red little cunt watching her shake and gasp and juice on my ass. On my hands. And when I entered her, the power of the contact—the soaring release from reality—spun me out. I humped her across the floor on her back—pushing her around the room with the force of my prick—like a human earthmover—I fucked her across the carpet. Screaming. I heard my own screaming. Growling monster man—using my prick to stop my head. Fucking away reality. Fucking into safety. Nothing matters but this. This wet little blur with her panda bear and her dancing ass. I came forever. And never stopped. I fucked my wilting Rose all day. Dracula. The Wolfman. Godzilla. And she was never afraid. Her back was seared with rug burns. Her arms bruised and bitten. Her neck and titties a mass of hickeys. Her lips bloody and swollen... fuck a madman a day, keep reality away. And I could not stop. I did not stop until I passed out. I. The master of self-control. Daddy cool. I fucked her into unconsciousness. Fucked her beyond my control. Left myself unconscious. Vulnerable to any attack. Out cold. Naked. Haggard. Stubbled and semen-stained. Passed out on the floor.

> Soon I must wake from this dream and play a round of golf. It's all been very interesting, but it is, after all, only a nightmare. Must have been the choucroute—that sauerkraut does it every time. Soon I must waken and have my car waxed. Put things back in place. Get on with it. It's been a most unusual dream. But it has nothing, of course, to do with real life. Not with my real life. Soon it will all be gone. And I will have a Cappucino or Cafe Royal and maybe a fresh corn muffin—or a brioche—from that little bakery my wife likes. And read the paper. Soon.

Just as soon as I wake up.

Rose woke me up. I was talking in my sleep. I looked "scary." It was dark.... She was cold. She was a mess. I was a mess. And I fucked her again. And we fell asleep in each other's arms. We did. Not a corn muffin in sight.

The phone woke me again. And something in my nose. Hair. A stiff piece of orange hair. My body buckled in panic. Rose was plastered to me. It was freezing cold (so much for climate control) and sun was pushing through the blinds. Rose was dead weight. The way babies sleep. No resistance. I rolled her over and jumped up, my heart thrashing. It was Reg-baby. My wife was ready to be discharged. Could I please come over and sign the release forms and take her home. (Of course I could.)

Rose, Randi—wake up. Time to go home.

Oh, Artie. Do I have to? I'm having such a nice dream. I feel so comfy.

I know, my dear. But I have something important to do. A patient. I have to go to the hospital. And I want you to go home and wait for me to call you.

Oh, no fair.

She stretched her bruised white body. Oblivious. I opened the curtains. One look at her in the light and I knew she couldn't leave like that. I would have to fix her up. I would have to leave her here alone. What to do first? I showered, shaved and dressed. Rose still lay on the couch, yawning and murmuring to herself. Nothing existed for her except that very instant. I envied her. I prepared one of my famous Quaalude cocktails.

Randi, dear? Sit up now. I have a surprise for you. You don't have to go home. You can stay here until I get back. But I want you to take some medicine. You don't look well to me.

I feel just peachy. Mmmmmm. You feel peachy too.

(Her hand—needless to say—had found my crotch.)

I mean it, now. You take your medicine or you can't stay here.

Okay. Don't be grouchy.

She sat up. Welts had formed on her breasts and arms. I watched her take the medicine. I brought a washcloth and wiped her face. I sprayed Bactine all over her squealing body. ("Uw, it's cold—it tickles.") And put her clothes on her. She was out—before I finished. Limp and trusting. I laid her back on Ol' Brown and covered her with my handmade afghan. I called the answering service and told them to hold all calls—I was on an emergency. And if a Dr. Dix called to tell him that it was urgent that I reach him and to please leave a number.

My wife sat in a wheelchair wearing a demure flannel bathrobe—that I had never seen before. I kept my eyes from her wrists. Or I tried. They kept shooting downward. Controlled by spastic rubber bands in my head. Wrists. All wrapped up. White and glaring. No one could mistake it. Couldn't she at least pull the fucking sleeves over them? Of course she couldn't. She had waited a long time for this moment of glory. The martyr's most memorable moment.

I kissed her cheek. (Reg beamed.) I wheeled her frigging chair. I signed the papers and wrote a check (that would soon bounce). I helped her into the car. And off we went. Home.

We had still not spoken one word to each other. No accusations. No tears. No threats of divorce. Nothing. I swallowed. I had to do something. Just to buy time. I could not bear another minute of this. I was too used to the game. The life-style. The form. I had to smooth the surface. Screw the underneath part. We had no underneath part. I needed the surface. I needed the outside. What could I do? Lie.

"Judy, I know how you must feel. How you must hate me. But I want to tell you something—and maybe in time you will forgive me. There has been another woman. But not the way you think. I guess it's just nearing forty and all. I needed a fling. I've been so guilty and upset about it—I just didn't know what to do. She was no one—a young girl—a tennis teacher. I guess it was just my ego. Feeling over the hill—all of that male menopause stuff. But it's over now. I had no idea you were so upset. We—I know we've drifted apart. But I don't want to hurt you. I think maybe—you need some help with this—and so do I. I..."

"I want to go to Puerto Vallarta to recuperate."

She looked straight ahead. She never turned her face. Her mouth was tight. So it was to be like this. So she saw, too. She knew I needed my little prototype. She had cut more than her wrists—she had cut through the delusion. She had shoveled into reality. Same game. New rules. Blackmail seemed to have moved to the forefront of my life.

"But darling..."

"Two weeks. I'll take David. I need to regain my strength. When I get back, we can talk."

"Judy, I can't afford it."

"I don't care. You owe it to me. Sell something."

(That suggestion was becoming increasingly popular.)

"All right. If it will make you happy. Go. But I am not kidding. I am in serious financial difficulty. Part of my breakdown or whatever I've been having. We are going to have to be very careful for a while."

"I don't want to hear about it. I've been through enough. It's your problem. You're the head of the house. You take care of it."

(Do I need this? What am I doing? Trading a room with little Rose for this brittle bitch.)

Rose, who never complains—maybe I should marry Rose? Get out of all of this. Dump Wife Person and son—they hate me anyway—screw dinner parties and Mouton Cadet. A room somewhere with my love slave. Live on my wits. And the money from selling everything... maybe ... but this was madness. Life in a room with a decaying floozy? Stop this Arthur. This insanity must stop. Rose must stop. If you get rid of the symptom—who cares about the disease?... You need the protection of this life you have paid so dearly to achieve. You must get off this train. Start rebuilding your practice. Doing your aerobics. Get it together, Doctor. You've had your fun. Now. Enough. Better dead than out of character.

"You're right, honey." (The word scratches my conflicted little throat.) "I will take care of it. I'll make the arrangements. This afternoon. Everything's going to be fine. We'll be back to normal in no time."

She doesn't answer. She raises her bandaged wrist to fluff her trendily cut hair. I pat her other hand. (A feat worth noting.) And so it was settled. I had chosen. Damning to hell having to choose. I must find my way back to plasticland. Before it was too late. Pay Lawrence and get rid of Rose. And pick up the pieces of my splintered life. Ole.

22

I heard music as I opened my office door. The tape machine was on. "Volare." Rose was sitting in a Breuer chair smiling at me, one of my textbooks in her hands. She was all fixed up. She was fine. I was amazed. And she looked so happy.

Oh, Artie, I'm so glad you're back. I woke up and it was so lonely. And then I thought, I'll surprise him. I'll get all freshened up and clean up everything and make things nice for my lover-man when he gets back.

(The thing about it was, she was really so simple and so nice. What a nice little rose. Cheery. And she looked so fresh. She walked over to the tape machine, her ass wiggling against tight green pants. Maybe just once more, I thought.)

Oh, honey, you had a phone call. I'm sorry—I didn't mean to answer it—I felt awful funny from the medicine—and I forgot I was here. He had a real cute voice—kind of like the South—he left a number for you.

Dix. It must be.

Oh, he said to call him at 7 p.m., not before.

It was only a little after one. I felt anxiety rising. He had become a mountain. Only way out was over it. He was my only way out. I had no ability to sort. No choices. Dix was my only chance. Six hours. I looked at Rose. I should hypnotize her now, start desuggesting her. Then the whispers in my clogged little ears: "Desuggest her—you fool—she's not in a trance—she's just madly in love with you—you can't turn that off. She'll cry and carry on and come banging on the door. You will have to start all over—try to distort yourself to an evil, awful force. But worse, she doesn't want to believe that—you have nothing to work with. You..."

> Artie, honey—could we go to a movie? I haven't gone to my movie in months. Pretty please. I won't ask for anything else ever again.

> All right, Randi.

(That was me. I did say it.)

> Oh, boy! Oh, thank you!

She hugged me. She kissed my hands. And then she just looked at me and said:

> You're the best man in the whole world. Better than my poppa, even. Better than the President. I bet God's like you. You know, I never really told you the whole truth about me. I mean about me and men. I mean, sometimes—well, lots of times—they weren't always so nice. They'd promise things. They'd tell lies to me. Sometimes they'd call me names. I know I'm not smart—and I am a little older and all, but I don't think people should be mean to each other. I like men. I like everybody. But you're the best one. I'm sorry if I hurt your feelings in the beginning—I mean about not being tall and having curly hair and stuff—I guess I've always been a very silly girl. But I'm different now. You've helped me. A lot. I never had a friend like you. And you can do anything you want with me, forever. And I'll never leave you. I'd die without you. I think I just would. You make me so happy.

(Soon I will wake up—take a hot shower and squeeze some fresh grapefruit juice. And maybe some rye toast with butter—sweet butter and marmalade.)

I took Rose to the movies. We ate popcorn and held hands. It was a very seedy neighborhood movie. The kind people who don't have a daily life go to. We saw reruns. *A Touch of Class* (no mercy was to be shown) and *The Bad News Bears* (which hit every withering neerve in my quivering little body) and a Woody Woodpecker cartoon and previews. Rose held my hand. She held my knee. She blew in my buzzing ears. She pushed her thigh against my thigh. She kissed my cheek. She patted my cock. I had given her ecstasy. With popcorn thrown in. A tray from Cartier. Smiles oozed from her powdered little aging princess face. It was kind of nice.

When we got back to the office it was only five. No one had called. I pictured my wife surrounded by family and friends. Being fed and patted and fussed over. Victim of the hour. And me. Here alone with Rose. I thought of their faces seeing me here with my girlfriend.

> "All right—all right. I can pretend no longer. I am still unfaithful, it is not over—I have found a woman who drives me mad, who excites me to the point of frenzy—I must give up my crown—forsake my kingdom. I want you to meet the Woman I Love—my darling, my Rose Liebschitz." (Rose sweeps in—hickey marks and bruises on her neck and arms. Orange hair glued to her head—wearing her nylon robe with the chicken feathers and her Arabian Nights slippers. The room is quiet. My wife's tightened little lids widen and snap shut as she faints. My son throws up. Our friends who hate one another reach for each other's hands. All the elegantly clad legs cross.) "The man is a maniac."

I look at Rose. She has lain down on her cushion and is humming. Her hips and ass gyrating softly as usual. Like leaves in the wind. Natural motion. Inevitable. Ass hits couch. Body moves.

Artie, I feel so nice. Let me make you feel nice.

I let her. She makes me. And then we send out for a pizza (pepperoni, because I like it—she picks the little sausage circles off hers). And it is only six-fifteen. And so I move over to her again. Only this time we do something very weird. We make love. Or I do. I close my eyes and make love to her. Nicely. Like lovers. Tenderness is involved somehow. And when I come, tears pour from my eyes. And I am very scared here. It is six forty-five. I must be alone before Dix. I help her up. She is a puddle. She is a wilting soft little posy. She kisses me a hundred butterfly pecks. And wiggles out the door.

Artie?

Yes, my dear—quickly now, I have some work to do.

I know. I just wanted to thank you for the very best day of my whole life. Better than when I won the back contest. Better than the samba thing, too.

You're very welcome, dear.

And I am alone. Silence and cold pizza. And me. And a little piece of paper with a phone number on it. The most important number in the world. My only hope. It has become. And that seems perfectly normal to me. Rational. And without contest.

It is exactly seven o'clock. I pour myself a drink and sit down. I reach for the phone. I push my tape button—and dial. It rings. It rings.

Hellooo, Arthur, my friend. Always so punctual. Such a good boy.

It is not a hospital. It sounds like a bar or restaurant. A phone booth. Clever devil, he is. Really doesn't want me to know.

Thank God. Dix, I don't have time to fool around. I'm in trouble and I need your help. Please, just listen to me, just bear with me for a while.

Sounds very serious, Doctor. Maybe you'd better hold on while I bring over a little refreshment to keep me company.

Okay. But hurry.

I have waited too long. I am too anxious. I take a sip of my drink. I take deep breaths. My heart bangs against my throat.

Okay, Doctor, I'm not going anywhere—start at the beginning and tell Uncle Dix everything.

You're going to think I'm crazy.

Arthur, Arthur—you forget who you're talking to—think about casting the first stone and all—I am hardly in a position to judge you.

All right. well, I have gotten myself into something here that I can't handle and I can't see a way out of. And I'm going to crack if I don't solve it. I've been screwing a patient. But not like an affair—I mean, I used her. I used drugs and hypnosis—I worked on her. She's—well, she's not like anyone you've ever known. She's in her fifties—hysteric —very childlike. It started like—you know, an answer to a prayer. No demands—act out my fantasies—shit, I don't know what, she released something in me—this lust—these feelings I thought were dead. And I got in. And my practice has gone to hell. I'm broke. My son's in crisis. My wife slit her wrists. And worse, Dix, worse, this woman—Rose— that I've been banging into oblivion—my oblivion, at least—well, she's got these crazy relatives. Anyway, one of them—her nephew—a paranoid psychopathic little sadist—he's blackmailing me—he wants twenty thousand dollars in two weeks or the sirens go off. The APA. Judy. The whole apple. And he isn't kidding. And I am in no position to negotiate with him. And I'm broke. And then with Rose. I've got to get rid of her. I don't have time to spend weeks of intense countersuggestion—and anyway, she's not layered enough, not motivated. She says she'll die without me. And besides. Oh, shit, this sounds so absolutely insane. But I can't be around her without my prick literally exploding. She triggers something. She walks in and I am less and less able to control myself. To manipulate. I even took her to the fucking movies today. I am totally isolated. I've cut everything else in my life off. She's like, my only friend (ha), the only person I trust—and the sex—I can't tell you—and anything I want—and I can't make myself stop. But if I don't, I'm going to blow everything I've worked for. My whole life. My kid's in trouble—my wife—jesus, and she's already making me pay. And my work's going. I've got to get my shit together—get back to reality. I know you don't approve—I know that the way I live cost me a lot. But it was what I wanted. I didn't want to be vulnerable. I had it all worked out. I could handle it. It may be an empty, unsatisfying little box—but I decorated it myself—you see, it kept me together and I've got to get it back. I need your help, Dix. Please. Tell me how to do it. Please.

I am gasping for breath. There is a long steady silence—a thinking silence. A necessary silence.

I am going to send you thirty thousand dollars. Pay off the creep fast. Will he be back?

I don't think so—my instinct is, no.

Well, trust it. Pay him.

Dix—oh jesus. Dix, I . . .

There's more, Arthur. That's the easy part—money always is. Actually. Lighter her.

What?

The pussy. Burn her.

Stop it.

I am not joking, Arthur.

You—I don't believe this. I am fucking dreaming this. You—the humanitarian, the saver of souls, the original "bring me your sick, your wounded"—you are suggesting that I kill this person?

It's your dime, Doctor. You don't have time to do anything else—you said so. And I hate to agree with you about something like that, but you're right—you are sinking and that's the big leak and you hardly have time for three years on the couch and you are in no shape to handle her or anyone else. Besides, I think somewhere inside that complicated cutoff little brain of yours you have been heading for that anyway. You always knew she was expendable. That is why you chose her, my boy. And she is. And if I were you, it is what I'd do. Shocking though that may sound. You see, Arthur, after years of living in here, I see things through a different filter. You have not been a good boy for a while now. And bad boys can do anything they want if they're smart. And you are. And if you don't, you're going to fall down hard, Doctor. You might even break something. And you are right about yourself. You are clear about one thing. You need your little nest out there more than you need anything else. That's just the way it is. And you are blowing it. And the reasons for why you're in this predicament are not important now. All that's important now is cutting the cords. And saving your endangered little ass. Burn her.

How? How could I do something like that? I wouldn't know where to begin.

Doctor, you are being coy; if you could suck this little snowflake in, you can certainly melt her. Use your medicine, my boy. Nobody knows about you two?

Nephew—her nephew.

Forget that. He doesn't know shit—that's not why you're going to pay him. And the only witness will be gone anyway. Use your head—you'll get it. But do it soon, Arthur. I don't want to scare you—but you are not in terrific shape. You're going to have to hang on—to medicate yourself—get your nerves settled—get hold of the old cold cunning that made you famous. Use your tools, Doctor. I'll send the money. Send your family away—pay your debts. Did you tape the nephew?

Yes.

Good. Are you taping this?

NO.

Good.

Dix.

Yep?

You're sure?

Yep. I don't prescribe this sort of treatment out of hand, my friend. I listened. I heard you. You see, I have some rather oblique ideas about society—about rules. I live outside. And it's one fucking big yard out here. You people inside—you don't know shit; somebody told you about the world—about "obeying the law" and all that cow-chip jive—and you spend the rest of your lives trying to do it the way they told you to. It's sort of like there's this huge open plain and everyone lives in a little parking lot. So, Arthur, you are about to break out. Actually, you are out—when you put your prick inside that strange little pussy, you left the lot, boy—you wanted to and you needed to, but you're too indoctrinated to stay out. Only problem is—to work your way back in you've got to go further out. Ironic, but true. So yes. If you want my opinion—as badly as you seem to—then I have given it. Do it. And do it good. And do it soon.

I'm scared. Jesus—I'm scared.

You'll get over it. You're more scared of not doing it.

And I'm fucking angry.

At?

At the prices, baby. Emotional inflation. Don't like the prices.

Ah, yes. You'll get over that too. Must pay up and let it go. Because there is not a thing in hell you can do about it.

Can I reach you at this number? Can I see you?

No.

Shit, Dix. Come on—I need you.

I have given you all I can, Doctor. I cannot allow myself to start thinking about you. I cannot let you lean in on me. I called you—hoping maybe you had something to give me—but I am giving you. I don't want that. I have my own whirlpool going. And I don't want to be involved in yours. I found out all I needed to know. I have nothing else to offer you. And you have nothing whatsoever to offer me. And that is fucking sad. But it is true. Don't try to find me, Arthur. Let it go. We'll talk again someday. When it's right. It's not right anymore now. Good luck, my friend. Do me proud. Do it right.

Please, Dix, please—don't cut me off, please...

The phone was dead in my ear. The bastard. The spooky bastard. And that was my life model? Brought tears to my twitchy little eyes for fourteen years just to think of him? It got to him worse than to me. Or did it? Because I did know...did really know that he had given me. That he was right. For the situation. For this impossible, schizoid situation. He was right. And about me, too, he knew. I *was* being coy. I *had* always known. She *was* expendable. Good choice of words, Dix. What I hadn't known was that I would lose my contempt for her. I never liked *anyone*. I thought I was safe. Who could have possibly known that I would choose her—this flea-brained cunt—to like? To crave. To need. He was right. Rose must cease. Her or me. Her. Burn her. Blow her away. Take her out. Dead. Poor Rose. Poor Dix. Poor me.

23

It is now 8:23 p.m. I slept again. My nervous system has been over a chemical track that could qualify at Indy. But I feel absolutely clear. Too clear. (I am opening a beer.) I dreamt something. Which is unusual for me. I dreamt that I was playing tennis in Germany. There was a big sign over the court. It said, "Every worthy person is welcome at the Stuttgart Country Club." I am feeling very happy to qualify. I am playing with lightning speed. Skill and ease. I am young and tall and handsome. I am smiling. Then suddenly—my racket turns into jagged wire, barbed wire in my hand. I am walking, stumbling in a line of people—I am in a concentration camp. I am holding this wire in my fist—as if I had torn it from a fence—I am old and am crying. We all stumble along toward this big door (an oven entry if ever there was one). And I keep saying, "No! No! There's been a terrible mistake! I am a worthy person! I am a member of the Stuttgart Country Club! I am playing tennis! I don't belong—here, this is not real! Take me back at once!"

One day you're playing tennis and the next you're walking into an oven. And we adjust to the changes so well. It's scary. When the little green men land, everyone will run around screaming and yelling on Tuesday—and on Wednesday we'll be trading recipes. How we stretch. Reality is just one big fucking rubber band. It astonishes me how I stretched. Moved all the way from mildly perverse middle-class morality to sadism, deceit and murder. (Made sense to me). I just bought into a new piece of elastic. Therefore—I was cast into destiny. Or, more aptly: I tossed myself onto the tracks, lay down and waited for the steam engine. My racket had turned into barbed wire and it never occurred to me to just drop it and leave the court.

So. There I was. Dix had abandoned me (whine, piss, moan). And I was truly alone. Even for me. All alone. And it was hardly something

I could discuss with Rose (my only friend). I had to wait for Dix to send the money. And I had to come up with a foolproof plan. A mesmeric plot. Actually it was engrossing. It was fascinating. It became a challenge. A game. A mystery story.

"Supposing (hypothetically, of course, doctor), a psychiatrist wanted to dispose of a patient in such a way that he would never be caught. Supposing said patient had limited access to the world. Parents dead. One sister and one brother—who posed minimal threat. But one pushy nephew. But—what could he prove? Without incriminating himself. Nada. All right. Patient is passive, submissive and madly in love with doctor. Solution? Obvious. Make it look like a suicide." And it fell into place like hands and gloves, baby.

I would create a session-by-session work-up of Ms. Rose Liebschitz. I would invent her neurosis. "Manic-depressive with strong suicidal tendencies." I would write the story—building step by step to the point where, my formidable skills exhausted, I was considering hospitalization. Meanwhile, I would be making phone calls to colleagues— asking for their opinions on a "difficult case." And I would gather together enough toxic chemicals to drop Wonder Woman. No prescription record (I had my sources). I would be covered. Convincing the prospective victim to swallow her poison candy. Seemed cinchy. And because she was expendable, no one would exhaust themselves questioning the event. Lots of middle-aged spinster types call it a night. Happens all the time. And a note. In her own handwriting. I saw no problem with that. And pow. It would be all over. These creatures from another reality—these stumblers would disappear—go back into dreamland—and I would emerge, the shining star of Stuttgart society. Unscathed. I would resume. My racket miraculously reformed in my tan, steady young hand. So my days would be spent creating this neat little pile of "reality" and my nights would be spent—home. Atoning. Being a faultless husband and father. Until the money came. Then off would go Wife Person and son. And I would set the timer. Ticky. Tick.

Of course, I would have to deal with Rose. Simultaneously. And think up some highly Calvinistic yet cosmopolitan propaganda for Nephew Lawrence. But after all—that had always been my self-proclaimed forte. Mind massage (Master of). I felt better. Hypothetically foolproof. Dix was right. I could do it. A walk in the park, babycake.

And so I began. At once. I was taking amphetamines to keep my mind moving, which of course did nothing for my nerves but kept my spirits so high, so delusively delicious, that I didn't mind the palpitating heart, the shaking hands, the night sweats. I wrote a case history of diamond-point accuracy. Brilliant. (I almost believed it myself.) I did tapes of my opinions and impressions. I even telephoned the internist who had referred her and explained the situation. (He thanked me for my professional courtesy.) I was doing fine, except for one little rub.

Rose. She didn't know anything had changed. Rose was calling twenty times a day. I had to control her. And I had to keep her happy. And I was afraid to see her. But I *had* to see her. So I prepared myself. How? You will love this, class. I jerked off until my cock fell from my hand in absolute surrender. If I could see her without lust, I would be fine. I could be objective. Get my contempt back; hone my instinct for survival to the necessary sharpness. I would survive. I would win. And I would go on with my life. So I beat meat. I pounded it dry. I could handle her now.

She came back Thursday morning. It had been only a workweek since our "outing." It seemed like centuries. I had, of course, prepared a story for her. (I was ill—the doctor had forbidden me to make love for one month—which seemed sufficient time—but I loved her madly and would see her and take care of her and blah-de-do.) I knew she would not question me. And I could work on her without being vulnerable. I took deep breaths. I felt cleansed of all desire. I heard her little knock at the door and moved to answer with confidence and serenity.

She stood in the doorway smiling at me. She was wearing a big furry turquoise coat and high heels. And a little yellow bow in her hair. Ludicrous, I thought. What a dowdy little toad. Arthur—you have seen the light. She said she had brought me a present. I invited her in and switched on my machine (for posterity).

> *Oh Artie, darling, I've been so lonely. I've missed you so much—I started to get a wrinkly in my forehead from crying into my pillow at night. What's wrong? Is it something I did?.... What's happening to us?... Please tell me...pretty please with cherries on top?*

> *No, no, my sweet. It has nothing to do with you. Come here, Randi, dear. I want to hold your hand for a moment. It will make this easier.*

> *Okay, my lover-man.*

(She wiggled across the room and sat on her knees in front of me and put out her little white hand with the clear buffed nails. Only understated thing in her repertoire—those clean-sweet-innocent little hands

—and the matching pussy of course.)

> Randi, dear. I've not been well. I've been ill and I didn't want you to know. I didn't want to upset you.

(Her face is stricken with something—caring—I think that is what you would have to call it—caring. I say I am ill and someone's face is stricken—a stricken victim. I swallow sour tastes.)

> Oh, oh, Artie. What is it? What can I do to help you? I'm very good at taking care of sick people—I took care of Mama and Papa till they died. I could take really good care of you.

> No, no, dear. That won't be necessary. It's not that serious. I will be just fine. Only, well, I will only be fine if we do not make love for awhile. The doctor was very firm about that.

> Oh. Oh my. Oh, that's awful. Oh, poor us. Well, I mean—it's okay. I mean I love you and I want you to be healthy and happy. And if that's what the doctor says...well, that's what we'll do. It's okay...I don't mind...(She giggles, a shy secret giggle.)

> What's so amusing, Randi, dear?

> Oh, well, it's nothing. It's just that my "present" won't mean anything now. I just feel kinda silly.

> I don't understand.

> Oh, never mind. It's just silly.

> No, no. Share it with me, no present from you could be silly.

(I am feeling good. It is working well.)

> Well, okay, I'll show you—but you have to promise not to laugh at me.

> I promise.

(She gets up off her knees, still holding her coat together. She places a cute little hand on each lapel and throws open her fuzzy coat. She is nude. Around her waist is a great big pink ribbon.)

That was my welcome back present to you.

(Need I say more. I made a sudden, remarkable recovery.)

Oh, Artie, Artie, you mustn't—I'd never forgive myself if you got sicker or died or anything because of me...no, no...it's not good for you.

Her resistance inflamed me. It was something new. I grabbed her from behind and pressed her fat white ass against my reconstituted prick. (Just add Rose and mix. Remarkable.)

Just once more. He said I could make love once more—to clear my ducts. Trust me—it's all right.

Oh, oh, ummm. Oh, Artie, if you're sure. It sounds like a good thought—clear the ducts out—sounds very smart...umm.

I cleared things out that I never knew were in there. I opened my present and it fit perfectly. Like a drunk. Like a food freak. Just one more piece and I'll never touch the stuff again.

It was the first time since she had left that I had forgotten myself. Forgotten to think. Felt anything loosen inside the steel bands of my panic.

24

I did go home that night. Bracing myself with two très sec *vodka* martinis and some Colombian. And smelling of Rose. (Somehow the smell never washed off. Maybe it lived inside my membranes now. Cheap perfume and pussy smells. Inside my sinuses forever.) Wife Person was sitting in the living room watching Walter Cronkite. Son was in his room doing whatever thirteen-year-old boys do when they're supposed to be doing homework. (My favorite was *Confidential* magazine—a true child of the fifties.)

Wife Person was also in her cups. It is amazing how white wine can slop you out with such acceptable panache. I knew she was loaded, because she accepted me as being perfectly okay. And I was shit-faced.

The fireplace was going. Beefy smells filtered in from the kitchen where our new housekeeper/cook was preparing dinner. (The cook idea being part of Wife Person's post-operative cunt-faced extortion.) This was to be our first real *Life with Father* evening since the "unfortunate incident," as her slashing was currently being referred to.

I took deep breaths. I approached the couch, where she sat ignoring me. I leaned over and kissed her dry tight little forehead.

Dry and tight. My wife (I think I'll keep her). Every inch of her exercised, pampered little body was dry and tight (with the exception of her pussy, which was dry and loose). Even her tongue was dehydrated. And all of her friends looked exactly the same way to me. An army of mid-thirties stylish matrons. Up-to-date. Current. Trim little haircuts. Trim little waistlines. Facialed and massaged and tanned and tennised and white-wined and frustrated. They all looked alike to me. Often at parties I would approach the wrong one from the rear and start to say, "Come on, dear, let's go home." Even face to face I could make mistakes like that.

My Wife Person. Who was she? This Wife Judy, that I had so currently rechosen. This person that I was giving up Roseland for. Committing murder to return to. Who?

So all right. It wasn't *really* because of her. But she was the winner. She and I would waltz through Droughtland 'til the end. Or at least till an acceptable option appeared. So maybe I should try to find out about her (fifteen years late, but not too late).

I realized as I planted my moist little lips on her frigid little brow—that I had never been the least bit interested in who she was. Or what she thought. Or anything about her. I was not even sure that she had always been this brittle. This cold. This boring. Maybe, with my considerable charm and unique sexual prowess, I could refocus on her. Turn her around. Turn her on. Like an old movie:

I begin to find out about her. She begins to see how I have changed. She pours out her heart. I listen with compassion and remorse. Accidentally our hands touch. Our eyes meet. A long, steady look that begins with surprise and builds, moment by moment, to disbelief—Can it be? Is it true?—to softness, fire, passion. I lift her in my arms and sweep her gingerly upstairs to our room. Where a miracle occurs. As if she is raining inside out—her whole body moisturizes—a human humidifier. My wife thaws. Rose on her best day—could not equal this end of the Ice Age. All anger is gone. We love each other with ravishing tenderness and, alternately, brutal passion.

It's my story—I can have anything I want. If this was my choice—this copout, this return to home and hearth, this reawareness of Walter Cronkite and roast chicken—bloody well might try making the best of it. Paint a mural in my cell, so to speak. Learn the lay of the land.

Ah-ha. So this is how they do it. I get it. Come home at night, have white wine. Read the paper. Watch the news. Ask wife and child pertinent questions about daily life. Smile benignly. Do a lot of patting on child's shoulders and cheek kissing on wife. Be friendly to the maid and the dog. (Did we have a dog? I didn't think so. Better write that down. Must get a dog. That would certainly help. A real family dog. A "Hills Brothers campfire and river-trout dog." An Irish-setter-type dog. That would help. "Here boy!" I would shout loudly as I lit my pipe—write down: buy pipes—and changed into my slippers and red-and-blue-checked Pendleton shirt. "Come now—Pop's home." He would race across the thicket of freshly mowed grass, tongue wagging. (Or is it the tail that wags? Tongue lapping? Tail wagging? Well, whatever.) He would leap into my waiting, serene but powerful arms. A man at home. With his dog. And his family. Norman Rockwell would cry.

But first things first. Too much change too quickly would arouse suspicion. After years of chronic alienation of affection, followed by months of acute alienation and physical removal—I couldn't very well bounce into the living room with my pipe, puppy and Pendleton, with no warning. Had to cool it.

I had even charted it. Night by night. I had Plan A, which was my Rose work-up. And I had Plan B, which was my family work-up. And there could be no false steps. Trust had been shattered. Millions of glass splinters, and me in my bare feet. But fueled by my amphetamized delusion, I felt surges of great confidence. I *could* do it. I could do *anything*. It might even turn out in hindsight that I had had my cake and eaten it (only not on the same day). I used to believe that you could have everything—now I believed that you could probably have everything—just not all at the same time. Funny little tricks that life plays.

So, here I was. I would go slow. I poured myself a glass of white wine and settled down next to Wife on the settee. I feigned deep interest in Cranktight. I felt her tension. ("Body language" in the trade.) Wife's body language was easy to read. It read: WHAT'S THE GAME, ARTHUR? WHAT DO YOU WANT AND WHY DON'T YOU GO AWAY? WE HATE YOU HERE. JUST SEND MONEY! TAKE YOUR HOT AIR AND GO BLOW IN A BOTTLE!

The cook/housekeeper entered. A tall Panamanian girl with a really superior ass. (No, Arthur.) Dinner was announced. I offered to bring Son David down. I whistled as I went. (Was that too much? Was I pushing? Whistling up the stairs in person to call Son for supper—that was possibly a bit too Ozzie and Harriet. At least I hadn't changed from my sport coat to a three-button alpaca sweater and tie. Anyway, one mustn't become too bogged down in details. No one had stopped moving. No whispers in the kitchen—"He's whistling up the stairs. Call the police.")

The only way to describe the look on Son's face when he saw me in the doorway to his room would be the way you would look if you had just swallowed a mouthful of sand. I pretended not to notice. He got up and followed me downstairs with passive resistance. I did not repeat the whistle. And chose not to touch him. The shoulder pat would have to wait.

We entered the dining room together. I pulled out my wife's chair (a gesture that gave me a sweet inner sense of well-being) and dinner began. The conversation had holes the size of air balloons. I filled them with my speeding patter. I made things up. Made up patients I had seen. Made up what I had for lunch. It was incredible. (Something about what Dix said—when you're out you can do anything, because there are no more rules. If I didn't care about telling the truth I could do anything. Lie on, King Arthur, the enemy awaits.) Several times as

I paused to chew or cut something—I felt their eyes on me. It was quite interesting. She would steal a look. Swift, but terribly intense. And so would he. But they did not look at one another. They were not behaving as a team. That was very helpful information. What it showed was that, like most everyone, they wanted to believe me. They were allowing a trickle, a tiny, teeny dot of hope. Which was all I needed. They wanted to believe that it was possible. A miracle. A middle-class miracle:

> The wayward husband, driven to despair by his wife's suicide attempt, wakes from a deep but troubled sleep and feels a presence in his room. A breeze. A cool, gentle blowing. A face appears. The most splendorous, omniscient mug in town. The husband falls on his knees sobbing. In the morning he awakens, a new man. A glow surrounds him. His shoulders are straight. His step firm and directed. A reborn Jew. He has seen the Face in the Light. He has become the man of his family's dreams. The devoted, indefatigable, all-knowing, understanding-compassionate-strong-and-loving father/husband. Carrying the globe in one hand. Problems will not touch this house. Bills will fly out of the mailbox. No one will ever be dealt a bad hand here. No problem will be bigger than a bread box. And whatever—he can handle it. Lean—lean one, lean all. Arthur has changed. Arthur has found his Hercules suit. No one need snarl, ever again. I have returned. Cry and kick and scream. Fail algebra—hit menopause—overdraw your checking account—anything. I AM HERE. LEAN. My love is endless. My capacity limitless. Robert Young and Fred MacMurray are running scared. I AM HERE.

I felt those eye darts. I sensed the hope. I had, after all, spent years listening to people delude themselves. Churning themselves into the high-priced spread—trying to make reality come out the way they wanted it to. Holding on to illusion like a death grip from the seventieth floor. Step on my fingers, anything. I won't let go. I had seen it before. People babbling out words without sound. Words that ran together, that could not be heard. I will talk so fast—I will make what I say true. "He really does love me...she really is changing...my marriage is a lot better than most..."—words soaring by—swish, zoom, crash. Hope. Tricky little bugger. Not even real hope. But a kind of cowardice. "If they change—*we* won't have to do anything." So. All right. I was good at that game. Want a little Hercules with a touch of Dagwood Bumstead? Fine. Whatever makes you guys happy. I saw that eye number. And they both chose to focus on me. Not on one another. A spark. A glim. Of hope? I could work with that.

We finished our lemon chiffon pie with relative ease. Wife said she was tired and went up to bed. Son went back to whatever he does in there. I had a nightcap and watched *All in the Family*. Tomorrow I would sort this all out. I felt rather pleased, overall.

25

My wife and I did not touch that night, but somewhere near morning in the fog of half-sleep I ever so casually moved my leg next to her leg. She did not pull it away.

Breakfast was considerably more cheerful (I even got my corn muffin). Not so bad, I thought; once again, surfing along on my magic smug rug. I suggested that we go out to dinner with friends. She agreed to consider it. Holding her own, she was—I must give her that.

And so, it was back to the office. I was still speeding. My skin seemed to be invaded with electric current. Jumpy and charged. As if my body knew something—was braced for some assault that my mind had no access to. A strange, unsettling state. I took just a quarter of a Quaalude, to slow it down, and began to work on my Plan A documents. I found myself immensely satisfied. It looked good on paper. Now what I needed was some thought time. Time to find a way back to my work. How to attract some patients—shore up my framework. Who to call? As I sat pondering, my light went on. Someone was there. A knock followed. I followed the knock.

A man in a cheap brown suit with a briefcase in his hand and unfashionably long sideburns, shading vacant but shifty eyes, stood, army drill fashion, in the waiting room.

"Dr. Arthur Freedman?"

"Yes."

"I have a package for you. May I come in?"

"Certainly."

(My tranquilized heart was thrashing in my electrocuted chest. He moved ahead of me with the kind of solemn sobriety usually associated with morticians.)

"May I see some proper identification, please."

"All right."

(I gathered together the entire proof of my existence. A gold American Express card; Master Charge; Driver's License; Standard Oil and my passport. All of which I kept handy in case of enemy invasion or random paranoia in the supermarket. Sid Serious scrutinized each and every one. Eyes flashing up to my guilt-ridden face—and back to the evidence of my existence.)

"Okay."

He placed his briefcase on my desk and opened it. A large double-wrapped manila envelope with my name and address on it was removed and handed to me.

"Do you want me to sign for this?"

"No, sir. I was told not to ask for signature. Just proof of identity."

"I see. Well, thank you very much."

I pondered tipping him. Somehow it seemed inappropriate. Like tipping a cop for not giving you a ticket. He nodded his head toward me and snapped up his briefcase.

My heart had run the mile in fifty. I locked my door and tore open the envelope. Inside the envelope was another envelope. Inside that was a plastic bag. Inside that was a lump of something encased in aluminum foil. Inside that was thirty thousand dollars in cash. Dix. (The dear.) There was no note. Nothing of him. My kind of loan. Take deep breaths, Arthur. What to do first?

I could not do anything about Nephew Lawrence until he called (which was thankfully only three days away). I took twenty thousand dollars out of the pile—recorded all of the serial numbers (saw Efrem Zimbalist, Jr. do that once)—and put it in my locked steel desk drawer with my dope and the dirty pictures. Five thousand I would put into several different checking accounts. Not enough to arouse suspicion. The rest I would keep in my shaky little hands.

Next, I called our travel agent and made arrangements for Wife and Son to fly off to Mexico. I could see their thawing little pusses now as I swept into the house tonight with real live airplane tickets. Keeping his word. The man is becoming a saint.

So, that left the heroine in the piece. I telephoned and asked to see her. It was not really one of her days. She was going to have her hair done. She canceled it. First her dressing table and now this. Love conquers all.

So. What was I to do with her? Start hypnosis. Work on her anxiety about getting old. Yes. I must make her feel insecure enough to guarantee her taking whatever I want. I diagrammed my attack.

And then I began to slip. Lost my balance and fell off my rug, flat on my smug little face. A breaker of fear hit me like a rock in the gut. Just thinking about her—and I was swelling.

And reality.

This is not a game, Doctor. It is not television. The dead people don't get up, collect their residuals and go home. Rose will be gone. You will be all alone with those strangers. Who do you think you're kidding? How long do you think you will be able to pull off these corpulent lies? And if you can't, you will be used. Stripped bare and cast out. A crippled ballerina prancing on your mutilated toes to the tune of "Gimmee, Gimmee"... You do not know whether you can ever screw Wife Person again. And it is a little late to start scout leading and Little League. And alone. No cock-tingling ecstasy. No easy, adoring, simple Piece. No friend. No haven. And more. A secret to carry.

Killer. Betrayer of creed. No shoulder to cry on. No confessional for the aberrant. No place to let go anymore.

I was felled. This was not supposed to happen to me. I had worked all of that out. I had recaptured my "old cold cunning," as Dix called it. I had moved through all of this vulnerable nonsense. Except for yesterday. HA! It was only yesterday that you could not exist in the same space with Rosie for fifteen minutes without blowing your entire anal-tight little "plan." You were a big shot at home, my boy, because you had gotten your fix. Your injection of Rose cream. Let's see how well you do today. Without that. Let's see what a smart ass you are at home tonight. And all the nights to come with no more Rose. No more bathtub boogie. No place to balance the bullshit. Let's see about that, hot stuff.

Fire behind my eyes. My head was filled with blaze. My throat burned with fear. This was not supposed to happen now. Things were going according to plan.... I was back in control.... Sure I was.

Flames inside. And thoughts. Currents of paranoia. Madness. I saw Rose, snickering at me. She and Lawrence were sitting naked at her dressing table. He was saying, "Okay, baby—just a little while longer—we'll have the cocksucker's twenty thousand dollars and ride off into the sunset. I know how hard this has been for you—pretending to like that four-eyed old fart—but it worked, honey. Twenty thou and we're off." She laughs, malicious Nazi whore laughter, and spreads her legs. "Oh, Lawrence, lover-man, fuck me good—so I can fake it with the poor paunchy pricktoe." Lawrence inserts the hugest penis seen outside a Brahman bull mating stable. And Rose gives him everything.

Thoughts like this, scorching my mind—my eyes smart from the smoke... I am lost in the fantasy. Vials of wrath pound in my body. I'll kill the evil bitch. I'll show them who's King... chicanerous whore! No wonder I never let any of them touch me. No wonder I married safe and stayed outside.

I knew. I was right. Women were killers. Medusas. Luring you in by your innocent little prick and grabbing all the power—choking off your ability to see. To think. To control your passions. Every man in his right mind protects himself against cunt/whores. I was smart. Marry safe. Keep cool. Lust is a demon. Love is a witch. Can't trust any of them. Must stay away from anyone who perks you like that. I have left myself unarmed here. Betrayer! Venus flytrap! Malingering bitch! Never again! I had beaten women at their own game for thirty-nine years. So I had a little slip. Every man does. Mine was somewhat costly. Still, better to murder her than to have married her. A spell. They weave a spell. Wiggle of ass-warm pussy. Smile and say "You're the best man, Arthur!" Liars! Judas kissers. I bet she put him up to it. They all want our balls. We give them everything. Work our butts off—and they screw us. All the way. Well, I'll show them. I will never give one of them what they want again. I will use them with new depths of cynicism. I will pick them up and put them down like mice on a snake's tongue. They *cannot be trusted*. Never let your guard down, men. Never again, Arthur! A hard lesson. LEARN IT!

I was spinning. I was toppling. Gucci heels over balding pate...lost in the burning, choking power of paranoia. A captive of my own army.

Somehow, however, I was getting what I needed. One of your ever popular paranoid breaks to get me through the night. So, as this phantasmagoria exploded in my head, I began to strengthen my hold on my obsession. Yes, I said it. I had just really begun then to admit it. Obsession. I was obsessed with this dingy red cunt. And the betrayal hurt. (I believed what I had just made up in my mind. I made it up and ate it up and now sat suffering the stinging, crying outrage of the cuckold. Rejected by my own creation.)

And then she was there. I always felt her enter. A kind of lightness would move up my spine. Rose. Waiting patiently outside. Sitting primly with her pocktbook on her knees and her legs together like a lady at the bus stop. Passive and accepting. If I kept her sitting there all day, I doubt if she would be audacious enough to knock.

I stormed to the door, gulping down the froth of my anger.

Okay, bitch, we'll see who wins. It's my game—I can pick up all the marbles and go home anytime I want to.

> *Helloo, Artie, darling. I brought you some soup. For your sickness. I've been so worried about you. I felt so bad, like maybe what we did wasn't good for you, even though you said. I mean, maybe what the doctor meant was just a little, but not...you know...*

> *No, no, my dear...I am fine. Just fine. In fact, I am cured. It surprised*

the doctors too, but it just all went away.

(I'll show her—now it will be real rejection—no more sweet little abstinence plan—don't have time—now I want to move quickly—get rid of it fast.)

Oh, good. Goody-good.

(She giggles and reaches into her green plastic pocketbook.)

(I have something so silly. I made you something. To wear until you got better. It's so silly.

(She wiggles toward me, perfume invading my flaming nostrils, little nipples popping around inside her tight white angora sweater.)

Close your eyes.

(I obey. I can afford to be patient—with one so soon to die.)

Okay... open!

(She jumps up and down in front of me, holding a small red and blue crocheted object in her hands.)

What is it, my dear?

Oh, it's so silly. It's a little coat for your thingie. I though it would make it feel better... warm and cozy. I made it myself.

Well, aren't you sweet.

(I feel some movement in my dementia—NO! I cannot afford to think. I must not see this little token. She is trying to trick me. I must be careful. Extremely careful.)

How adorable. And what a lot of work it must have been. You must have been up all night.

(I examine her face critically with my steely eyes.)

Unh-unh. It was easy. I put my sleepy shade on and slept like a baby. I guess it was feeling so nice from yesterday. Because usually, you know, without you I can't.

(She puts her arms around me and presses her little mound against my groin. NO! My cock instantly responds, which encourages her. I am hanging on the far edge of my control—I cannot afford another slip.)

Randi, dear, you don't look well. I think you're more tired than you're telling me. I don't think we should play around when you're not well.

(Her face puckers. Index finger goes immediately into mouth.)

Oh. I thought I looked really nice. Got my beauty sleep. I even wore my new sweater. I'm sorry you don't like me today.

It's not that dear. It's just—well—I see some little lines around your eyes, and a woman your age—you must be careful. I think maybe you haven't been obeying me. But you know, I told you, I only treat the most beautiful, most sexual women in the world. And that's why they come to me. To stay that way. To follow my instructions. Otherwise bad things can happen to them. Of course, we have a personal relationship. But you are still my patient. Don't forget how sick you were before our first weekend together. I saved your life. And I saved your looks. I think maybe—you're not doing something. I want you to go home now and take this medicine. (It is the old stomach agitator.) *And this other bottle.* (Lithium to cover my manic-depressive story.) *Don't take any—just put it in your medicine cabinet and leave it there until I tell you what to do with it....*

(Her face is ashen. Her lower lip is trembling visibly. She drops to her knees and throws her little furry arms around my thighs. Thus putting her shaking orange head right against my prick. NO! I try to shift her weight. She holds firm.)

Oh, Artie. Please...please...don't send me away...you're scaring me...I love you so much...I'd die without you...I'll do anything ...please don't let me get wrinkly...and old...don't leave me...please.

All right, dear. All right. Calm down. I don't want to. But I see the signs. You will have to do exactly what I say. And not tell anyone.

I promise. Cross my heart. Anything...

(Her mouth breath moistens my fly. I am swollen. She knows. Shit. Well, maybe. I've done my work here. I am safe. She does not know that I suspect her deceit. If she wants to play, why not? I've got the cat's-eye in my pocket. She can't win now.)

Oh, Artie. Oh. See? You still do like me. I still make you happy. Let me give your thingie some kisses. I promise I won't do anything else. Just for a few minutes. And I'll go home and do whatever you say.

All right, Randi. If it will make you happy.

I stand, hands on hips. The Master and the Slave. She daintily opens my pants and out springs my jack-in-the-box. Boing! I watch. Little hands holding my balls. Little pink tongue licking. Little lips and teeth sucking. A magic mouth, this one. Happy as a hamster. I am allowing her to touch me. My thighs bend. My ass tightens. And as I come, my hands reach out involuntarily and stroke her hair. This intolerable tinge of tenderness that has entered the scene. I snap them back. But it is too late. Hope again. Give them a speck. At work—at home. Give the victims a glint and you can have anything. "Thank you, thank you."

She is happy. I have allowed her to give me pleasure. It is too bad I do not have time to clone her. For posterity. What a find. I fight for my paranoia. It is mixed up in there, with other things. I do not want clearing. But it's starting. Get her out quick. Before I lose any more ground.

Now, Randi. That was enough for you today. I can see your jaw muscles weakening. You go home. Take the little pill and get some rest. I want to see you the day after tomorrow. And I don't want any new wrinkles. Do you understand?

Oh yes. Yes, my lover-man... you'll see... I'll be fresh as a daisy. I promise... you'll see.

(She throws herself in my arms. I can feel the fear. Losing me. Lovely me. Poor dear. I can sympathize.)

26

Driving home (how strange that sounds, "home"), returning to my other life that night (that feels better)—my head a mass of third-degree burns and ashes, depression clutching at my gut—I realized, once again, that I had not succeeded. I had still not been able to spend one hour with Rose without lust. Not since that first day when she giggled her way into my world. Not once. So, okay. All the more reason to get rid of the source. I was determined to see her as the source of my problem. Recreating my "previous" life in a sort of poignant all-American reminiscence. It was *she*—that calculating tit-face hag. She who had ruined my life, short-circuited my coping mechanisms and brought me to the verge of financial and emotional (not to forget professional) ruin. And I was not strong enough to stop. So she must stop. Forever. Seemed absolutely clear.

And I decided something else. I must fuck Wife Person. The way to her dry little heart was through her arid little hole. After all, they found oil in Oklahoma, I should be able to squeeze out a pint or so in my own bed. If I could do that—I could let go of Rose. (I was, you see, still enough of a shrink to remember about twitching limbs. People clinging to fantasies of loved ones long since turned to dust.)

And so, I set the stage. We went out to dinner, alone. I talked earnestly and contritely. I poured a lot of white wine. And when the stretch of doubt in her tucked little eyes loosed ever so slightly, I pulled the plane tickets from my pocket and placed them in her hand.

And she smiled at me. She said thank you. Like a real woman. And part of me was absolutely amazed. At how little we settle for. Here was a woman (whatever her limitations)—a person who had lived without any nurturing, any sexual gratification, affection, warmth or communication for most of her adult life (and I can safely say, given her family, *all* of her childhood). The payoff was a nice "life-style" and two red scars on her wrists. And a few golden syllables and an airline ticket could bring softening to those frozen brown tones. How we settle. How we wither. How we go gently into that shitty night. It made me feel quite sad.

When we got home, I poured us a brandy and followed her upstairs. For this overdue moment of truth. I was no longer afraid. I would think of someone else. Pretend it was...who? Rose? No. That would be defeating the purpose. I would focus all of my concentration on her. I would call her Judy. Judy. Judy. I would pound that name into my brain.

She got into bed and patted my hand (an overwhelmingly encouraging gesture given our recent history) and I made my move. Gently I began to stroke the back of her neck. Softly I caressed her shoulder. "Oh, Judy," I sighed. I kept on. Stroking whatever part I could reach. Not quite confident enough to turn her over. She lay still. Not resisting (but not exactly gasping in ecstasy, either). I kept it up for what seemed like hours. Finally, I pressed myself against her flat little ass. And rubbed myself around her, slowly. Two things happened. She started to cry and I faced the cold hard truth. Which is to say, the cold limp truth. The sex god of modern psychiatry couldn't get it up. My cock lay there like it had been pinned on for decoration. My mind was turned off. My everything was turned off. So I used her tears to save face. And to keep her from knowing.

"No, no, Judy, dear. It's my fault. I'm pushing you. There's been too much anger. I'm so sorry. You need a rest from all of this...After you get back from Mexico, we'll see. Or we don't have to make love. That is not the most important thing. Saving our, uh, home is what's important. I just wanted you so much. I was being selfish. Go to sleep, now. It's all right."

Spoken in pure manipulative perfection. She slept. She never said one word. Or touched me. Or turned over. I lay there. Rigid. It's Rose. She's put a spell on me. I may never have liked it much, but I could always get it in there and poke it around for a while. I could get off. She's got to go, fast. I can't stand this pressure any more. Tomorrow. No, I can't until I get rid of Lawrence. The day after Cowboy Joe. She goes. This is not funny. I am not enjoying this all. She tricked me today. All of that hugging and falling on her knees. The red witch. She weakened me. A little Samson Sonata number. She's doing it on purpose. To make me crazy. To keep me from fucking anyone else. This is not funny! She knows what she's doing. Dirty cock-tease. She did it again. Sucked me in. Well, no more, babycake. You're not going to have Artie to push around anymore.

I lay there all night. My mind speeding. Flashes and fantasy. Paranoia and reality. Enemies within and enemies without. Teeth gritted. Hands clenched. And this little limp excuse for a penis. Flopped over in meaningless surrender on my proper dress side.

What had happened, in fact, was that I had now totally stopped knowing myself.

The center had not held. Whoever it was walking around in my skin suit, he had eaten the core and left the apple. And what remained? A delusive, terrified, paranoid madman who had bombed his own bridges and torn up his flight plans. I was set on a dead-end course with open roads all around me. Never saw a one. I am choking on self-pity here. (I will reread *King Lear* and *Othello* with new levels of compassion.)

The day after my aborted attempt at conjugal bliss is a blur. Travel talk kept us operating as a unit. Packing was going on. Hairdresser appointments. Medicine for the Taco two-step and other potential irritations. I saw two new patients. And did not remember their names or one word they said. Rose called thirteen times. (Her stomach hurt—she sounded whiny and scared.) And then, mercifully, it was the next day. Wife Person and Son were taxied off to the airport. And I was in my office by 7:00 a.m., waiting for my extortionist.

He was on time. The money was ready. The tape was running. He knocked. Or rather he pushed his fist against the door. A contemptuous rap. Once. Cocky son of a bitch, this was. I would not get up to greet him.

It's open. Come in.

He entered. Looking ugly and menacing. A cigar held between his teeth (now, really). Hands in jeans pockets. Stained (probably with horseshit) boots.

Up bright and early, huh, Doc? Got a lot of heads to shrink? There's supposed to be a full moon tonight—all the loonies will be rattling their chains...

We hire werewolves to take care of things like that.

Funny. That was very funny, Doc. You're a quick man with a comeback...I'll give you that.

All right. Let's cut it out and get this over with. I have your money. I also have a couple of conditions of my own. Whatever you think you

> know—you do not know the truth about your aunt. Or about your family history. I think you should, before you leave.

(His jaw tightens—I am going to enjoy this little scene.)

> Hey, what are you talking about? We have a simple deal. You pay. I split. And keep my mouth shut. Simple.

> Not quite. I think you should know that your aunt has a genetically inherited psychobiologic imbalance in her nervous system. So do your mother and your uncle. And most likely you do too. I have used some rather experimental treatment modules to try and help your aunt, but they are not working. The suicidal impulse is very strong in her. In your entire family. And I saw it in you the first time we met. Often it lays dormant for years—and then some turn of events triggers the chemical reaction in the brain—and the patient begins to act in a self-destructive manner. I may have to hospitalize your aunt to stop her from destroying herself. I am telling you this because—as a doctor—I can see your actions as the beginnings of a primary manic-phase decompensation. You must be very careful. Take this money. And keep your promise. To do otherwise could result in activating the chemical reaction in your mother or your aunt or uncle. Or in yourself. If I were you, Lawrence, I would use this grubstake of yours to leave town. Go to the mountains. Stay quiet and close to nature. Don't come back here... for your own good, as well as for mine.

> Oh, come on, now, Doc. Cut the shit.

(He is trying to be cool—but his fists are clenched and his right eye is twitching. Self-fulfilling prophecy—fate neurosis—I knew I had hit it. I stood up and unlocked the drawer. Slowly, with great calm and sepulchral quiet, I remove the money and place it on his lap. He does not move. He is shaken. He wants more. Wants to toss a new pair. Fat chance, Turkey Tongue.)

> It's all there. Twenties, tens. Clean money. Now go and never come back. I hope you have listened to me. I am telling you the truth. Your aunt may not survive her sickness. Don't play around with this. Go away. Buy some land somewhere. If you find yourself drawn toward any form of selfdestructive behavior, seek help. You are playing with fire here—given your family background. You pride yourself on being street-smart—well, if you push your luck here, you're just goddamn dumb. I can show you research on this sort of dysfunction. I can show you your aunt's case

history.

(He literally jumps out of the chair—grabbing at the foil package and clutching it to his chest.)

> *Hey—I said cut it out. We made a deal. The code of the West, Doc. I won't bug you. I ain't that greedy. Just lay off the word game. I ain't interested. It's all a lot of cow crap. You stay off my back—I stay off yours—we don't ever have to cross paths again. Just shut up with all that jazz. I'm no patient.*

> *Of course. I was just trying to warn you. It may be of help to you some day. And if your aunt should kill herself—despite all our attempts to save her—it may help you avoid a similar fate.*

> *Listen, what that floozy old broad does has nothing to do with me. Not that I believe this shit for a minute—but my motto is Every Man for Himself. And that goes for my mother and my uncle too, Doc. I look out for me. And that's all the looking I've got room for. So just choke it off.*

(He is backing out of the room. Holding the money bag against his chest).

He stops, looks down, then at me. Startled to have lost his footing. I can afford to be generous.

> *Don't you want a bag to carry that in?*

(I pull a manila envelope from my desk and hand it to him. He grabs it from my hand, struggling to fit the money in. His face is blotched with anger. Blew his covers off. The poor kid is sleeping in a draft and he don't know how to remake his beddie-boo. He turns his back on me, without a word, and lumbers (gone the swagger, gone the game) out, slamming the door behind him.)

I let out the longest deepest breath in the history of anxiety. And lie down on the couch, exhausted and amazed. How easy it was to intimidate. But it hit *le nerf*. He never even challenged me. And he gave me all the ammunition I needed. Told me himself—where to insert the knife. "Just slip it in here, Doc—near my mother and being an only child in a house full of hysterics—ouch—that's it, thanks."

I felt relief. Suspended for a moment from the real test. The work of the day. Rose. I would sleep for awhile. Replenish my supply of deadly bon mots and continue with my journey to the end of the earth.

I slept, dreaming of roses. I walked through a vast, wondrous garden of bright red roses. The wind gently caressing my face. I breathed in, deep satisfying gusts of flower scents. Every now and then I would stop, bend down and put my nose into the petals. In the center of each was a sweet little pussy. It would tighten around my nostrils and give me the sweetest, warmest, moistest little kiss. Nicest dream I ever had. When I opened my eyes, I was smiling. And then, the thought.

Rose dies today. I sat up quickly. Too quickly. The room spun. I felt faint. All of that deep breathing, all of that Rose gas.

I sat on Ol' Brown for several minutes, my head between my legs—trying not to faint. And then I heard her open the outside door. My little pussy petal. Our last rendezvous.

I stood up. My head hurt. I walked slowly toward the door, trying to get into character. Ariel or Caliban. Not enough rehearsal time.

She sat. Holding a big box with yellow and blue wrapping paper. Another "present" (awfully big for a thingie warmer). She looked tired. And fragile. I had made her unhappy. I could tell. One of her eyebrows was penciled too high (a dead giveaway).

Hello, my dear. May I carry that for you?

Oh, no. It's okay, Artie. It's just a little something for you.

You shouldn't keep buying me things. You must save your money—for your old age.

(Her face went chalk-white. Her eyes filled with tears. Bulls'-eye.) She stood in the middle of my office. Disoriented. Not knowing what was expected. Possessing no guile. No cunning. No game book. Gotten by for fifty years on a wiggle and a tongue slide. In over her head. Playing with the big boys.

I did everything you said, Artie. But something's wrong—my poo-poos were funny again. My tummy hurt. I tried and tried—but I couldn't sleep. But I did lots of exercises. I didn't get any more wrinklies. I'm still the same.

I penetrate her fear with my intractable stare. And slowly shake my head.

I'm sorry, my dear. But something's changed. You are going to have to do more. If we are going to try and save our relationship, if I am going to keep you safe and young. I want to hypnotize you today. Lie down and take off your clothes.

Yes. Yes. That's a good idea. Hypnotize me. That worked real good before.

(She is pantingly eager. She sits down and daintily begins undressing. Just look at her once more. The Last Dance and all of that romantic nonsense. She shimmies her way out of her panties and garter belt (God love her, a woman who wears a garter belt). She looks very pale and soft. Most of the marks and bruises have faded away. She's just about ready for another round of rough stuff...NO! Arthur. My prick stiffens. I cross my legs. She lies still. Her eyes closed. Her fuzzy orange bangs resting on her eyebrows. Her little purple lips pursed. Her arms are crossed over her chest, like a mummy. Her little yellow feet are pointed straight out. She looks so sweet. So innocent. So cuddly. And all I have to yell is..."spread 'em, baby"—and she becomes a wanton whore. True child-woman—a trusting innocent who fucks like a cunt. Yeahhhhhh. I'll do for the *Reader's Digest*—My Most Unforgettable...I had her. Every boy-man's fantasy. (Boy/man...child/woman.) So simple...when it comes out right.
She lies still, waiting for my command.

All right, Randi, dear. I want you to think of something very peaceful and happy. Clear everything else out of your mind. I am right here. I am with you. Now start counting backwards from one hundred..."

(She is under by 98—such a good girl.)

I open her purse. I need stationery. Her own. There is a little red pad with notepaper. Little blue pages with bunches of flowers on the corners. An eight-year-old's stationery. I tear out a sheet and replace the pad.

Now, dear, I want you to sit up. And open your eyes. I want you to write something for me. You will write it and take it home. Tonight I am going to give you medicine. Lots and lots of medicine. The more you take, the better you will look and feel. If you take it all, like a good girl, I will love you again. Everything will be wonderful. Better than before. We can go to the movies again. Everything. But if you don't take all the medicine—you will get wrinkled and old and ugly—and I will not be able to help you and I will have to send you away forever.

(She sits up. Her eyes wide and frightened. I have planned this well.)

All right, here is the paper and pen. I want you to write exactly what I tell you.

(She nods. Her titties bob. She sits, knees together, looking professional. Steno in the blood. A born order-taker. A true man-server.)

Okay. Now write: Dear Family, The Doctor tried. I can't change my ways...I just want to sleep...Forgive me, Rose.

She writes slowly. Mouthing the letters to keep her concentration. She never pauses or seems to question the words. When she is through, she sits, a mechanized dolly waiting for instructions.

Now I want you to fold that up and put it in your purse.

(I walk to my desk and bring forth my arsenal. A mixture of barbits and bombers that could stop Rocky. I put them in an unmarked vial, wipe it clean and press it into her hand.)

All right dear. Here is your medicine. Now, tonight I want you to take out the note—but don't open it. Put it by your bed. Then you pour yourself a big glass of water or milkie for your tum-tum. And you take all of these pills. They will make you very, very sleepy. You will sleep like an angel baby. You must take all of them. Lock your door. And take your phone off the hook. I don't want anything to disturb you. Do you understand?

(She nods once. A sweet little nod.)

Tell me you understand. And then you repeat, word for word, exactly what I told you.

I understand. I will go home and lock the door and take the phone off the hook. I will take the note and the medicine out of my purse. I will not open the note. I will put it by my bed. I will pour myself a big glass of milkie or water and take all the medicine. I will be very sleepy...like an angel baby. And when I wake up, we will be in love and happy again— and I will be beautiful and you will take me to the movies.

Very good. That's my good girl. All right, now you lie down and sleep for a while. I have some work to do. I want you to keep repeating to yourself what you must do tonight. And remember, it is our most private secret—no one must know... or it will not work.

No one must ever know. It is our most private secret.

That's right. Now, you just lie there and doze. I will tell you what I want you to do next in a few minutes.

She snoozed. Gentle sweet-lady snores quivering at her nostrils. Her mouth working silently over my words. I sat. I just sat, watching her. As if I were a human printing press, a computer with eyes. I would record her forever in my mind. I touched her belly. Soft and warm. I gently spread her legs and looked at her cunt. Lovely little petal. Not a woman's cunt. A girl's little bud. I sniffed it. I gently licked the clitoris. She moved, murmured something, sighed. Happy. Relaxed now. All fear gone from her white and red-rouged face. I put my nose between her toes and sniffed the talcum (clean, so clean). I poked and played over her like a boy with a baby chick. My first pet. I remembered. A warm little yellow chick. Could feel its heart flicking against its fragile little carcass. Its little beak tickling my fingers. I would sit for hours, just holding it. Sniffing its warm feather smell. Feeling good. Big boy now. Sniffing my dying chick.

It was getting dark. She must go soon. I swallowed stones in my throat. She sighed and turned over on her stomach. Such a dear. One last rear ass view. I throbbed. I began to unzip my pants. No. Semen stains in the autopsy. Not wise. And I stopped. Still hard. I stopped. And not just because of that. Something else. Humanity? Let her go out with some pride. I stopped.

I paced the room. "Let go, Arthur." I felt frozen. Not frightened. Just paralyzed. Unable to release her. Unable to say good-bye. I had not thought of after. No thought of finality. No image of end. Of death. I just could not say good-bye. "LET GO, Doctor!" My head hurt. My eyes itched from the inside. I swallowed albumen-covered stones. And moved. Pushing myself forward. Using all my will.

Randi, dear—can you hear me?

Yes, Artie darling.

All right, then. I want you to wake up now. When I tell you—you will open your eyes and sit up. You will go straight home and follow my instructions. You will speak to no one. You will remember to take your

phone off the hook and lock your door. You will feel happier and more peaceful than you have ever felt before. All right, when I say the number five you will wake up. One... two... three... four... (I stop. Physically unable to utter the sound. I fight back panic. I feel holes widening in my stomach—lumps growing in my throat—fists squeezing at my heart. LET GO, ARTHUR!) *five.*
The hardest word I have ever spoken.
She sits up and stretches. She opens her eyes and smiles at me.

Boy, I feel great. See, Artie, I knew that would help. I'd better go home right away and take my medicine.

She stands up and begins wriggling back into her clothes. The dream ass disappears inside her undies. The warm jelly-belly. The redhead cunt. The fuck-me titties. Bye, pussy. Bye, belly. Bye, tushy. Bye, little tits. I stand still. Watching. She is humming. "The Man I Love."

Oh, Artie—I almost forgot—your present!

She skips over to my desk and hands me the big yellow and blue box. I sit down in my doctor chair and unwrap it slowly. Everything seems to be moving underwater. So slowly... still life. Not real. A water nymph and a guppy. Diving and paddling around. The paper inside smells of mothballs and stale Old Spice. It is a faded white tuxedo, the satin piping yellowed and dry.
Rose is bouncing on her toes. Joy shines from her peaceful, clear face.

It's Frederic's tuxedo. Like I promised. I found him. Well, not him exactly, he's sick... I found his sister. She was real nice. I told her about it—and she said that he'd had a stroke years ago and was like a vegetable—and was in an old people's home—and that she was sure it would be okay with him if I took it. She said maybe it would bring someone good luck—like it used to for Frederic. Try it on. Please, Artie. Pretty please with cream on top? Just once, before I go.

The last wish. On death row it's always steak and baked potatoes. In Freedman's row—it's a mothball-tainted fashion show.

All right, Randi, dear. Just for you, I will.

I rise. I strip off my clothes, from inside the diving bell. A water ballet. A guppy fighting for his way toward froghood. It is too small.

Frederic of the tight tummy, the big dipper. I suck in my quavering gut.

It's stunning, Randi. A perfect fit.

Oh, goody. Good. I just knew it. You look so handsome. Better than he ever did. After I'm well again, I'll bring in my pink dress and maybe we can go dancing.

That sounds just fine, dear heart. Now—it's time for you to run along. You have your health to think of first.

Okay. Artie, darling. Let me just give you one kiss good-bye.

She rises on her toes and plants a wet warm little smacking kiss on my mouth. Then one on my nose. One on each of my unshaven cheeks. And pats my crotch. Then she puts her chubby white arms around my waist and gives me a great big hug. Albumen and rocks, gagging me.

Bye-bye, my lover-man. I'll dream of you all night.

Bye-bye Randi. Have a good sleep.

And she blows me a kiss and wiggles her luscious ass out the door. "And what do we care...at the end of a love affair."

And there I was. A psychasthenic psychiatrist in a soiled white tuxedo, all alone in the middle of nowhere. Rose scents infested my sinuses. And soluble. Melting away into nothingness. I made myself move. There were things to be done. Burning. Things to be destroyed. I took the photographs from my locked desk. Rose and me and immortality. I burned them all. One at a time. Savoring the memory. Feeling my cock throb against my tight white dance pants. And then the closet. Out came the vibrators. Out came the handcuffs, the whips and the dildoes. And the pussy-hole undies. And the nippleless bras. And the dress-up clothes. Everything. And the chemical wonderland. Bye, Quaaludes. So long amyl nitrate. I put them all in my golf bag. And the tux. Stripped it off and tossed it in. So long, samba.

I went home. Quiet. Dark. Housekeeper's day off. In the yard, I built a fire and burned everything but the handcuffs and the vibrators. The whip scorched but would not succumb. What was left I put in a plastic garbage bag and drove to the city dump, tossed from a moving Mercedes into the rubble. And now there was waiting to do. Where should I go? Should I be at home?

> The cerebral and successful mind-healer, spending a quiet evening at home with his invisible Irish setter, his invisible pipe and Pendleton Shirt—and invisible family—by his nonexistent roaring fire, is brought back from the quiet reverie of Sack sherry, Horowitz playing Rachmaninoff and the darkened delicacy of Faulkner by the ring of the telephone. He rises serenely—rubbing the shiny coat of his make-believe pup—and answers. Oh NO! A patient has been found dead. An apparent suicide. Dear ME! A tormented scientist. "I will be right over, officer," he offers, in the most grave and professional tone of voice. Throwing a fleece-lined suede car coat over his log-cabin shirt—pipe held determinedly in his serious, white-lipped mouth—he races to the scene of the unfortunate accident. "Such a waste. We were working so hard. I felt sure. What's this? The lithium? She was not really taking the medication? My God! No, no! Of course I never gave her any sleeping pills. She was depressive. I cannot believe this. I was concerned, but lately we seemed to be making progress. I have failed a human being. Now I must live with my failure. Forever. Excuse me officers—if it's all right—may I go now? I am at your service...but for tonight, I would just like to be alone"...Of course, Doctor, we understand"...He walks off into the night. A lonely figure. Head down. The sensitive, brilliant healer, tortured by doubt. The end.

But I couldn't go home. I went to a bar. I drank. I went to a restaurant. I ate. (Risotto al frutta di mare, roast white veal, pecadino romano and pears, Sicilian wine, anisette and espresso dupio.) I went to a late movie. And saw a Marx Brothers film festival (without laughing once). And then I went back to my office. I sat on my brown beauty and drank brandy and waited for something to happen. To sleep. I did not sleep. To be called. The phone never rang. I sat there all night. Teeth like welded spikes in my head. Neck muscles clenched in tension. Eyes dry and dead. I couldn't get drunk. I couldn't pass out. I couldn't move. Peter Passive. Wired shut. It was the worst night I have ever known. (I did not know that it would become routine. I did not know anything about things like that—yet.)

By nine the next morning, I was desiccated. Drained, flailing, a humanoid blister looking for a pin. I took a tranquilizer. Something to steady my hands. Something to reset my iron mask. And I telephoned Morley.

> *Morley, this is Dr. Freedman. I hope I'm not getting you at a bad time?*

(So thoughtful, so elegant, so kind.)

Oh, no, Doctor, you honor my home. What a wonderful surprise. What is it that I can do for you?

Well, I'm sure it's nothing, but Rose missed her appointment this morning—and I'm getting a bit concerned. I have been meaning to call you—because things have not been going so well—but—I didn't want to alarm you until I was sure—however it's not like her to miss an appointment and I wondered if you or Louise could go over and see if she's all right. I can't reach her by phone. It seems to be out of order.

Oh my. Yes. Yes. I will go at once. It's funny that you should call this morning. I was praying for Rose this morning. I had a dream about her—a godless, terrible dream. I will go at once.

Thank you. I'm sure it's nothing—maybe she just overslept—she's been having some stomach trouble again—I hate to alarm you, but I am concerned about her state of mind.

Do not worry, Doctor. I will see. The Lord will be with me.

Good. Please let me know.

But of course. I will call immediately. God bless you.

Thank you.

I showered and changed into a three-piece gray wool suit, a pale blue shirt and navy-and-red-striped tie. The tranquilizer soothed me. I felt calm. Almost euphoric. Anticipatory. The game was moving toward climax.

I sat again. Just sat. What a bizarre experience. Sitting. I could not remember ever before in my entire life just sitting. Not thinking. Not working. Not watching, reading, chessing, backgammoning. Teeveeing. Yakking. Just sitting? Borders on the psychoneurotic.

"See that man over there?" "Yes." "Well, he's just sitting." "Just sitting?" "Yes. He must be crazy."

At twelve o'clock, there was a knock on my outer office door. I rose—The Creature Who Returned from the Dead—and went to open it. Louise and Morley stood together holding hands. She looked pale and red-rimmed. He was beaming. A huge Jewish savior. Beaming to beat the band. The guy who saw Christ rise. In person.

Doctor, may we come in?

Please. I've been waiting to hear from you. I've been terribly worried. Is Rose all right?

(Louise collapses in whiny sobs, her stringy black head bobbing up and down in her fisted white hands.)

Please, Doctor, sit down.

Morley (my man) is about to play his best scene. A once-in-a-lifetime chance. The archangel of angst. A shepherd with a new flock. Go for it, Morley. I sit, looking saturnine and rueful (a hard thing to pull off).

Dr. Freedman, our Rose has gone back to the Maker. She has committed a sin against God. She has taken her own life. I believe the burden of her wantonness, her rejection of God, became too much for her to bear—despite all your efforts. And ours. She is gone now. It is in God's hands. I will pray for her immortal soul. I do not know if I can be heard. To take your own life defies God's commandments. We must all pray for forgiveness, may she find peace and mercy in the house of the Lord.

(Louise screams, pulling at her hair and pounding her wet, white fists against her temples. I steady her and prepare a sedative. The thought of emotion—any raw, raging feeling—overwhelms me now, like nails on slate—screeching discomfort moving up my spine. Give me cartons—give me containers—give me dry ice, dispassion, repression, alienation, obliteration, numbness, blindness, paralysis, disassociation—anything but screaming pain, tears and sobbing. I will crack under that. Bring silence—bring coffins of control, take this emotion out at once. I force her to drink the sedative. She quiets. Sitting. Rocking back and forth on Rose's cushion.

I saw it in a dream. I saw it. I saw spirits—hovering around her—I saw sickness—bloody tumors and demons. Naked raving demons ravishing her...the aura was around her—it was too late...

What about the police? I hate to bring this up—but were the police there?

Yes, Doctor. We called them at once. They came. That is why we were so long. A note was left addressed to you. They took the body. We must go now and arrange the burial; in an Orthodox ceremony—the body must be prepared immediately. I imagine the police will be contacting you. The funeral will be tomorrow morning. I do hope you can come. I know Rose would want that. Pray for her soul, Doctor.

His beam grows. His lips spread in crescent-shaped smiles. His finest moment. How it shimmers, how it glows. The polyester prophet.

We shake hands. I help him, help Louise up. Louise staggers against me. I feel her hot little heart thumping against her moist black dress. She is dazed. He is aglitter. She sees tumors and naked demons, he sees the Gardens of God. Lucky Morley. He maybe knows something we don't know.

And they left. The Witch of Salem and Reverend Ike. And then the police came. Looking like rejects from the Redneck Review. Not a Kojak or Baretta in sight. Not a Columbo in the lot. I brought forth my Rose files, shaking my head and acting contrite (and terribly smart).

Even in the remnants of my paranoia, they did not seem suspicious. As I predicted...another old broad hits the trap door. And—chauvinists that we all are—what's one more piece of toneless tail? I gave them everything I had on my patient, Miss Rose Liebshitz, otherwise known as Randi Laine. They asked about the note. I was earnest and soft-spoken. And then they offered some descriptive background information, some macho gossip—if you will. They told me how they found her.

Rose. Lying on her bed with a panda bear in her arms and a sleep mask on. And a nylon robe with feathers around the neck. All of her makeup was on, and her hair was wrapped in Kleenex and covered by a big black net. Beside the bed was a half-eaten dish of peppermint ice cream with chocolate sauce over it.

"Damn weirdest looking suicide I've ever seen—she looked so happy. Almost cozy. Never vomited or nothing. Looked almost like an old kid or something. Really strange."

I thanked them for the information, feeling something heavy and warm building behind my eyes. Filling the sockets—pushing against the lids. They took my records and my carefully prepared tapes and left.

I went back to my couch. And sat some more. Until the pressure behind my eyes exploded and tears came. Salt tears from the Dead Sea. Loss. So this is what it felt like? Grief. Not guilt. Not fear. Loss. Rose was gone. Forever. And I had done it. I had destroyed my only friend. My only place of release. Of safety. Of love. My God...what a chilling thought. Of...love? Yes, Doctor. Off she went—with her panda and her chicken feathers. To Old Floozy City in the sky.

And now I was all alone. Forever. And worse. I knew that if Rose was watching now...if she knew what I had done...if she was up there in some Cabin in the Clouds listening to all of this...that she would forgive me...She wouldn't be mad at me, she would understand. I don't even think she would have minded. "Oh, that's okay, Artie—if it will make you happy—I'll do it—my life isn't so much anyway...lover-man."

My life seemed to have stopped. The future lay in front of me like a tired whore. Passionless. Rancid. Used. Jasmine and come in my nose. All that was left of being alive.

27

I went to the funeral. Louise was there. And Morley. And two Roselike ladies from her dancing club. And the cashier from her movie house. And the lady who fixed her hair. (Lawrence was not there. Lawrence, it seemed, had left town, and no one knew where he was.) It was a funeral's funeral.

They tore our clothes and we sat behind a curtain. Morley rocked back and forth in near-orgiastic fervor. Louise rocked back and forth in near-schizopodal hysteria. And we walked behind the plain pine box and watched it being lowered into the earth. I tossed the first shovelful of dirt over my Rosebud. And felt the heaviness behind my eyes. Not guilt. Not fear. Loss. (I repeat.) Grief.

And I wandered around for about a week. The police seemed satisfied. Lawrence did not appear. Morley and Louise wrote me a loving letter filled with iconic jargon and fervor. My colleagues were sympathetic. I began to resume. Wife Person called and asked for money to stay another week (how soon they forget)—they were having a wonderful time and had met some interesting people (I briefly entertained the thought of her having an affair and leaving me after all I had done for her...why-me, why-me). I sent it. Stupefactionville. (That's my new address.) I made every effort to fuel the engine. I played tennis four days in a row. I made a golf date and hustled some consulting work at the university. I bought a set of English briar pipes and began reading ads for Irish setter puppies.

And every night I sat. Sleep had gone to another party. I sat. And watched the heaviness grow until it pushed open my eyes—popping them in their dry little sockets and flooding my lost little face. Lonely. I was so lonely. When I did find sleep, in a bottle, in a capsule of blackness, I dreamt of Rose. Swinging on a swing with her sturdy little legs spread...blowing me kisses...sucking my cock. I would wake, forgetting—and reach for her. And then would come the flood. And the pain.

So this is what it feels like. All of those years of listening to lovers carry on and break down and rant and whine and wail—"She's gone, he's left...I'll die from the pain"—or death...or any form or fragment of abandonment...I had heard it all...an outsider, bemused and cynical...how unchic...all of that raw emotion...tsk-tsk...what a waste of energy....

So, this is what they felt like? And worse. I had done it to myself. That was the true madness. The real sickness. I had destroyed the only thing in my life that had meaning. Because I could not tolerate the meaning of the meaning. Not *that* kind. The ol' ember again. If that was my ember—forget it.

Only I didn't know I would have to pay like this. A few doubloons for the natives. A couple of anxiety attacks for the record. But not this. Loss. Grief. Hurt. Loneliness.

All of my life I had avoided that kettle. Leaping and darting like a first-draft quarterback. Not that bucket of barracudas. And here I was. Dropped in the middle, with the slimy little bastards nibbling at my middle-aged flesh. I did it to *skirt* this. So what was I doing here with all of these fucking petticoats over my head?

Irony. And so, you. I came back to tell my tale. It has been two months since Rose took her medicine and went off to Redhead Heaven. My wife and son returned tanned and cocky. (Somewhere in Mexico they joined hands—somewhere they became a team again.) And we are the meaning of form as a life-style. Three callous robots winding slowly down. And as for Eros. As for Freedman, cocksman nonpareil—well—fill in the blanks. The barracudas bit it off. Mid-life what's-its'-futz-it. Haven't gotten it up since Rose left. Once—not very long ago—I had a dream about her and my prick erected—but I woke just before coming. To come over a corpse. Sends chills up my brittle little back.

So. Here we are. It is now 11:19 p.m. I am alone. I am stoned. I am drunk. I am through with my story. The perfect crime. To commit the perfect crime, one must have the perfect victim...There aren't many around. I had one. (I'm just not sure who it was.)

That is what I did. Whoever you are...you can believe all of this or not. You can begin investigating—lock me up—shoot me—take away my doctor badge...pluck the strings from my new graphite racket. I don't think I would care much. And also, I still have not decided what to do with all of this. I think I must want to keep it on hand—for a rainy day—for an endless night—for the time when my invisible dog dies and my pipe won't light and I can no longer button the buttons of my Pendleton shirt over my sagging belly.

Everyone says I look well. And patients are returning—drawn by my indifference and ennui. Money is coming in. I heard from Morley and Louise the other day. Apparently Rose had made a will. She left everything to me. With special mention of Victor Mature and her dressing table. But she never blew her cover. No love words. The will read: "I leave all my worldly belongings, etc., to Dr. Arthur Freedman, for saving my life."

Some Life Saver. All that seems to be left is the hole. *Someone licked away all the candy and left me out here in the middle of this fucking night sea with nothing to hang onto.* Can't hold onto a hole for long.

Well. It seems I am finished. And just before the stroke of midnight, I can feel the waves of heavy saltiness forming behind my eyes. So, class. I will click you off now.

No. Wait. This is not the ending....What did I have in mind? Something...something about clicking you off is scaring the shit out of me....

You...? What is *you*? *You* are nothing yet. *You* are a machine. My machine. I turn you on....I turn you off...*I* am in charge here. *You* are just a receptacle. A confessional. A lifesaver. A friend.

No. You are not my friend. I will not click you off under these conditions. They are *not* acceptable. You can *not* be my friend. Just because you have sucked up my secrets. Just because you have seen me stripped raw and peeled bare.

No.

I push the buttons. You have no power. And no right. To pity me. To judge. Don't pity *me*. I...have gotten away with murder. I have lost ten pounds. I have kept home and hearth together and improved my tennis game. I do not like the tone of this. There seems to have been some gross misunderstanding here.

Maybe....The thing to do is begin again. Maybe you are defective, machine—intellectually, emotionally or mechanically. This echo of one hand clapping, this hollow hunger...is your fault. You are trying to take my plate—and I am still eating.

Obviously I am not through.

All right, class. We will rehearse this scene till we get it right.

Please.

Let me start over.